THE FATE OF AVA MILLER

HOPE E. DAVIS

This one is for you, Mme. Leslie.

ACKNOWLEDGMENTS

Cover Photo by Warren Designs
Edited by Joan Sands and Larissa Abdalla

PREFACE

In an article published in the year 2018, Parents.com has estimated that there is a child abduction every forty seconds in the United States. Every forty seconds, a mother is faced with the fact that she may never see her child alive again.

Police pursue these cases for months, oftentimes years, and sometimes never find a solution for these families. The FBI database for missing and exploited children keeps these cases open for decades. Some families give up and eventually decide to "bury" their children without a body. But sometimes, the decision can come too late—years after it has destroyed a marriage or a family member's mental well-being or even after it has torn apart the family itself. These cases are never easy. Not on the families that experience them, nor the police officers who have to ask the hard questions that can be even more difficult to answer.

A simple Google search can reveal hundreds of articles with statistics that most people already know. Most abductions are perpetrated by a family member, and an even larger amount by someone the victim knows. Even with what are referred to as "stranger abductions," the perpetrator will often have prior contact with the family, enough so that a parent or friend will remember seeing the person before the abduction. Then, of course, there are the abductions that happen completely out of the blue by someone who saw an opportunity and went with it. Either way, it doesn't matter how these abductions occur because they destroy a family.

Despite all of this, people often forget that missing children make up only a fraction of the missing persons cases each year. According to the FBI's National Crime Information Center, ninety thousand people are missing at any given time in the US. Over half of these missing people—or about fifty thousand—are adults over the age of eighteen. These cases are publicized a lot less and for not as long as child abductions, and could be happening right in your neighborhood. Of the number of missing adults reported every year, approximately sixty-one percent are found deceased. Another twenty-one percent are found living. The other eighteen percent are never found.

PART I

1

PRESENT DAY 2018

"Ava's dead, you know, it's time you let her go." Greg shook his mom's voice out of his head. This time, he wouldn't let her deter him. Sure, it'd been years since he'd dated Ava Miller, but he just knew she couldn't possibly be dead. She'd always talked about disappearing, and Greg had always figured that's exactly what she'd done five years before.

As he edged his black tie up his neck and straightened his black collar, Greg glanced in the mirror. Ava's funeral is today. After five years of looking, her parents were calling it quits.

Greg didn't really know why he was attending, other than the fact he'd always loved Ava. Sure, they had broken up seven years before, but they'd been young. And Greg knew now that he'd said the wrong things at the worst times. Ava had been a free spirit, she'd wanted to see the world, so, Greg let her go—thinking she would always return —but she hadn't. In fact, after dumping him, Ava had been quick to date another man, Kyle. But, then, one day she'd just disappeared.

At first, the search had been vigilant. Volunteers out with flashlights, accosting every car that drove into her neighborhood. They'd searched gullies, the mountains, washes, anywhere, for the missing twenty-five-year-old woman. This continued on for a month or so.

Then, slowly, the investigation had stalled, until it came to the slow rhythm it had found in the past couple years, where every time a killer was brought in they would question him or her about the victims. Hoping beyond hope that one would be Ava. But nothing. The lead detective on the case had kept at it, refusing to acknowledge her death without a body. But after five years of sleepless nights, even he had to give up at some point.

At first, Ava's parents hadn't wanted to accept that their daughter might be dead. In fact, they had kept pushing the lead detective with weekly phone calls and monthly visits. But the years had been taxing on the whole family, and even her parents realized that maybe it was time to let go and finally lay their daughter to rest.

Greg worked as a traffic cop, though he'd hoped to become a detective—he was still waiting for the senior detective to retire—and, at this point, it could be years. Greg had also pushed for them to continue the investigation. Alas, his pleas fell on deaf ears. Two weeks ago, Ava's parents called it off and ordered an urn for ashes that didn't exist, and they reserved the gazebo at the park for a ceremony that was sure to be small. You don't disappear for five years and still have hundreds of friends. That's not how the world works.

Greg knew better. He remembered the summer day when Ava had turned to him and said the words that broke his heart.

"Someday, I'm going to disappear. And no one will find me, ever." Ava tossed her beautiful chestnut hair over her shoulder and gazed off into the sunset. Greg moved to put his arm around her, and Ava leaned on his shoulder.

"But how will you live? How will you make money?" Greg gently rubbed his girlfriend's shoulder. They were only nineteen but he was so in love with this girl and he would do anything for her.

"I'll figure it out. I can be a stripper, if nothing else." Greg almost doubled over in shock. He couldn't believe those words would ever come out of her soft pink lips.

"You know I'll never let that happen." Greg rubbed her shoulder once more.

Ava said nothing, brushed off his embrace, and then began to skip through the field. She turned back and gave him a glance, then took off running, her white dress flowing behind her in the wind, a smug smile on her face.

Greg smiled back and began to jog after Ava. Nothing was ever easy with her.

Greg shook his head to clear it of the unwanted memories, grabbing his large key ring as he headed towards the door. Ava wasn't dead. She couldn't be.

And now, as everyone else was giving up, he realized it was his duty to find out what fate had befallen her.

2

AUGUST 25, 2010

"Pop-tart?" Ava tossed a packet of pop-tarts at Greg as she hopped in his black SUV. Greg smiled at the sight of his beautiful girlfriend with her hair blowing every which way and her makeup not yet complete. As she situated herself in the passenger seat, Greg opened the pack of pop-tarts and began to eat one. He was never much of a pop-tart eater, but he was hungry and he knew Ava wouldn't let him skip a meal.

"Thanks, Babe." He smiled as his girlfriend adjusted her simple V-neck top and skinny jeans. She was wearing her favorite ballet flats that he never saw her without.

College had started last week and Ava, who had been planning to take the bus, had quickly discovered that she hated it. She couldn't stand the men leering at her, the drunks puking, and the mean old ladies snapping. Greg had offered to drive her since he, too, had classes on Monday and Wednesday. Although he attended a different college, Greg would do anything to keep Ava happy.

"So, will I see you for lunch today?" She turned her flawless face his way as Greg pulled away from the curb.

"Of course. I wouldn't miss it for the world." Their colleges were only a short train ride away and, honestly, Greg loved leaving the prestigious and often uppity students behind to visit the more friendly students at Ava's campus. Plus, more than likely, Ava had packed him a lunch in addition to her own.

Not that it was needed. Greg had a decent job for an undergrad and could afford to buy lunch every day if he wanted. Ava came from a much different background and often didn't grasp the depth of his money surplus. Not that he was rich. It was just that he definitely had more money than he needed for his low profile lifestyle.

When they had first started dating, Ava had been hesitant to suggest dinner ideas. Growing up in a lower income family, money was always close to her mind. Their first date had been at a chain restaurant where two people could eat for under thirty dollars. Over the past few months, he had taken her to some nicer places, and she finally seemed comfortable enough to suggest new places she wanted to try. Greg hoped she would continue to grow more comfortable and to trust him more.

Greg merged onto the highway, glancing over to the passenger seat briefly. Ava had the visor down and was applying mascara to her eye lashes. She made no indication that she saw his glance, as she was focused instead on trying to get her makeup just right. With a blink, she capped her mascara and slid it back into the makeup bag on her lap. Flashing him a quick smile, she leaned down to return the makeup bag to her over-flowing backpack.

Ava tried to be organized, she really did, but oftentimes her over-whelmingly busy lifestyle just didn't allow it. With two jobs and a household to run, organizing her room—much less her backpack—simply took the back burner.

Greg turned his eyes back to the highway in front of him that was practically a parking lot. If they didn't leave right at seven, they often sat in traffic for so long that it made Ava late for her first class. Luckily, they only had to be on the highway for about two miles before they took the exit for Ava's centrally located university.

"So, I've been thinking about dinner tonight?"

Greg smiled at Ava's way of bringing up a topic. She was far from demanding and often would pose her desires as questions instead of statements.

"Yes, Babe?"

"Well, what if we tried that fondue place? I've heard they're good and I have a coupon . . . "

"Sure, Babe, whatever you want." Greg smiled to himself once more. Ava was a coupon guru even though he often assured her they were unneeded. He could afford any meal she wanted. Ava leaned over and gave him a peck on the cheek. "Thanks, you're the best."

Greg felt his heart skip a beat. He had never felt as loved by anyone as he did by Ava. She was so sweet and always thankful no matter what he did. Granted, they had only been dating for a few months, and the glow was sure to fade, but he hoped it never did. Ava was the most beautiful girl Greg had ever met. And somehow, he had been lucky enough that she had chosen him, an average, not fat but soft built sort of guy, to be her man.

Finally, Greg inched the car off of the highway and onto the exit for Ava's university. He knew she was checking her watch in the passenger seat.

"You'll be fine, Babe, we're almost there."

"I know but, if I miss attendance again, I drop a letter grade." Ava was always so concerned about being on time.

Greg just shook his head and found himself smiling once again. It seemed as if he had never been happier in his twenty years of life on this earth. And he prayed the feeling wouldn't fade.

3

PRESENT

"Thank you for coming to show your support." The aged Mrs. Miller took Greg's hand and smiled at him. Her hands were thin and papery. Losing a daughter had made her old beyond her years. He could still see traces of her missing daughter in her regal features. Ava's face had the same high cheekbones and thin nose.

"Of course. You know I cared for Ava." Greg tried to step forward to allow the next person in line to give their condolences but Mrs. Miller held firm to Greg's hand.

She leaned closer as if to tell him a secret.

"She never stopped loving you, you know."

Greg felt his heart go pitter-patter in response but quickly tamped down the feeling. It was no use getting his hopes up. He opened his mouth to respond but Mrs. Miller had already released his hand and had moved on to the next attendee.

All in all, there had been maybe fifty people at Ava's funeral. For such a vivacious and friendly girl, it was almost an insult to see such a small crowd. In fact, Greg had been sure she had, at one point, been friends with upwards of two hundred people. Every day she would come home from work or school with a new tale, involving a new friend, with whom she now had plans to do something later.

It had been hard sharing Ava with her multitude of friends, but Greg had come to accept it as the small price he had to pay for her to be his girlfriend. As he headed for the door of the church, he passed a full-length mirror and barely recognized himself in the reflection.

When Greg met Ava, he had been a shy, mousy, high-school boy with ambitions higher than his five-foot-ten build. Luckily, he had continued to grow in his college years and he now stood at six-feet-tall. He'd also lost the last of the baby fat that had seemed to have a death grip on his face. The hard planes of his chin now separated him from the legion of boys. His shoulders also filled out, as he had grown taller, and his body composition had shifted to more muscle after attending the police academy. His hair was still the same mousy brown it had always been, but he had shifted away from the juvenile spiked look that had been all the rage while he was in school, and now styled it much more professionally.

These days, he barely had time to look in a mirror or go to the gym. His job often required him to work long shifts and sleeping through the night was an absolute luxury. With a sigh, he turned from the mirror and continued his path through the double doors leading to the parking lot.

Walking alongside his red truck, Greg's memory flashed back to his black SUV. How he missed that car. But a truck was now more practical for his bachelor lifestyle. He could cart around furniture for any damsel in distress who was in need. Although, as he grew older, the damsels in distress seemed to be fewer and farther in-between.

Jumping into his truck, Greg placed the keys in the ignition, trying to think of where he should stop and pick up dinner. As a long-time confirmed bachelor, he had quickly grown tired of cooking for one.

With a sigh, Greg realized he didn't really want to stop on his way home. Scrambled eggs, it was. As he started the car and backed out of his parking space, he began to wonder what had become of Ava's file. The Department had recently started going digital, but a cold case like Ava's would be set aside and put on a "time available" basis—which, in the Police Department, meant never.

Greg tried to stop his mind, as it continued down that dangerous path, but he found it was already too late to reel his imagination back. He wondered if anyone would miss Ava's file. Maybe he could borrow it for a while. He mentally smacked himself as he turned onto the main road and headed towards the center of town where his apartment complex was. He wasn't a detective, he was a traffic cop, and it was time to let Ava go. But he couldn't.

GREG AWOKE the next morning from a series of dreams featuring Ava, as he remembered her, but not *where* he remembered her. The last dream before he had awakened was of the two of them having a picnic in the Italian countryside. That was something he had always wanted to do with her.

Stepping out of his bedroom and heading into the kitchen, Greg made a pit stop by the fridge to pull out a gallon of orange juice, which he proceeded to bring to his lips and take a giant gulp. Breakfast complete. With a glance at his watch, Greg winced. He was expected to be in the office in fifteen minutes.

Bypassing the shower, Greg slid on his uniform and grabbed a bottle of water as he ran out the door and down the stairs to his truck. As soon as he got there, he realized he had forgotten his work laptop and he had to run right back up the stairs. At least he was getting his exercise in for the day.

Although Greg only lived a short ten-minute drive from the station, traffic was as unforgiving as it always was this time of the morning. In fact, it had become so bad recently that he was beginning to miss the night shift.

Most cops had to work the night shift their first few years on the job. Greg had, unfortunately, done so himself for almost four. And he knew the only reason he was even currently on day shift was because of his partner. Ione was a good cop, and he was very insistent that he would only move shifts if his partner, Greg, could come with him. The Dayshift Captain, Carl, had wanted Ione so badly that he had said yes to both transfers. And here Greg was, about to be late for the third, or maybe the fourth time, this month.

Luckily, he wasn't the only one trying to sneak in five minutes late. In fact, there were so many that it might as well have been as if they were all on time. Greg slid into his desk at 9:10 without glancing at his partner at the desk right next to him.

"You're late."

"Thanks, Sherlock." Greg grimaced. His partner didn't even look up from his computer. Ione Richard was a big bear of a man but with a heart of pure gold. So pure, Greg couldn't believe the guy was even capable of being a cop. Unlike Greg, Ione had no goals of becoming a detective. He'd rather be the cop to go visit kids' schools on a weekly basis.

"Kind of hard to get work done when you're not here." Ione was staring at his computer screen and diligently clicking his mouse but Greg knew better.

"Kind of hard to get work done when you're checking out the new secretary's Facebook." Ione's face broke into a smile.

"Well, now that you're here finally, I can get to work." Ione was of Native American descent, which showed through his raven black hair and a face devoid of facial hair even at the age of thirty-one. Women would fall at his feet when he smiled. Greg couldn't help but be slightly jealous sometimes.

Greg rolled his eyes. They were traffic cops and spent most of their time on the streets. In fact, the only thing they did in the office was file reports, and Ione definitely didn't need him to do that.

The day passed in its usual mundane blur—an hour or so of reports followed by six hours sitting in a car issuing traffic and jaywalking tickets—bookended by another hour sitting in the office filling out reports. As the day was coming to a close, Greg was shutting down his computer and gathering his jacket when a file was thrown on his desk by Carl, his boss.

"Do me a favor and file this on your way out." Greg glared down at the file on his desk. What did Carl think he was, a secretary? Carl knew what he was thinking.

"Marie already left, it's on your way out, please just do it." He rolled his eyes and left Greg's desk.

Greg grabbed the file, stood up, and headed for the door. Right outside the door to the main precinct was a desk for intake that had a great view out of the bulletproof front windows. A young woman sat at the desk, not even glancing up from her book as Greg entered. Instead of clocking out at the machine right above the intake desk, Greg turned and headed down the stairs to the Records Department. Sliding his badge through the card reader to unlock the door, he called out as he entered.

"Hello?" His greeting was not returned. The row of desks directly inside of the door was empty. It seemed the file clerks had already left for the day.

Greg checked the name on the file and headed towards the row of filing cabinets with the corresponding letter. As he did, he passed the letter M. Without thinking, he stopped right in front of the filing cabinet labeled "MIL."

Greg knew he shouldn't. After all, he had already been reprimanded for this once before, almost four years ago. But he couldn't help himself. He slid open the drawer and began rifling through files that contained the last name of Miller. It didn't take long, seeing as Ava was at the beginning of the alphabet.

With a look over his shoulder, just to be cautious, Greg slid the file from its spot and placed it under his arm. He quickly closed the filing cabinet and continued down the aisle to the cabinet where he needed to put the file that Carl had given him. The job was finished in a few seconds, and he headed up the stairs.

It took Greg's entire will power not to immediately open Ava's file and begin devouring its contents. He made himself wait until he safely drove home and parked his truck outside his apartment complex in his assigned spot. He didn't quite make it to his apartment, however. Instead, he opened the file across the steering wheel and began to read.

It was all there. Just as he remembered it. And it made him just as sure as ever that Ava was still alive. He had fully intended to head into his apartment and order wings for delivery but, instead, he found himself putting his keys back into the ignition and driving to a location he had been to many times a few years before. It was a restaurant. Specifically, the restaurant where Kyle Lund, Ava's boyfriend at the time of her disappearance, worked.

Greg sat there for almost an hour in his truck, willing himself to turn around and go back home. He had promised Carl he wouldn't do this again but his promise quickly flew out the window as six-foot-three Kyle passed Greg's window. He removed his keys from the ignition and stepped out of the car.

Greg had watched the videos of the initial interrogation of Ava's then boyfriend. Although Kyle had been cleared of all charges, Greg had never been sure of it. Four years ago, he'd been dying for a chance to talk to the man off the record, and it looked like he might as well do it now.

4

SEPTEMBER 15, 2010

It was nearly three in the morning when something roused Greg from his sleep. It took a moment for him to open and close his eyes and adjust to the look of the room. Intending to roll over and go back to sleep, he pulled the comforter closer to his neck. Immediately, he realized he had full control of the comforter. That was unusual as Ava usually completely burritoed herself into one end of it. Greg stretched his hand over to her side of the bed only to find that it was empty, and cold.

Greg felt overcome with worry. It wasn't like Ava to leave the bed in the middle of the night. He swung his feet over the side and headed across the room, poking his head in the bathroom. The lights were off.

"Ava?" Greg whispered as he flicked on the lights. The bathroom was empty.

Greg went to the bedroom door, turned the knob silently, and slipped into the dark hall. He could see blue light coming from around the corner. The TV was on. He could hear the muted voices of actors in what was probably a late-night sitcom.

"Ava?" Greg said again, louder this time, as he turned the corner. Then he immediately saw his girlfriend's slim body, sleeping in a sitting position on the couch, halfway covered by her favorite blanket. He walked over and touched her shoulder. Ava jolted awake. She seemed confused for a minute, then looked at her surroundings until her eyes made contact with Greg's.

"Hi," she said softly. Greg sank to a sitting position on the couch next to her. "Hey Babe, what are you doing out here?" She touched her chest and winced. "Heartburn. It's easier to sleep sitting up on the couch." Greg nodded and began to rub her back gently.

"Maybe we need to watch the spicy food."

"I don't know, Greg. I've been watching the spicy food before bed for the last month. This heartburn seems unrelated." She shook her head and closed her eyes.

"Maybe you should go see a doctor." Greg knew it was a long shot. His girlfriend absolutely hated visiting doctors. She would only go if it was an absolute dire situation and he doubted that this qualified.

"Maybe." Greg turned towards the TV, grabbing the second blanket they kept on the couch and placing it on his lap.

"No, Greg, it's okay, you go to bed. I'm fine here, really." Greg looked at Ava. Her eyes were heavy with sleep but she seemed genuine about wanting him to return to bed.

"All right, if you're sure." He got up from the couch, noticing that Ava's phone was plugged into the extension cord that ran behind the couch. Greg knew the phone was her alarm for the morning. Meaning she would be spending the rest of the night out there. Greg didn't like it but he knew better than to argue with his girlfriend once she made a decision.

"I am." Ava yawned and closed her eyes once again.

Greg turned the corner and walked back down the hall to his room. His apartment was small, only a one-bedroom, but he didn't mind. This apartment was only a temporary solution. He hoped to buy a house and have Ava move in with him by the end of the year.

Ava had originally been cautious at the prospect of them moving in together, even though they had been dating for just over a year. Greg had understood and, instead of pushing the issue, he agreed that they would live separately for the time being. However, Ava lived in a shared home with two roommates and ended up in his apartment more nights than not. They did occasionally spend the night at her place, but those times were becoming fewer and fewer. Greg took this as a sign that it was about time to bring up cohabitating once again.

As he slid back underneath his comforter, Greg could practically feel the emptiness radiating from Ava's side of the bed. He tossed and turned a few times before he finally found a comfortable position. He really hoped this Ava sleeping on the couch thing didn't last too long. As he drifted off to sleep, he couldn't help but hope that he would dream of Ava.

5

PRESENT

"Kyle!" Greg shouted as he jogged up to the other man.

The years hadn't been nearly as kind to Kyle as they had been to Greg. Kyle looked very thin, and worn. His skin was papery and it barely seemed to stretch over his bones. Greg wondered briefly if perhaps Kyle had gotten into drugs. Kyle looked up at the sound of his name, an annoyed look immediately stealing over his features.

"Leave me alone, Sanders."

Greg and Kyle had been at odds after the multitude of interviews Kyle had to go through regarding his girlfriend's disappearance. Greg had enflamed the situation by pushing for more and more interviews. Back then, he had been so sure that Kyle had killed Ava that he couldn't even see straight. As time had passed, he had become less sure, but that hadn't made Kyle like him any more.

"Kyle, I just want you to tell me the events one more time," Greg pleaded.

"She's dead." There was no emotion in Kyle's voice.

"You know as well as I do she may not be." Kyle turned away and Greg had to jog to keep up with the tall man's strides.

"No, I don't. And you need to let her go, too." Kyle stopped alongside his blue Toyota. He had been driving the same car the past seven years. Ever since he had started dating Ava.

"I need to bring her body home. For her mother."

"And you can do so without me."

"Just run over the events one more time. And I'll never bother you again." Greg knew he shouldn't bother to promise such things but he really wanted to get the man to talk. Off the record. He knew it was a long shot but he hoped he would slip up and say something new. Kyle sighed and ran a hand through his dark hair.

"Promise this will be it? You'll let her rest in peace?" Greg nodded. Kyle let out a breath and leaned his back against his car, sinking a couple of inches.

"It was a nice night. May eleventh. We were supposed to meet another couple for dinner." Kyle pinched his eyes closed. It was obvious he was reliving the night.

"We were meeting Steven and Cara. They were more my friends than Ava's, but she never seemed to mind that. In fact, she got on great with Cara, and she's not the easiest to get along with." Kyle suddenly stood up straight and looked around, as if remembering where he was. When his eyes connected with Greg's, he turned his back to the restaurant and leaned in closer to Greg.

"We decided to walk there, because it was such a nice night. We left my apartment at seven in the evening. About halfway there, we were along the busiest road on the route when I realized I forgot something for the project Steven and I were working on. I told Ava I needed to go back." Kyle took another deep breath and shut his eyes. It was odd for Greg to see a man his age fighting tears. But it was clear this night in question was full of regret for Kyle.

"She didn't want to go back. She was wearing heels and insisted we were already halfway there. I didn't want to disappoint Steven, so I told her I had to." A sad smile took over Kyle's face.

"She made a joke and said that she would stand there like a prostitute until I got back. I laughed and headed back the direction we had come. I crossed the street and looked back over my shoulder. She was just standing there, in this cute blue and white striped dress and black heels. She saw me looking and gave a little wave. I couldn't be sure, but I'm pretty sure she smiled. Then I turned the corner and went back to my apartment. I grabbed the bag I had forgotten. When I got back to where I had left Ava, there was no one there. She was gone." Kyle pinched the bridge of his nose.

"Going home had only taken me about ten minutes. I thought maybe she had continued on without me, or gone somewhere to sit, but I continued on our path to the Mexican restaurant and no one I passed and no one at the restaurant had seen her. It was like she simply vanished into thin air."

"Then you decided to call the police," Greg finished for him. Greg had the transcripts for this exact story in his truck and had spent the past two months memorizing every bit. Five years later and Kyle's story hadn't changed one word. Kyle nodded.

"And you know what happened next. We done?"

Greg wanted to press for more information but he had a feeling he would get the same responses he had seen on the police interview tapes. He was also worried he would get an adverse reaction from Kyle. And the last thing he needed was someone calling and alerting his boss that he had put himself back on this case.

"Thanks Kyle."

"You're not welcome," the tall man retorted as he folded his over-six-foot frame into his car. Kyle didn't even wait for Greg to move before he started the car and stomped on the accelerator, speeding out of the parking lot.

Greg sighed and returned to his truck and the file. The cops, after hearing the same story, had headed straight to Kyle's apartment building. Greg knew it was a long shot but figured he would head there and see if there was anyone left that remembered Ava.

Checking his watch, he realized it was almost seven in the evening. He would have to wait until tomorrow. Most apartment buildings in the area only kept skeleton crew on after five. He needed to go during the day if he wanted to interview the administration employees. If they even wanted to talk to him in the first place. Greg knew all of this could possibly be a total crapshoot. After all, this was a five-year cold case. Most people barely remembered the story of the disappearance of Ava Miller, much less the woman herself. He shook his head. He wasn't going to let himself get talked out of it that easily.

As he started his car and headed to the takeout wings place, where he intended to pick up his dinner, Greg wondered just what had gone so wrong. He had loved Ava so much. She had been so beautiful, and she had so many friends, but she'd always been so sad, depressed almost. Greg had always pressed her to express her feelings to him, but it had seemed that something had always been stopping her. He just wished he knew what.

Even now, Greg had to wonder if some passerby had picked up Ava on the street. Had she fought? Or had she simply resigned to her fate? Ava had fought so hard for everything she'd had in life. She deserved the world. But when Greg had tried to give it to her, she'd practically run away. With a sigh, Greg turned his attention back to the current task of driving.

"Ava, where are you?" he asked the universe. But the universe either didn't know, or was willing to keep her secrets.

6

OCTOBER 20, 2010

reg slid the gold key into the lock of his front door and turned it. Surprisingly, it lacked the usual resistance. The door was unlocked. He turned the knob and opened the door slowly.

"Ava?"

There was a sniffle and a muffled, "Here."

Greg felt his shoulders immediately relax as he opened the door all the way. Ava was sitting on the couch, a tissue pressed to her face. He quickly set down the groceries he was carrying and hurried over to the couch next to his girlfriend. He placed his hand under her chin and lifted her face so that her eyes met his. Her eyes were red and stained with tears.

"What's wrong, Babe?" Ava sniffled again and snuggled into Greg's shoulder. "I tried to apply for financial aid for school again."

Greg knew immediately that these tears meant she was once again denied. Ava had applied for financial aid for the fall term, only to be turned away and told to try again for the spring. Apparently, the spring was a no as well. He placed a protective arm around his girlfriend and brought the box of tissues closer with his other hand.

"Don't worry. I'll help you, Babe." Greg would say or do anything to keep from having to see his girlfriend like this.

"No, it's fine. I'll just get another job." Ava blew her nose one final time and stood up to walk across the room and throw the wad of tissues in the trash. Greg didn't like hearing this. His poor girlfriend already worked two jobs and he had no idea where she would fit in a third.

"Let me help you, please. I can afford it." Greg stood up and walked behind Ava, placing his arms around her waist.

"No, I have to do this on my own. You know that." Ava leaned back to rest her back against his chest.

"I know. But that doesn't change the fact that I wish you would let me help. How are you even going to work a third job and go to school?" Ava shook her head. "I'm not sure, but I'll find a way. You know me."

Greg suddenly had an idea and spun Ava around to face him. His action was so abrupt he almost knocked Ava off her feet and had to tighten his grip so she didn't topple over. Ava seemed unfazed. In fact, she seemed to enjoy the sudden dance-like movement and she giggled.

"Well, how about this? You move in here with me and what if you traded your lowest paying job for a better one?" Ava's main job as a server at a chain restaurant paid pretty well. In fact, she often brought home a couple hundred dollars a night on the weekends. However, her other job as a cashier at a pet store, barely paid minimum wage. Ava scrunched her nose up in a way that Greg knew she was thinking. After a moment of silence, she broke into a grin.

"I guess that's a decent idea. The restaurant is flexible, so, I guess I could get an office job or something."

"That sounds like a great idea, Babe. Let me know if you need any references. And you can move your stuff in here whenever." Greg smiled wickedly.

"All my stuff is pretty much already here." Ava squealed and ran into the bedroom, jumping over the bed.

Greg laughed and chased after her, jumping up only to land on the bed. He looked over and saw Ava crouched on the floor by his side of the bed. With another evil grin, he feigned a yawn and rolled over to the edge of the bed as if he were going to land on top of her. Ava laughed and put up her hands to stop him.

"You're gonna fall. I can't hold you up," she threatened. This only made Greg's smile widen.

"Oh, really?" he challenged. He rolled just slightly, putting a small amount of his weight in Ava's hands.

"Yes, really! If you roll any more, you're gonna hit the ground!"

Greg put more weight on Ava, only for her arms to start to give out. Greg was prepared, however, and caught himself on his hands as he "fell" on top of Ava. This only made her collapse into a fit of laughter. Greg looked down at his girlfriend from his position above her, glad to see no trace of tears remained on her face. The moment was interrupted by the grumbling of Ava's stomach. They both laughed in unison.

"Guess I should start dinner." Greg pushed himself up into a sitting position, brushing his hands to try and get rid of the annoying carpet imprint.

"You're going to cook?" Ava sat up and eyed Greg incredulously. He nodded. "You bet. You're always cooking around here. It's about time I gave it a go." Greg had looked up a recipe for a mushroom pasta online. Finding one that he figured was easy enough, he had downloaded it and headed to the store. Now he only hoped he could deliver. Ava still seemed suspicious.

"All right. I'm going to watch TV while you cook, then." Greg feigned hurt. "What? You don't want to watch me cook?" His smile leaked through his demeanor, even as he tried to stop it.

"Watch a train wreck? No, thanks. I'll have the pizza menu ready, though."

"Oh, ye of little faith." Greg stood and headed for the kitchen.

"Mushroom or pepperoni pizza?" Ava called after him.

"Both!" Greg shouted back. Although he was sure they wouldn't need it. How hard could cooking be?

7

PRESENT

Greg knew better, he really did. But the next day he did it anyway. He called in to take a personal day and, instead of working from home like he told Ione he would do, he abandoned his work laptop and headed to the apartment complex listed in Ava's file.

On the drive over, he could hear his phone vibrating repeatedly. Probably Ione giving him shit for not coming in. As soon as he pulled into the parking lot right outside of the complex, he checked his phone for texts, only to confirm his suspicions.

Ione: "Why didn't you tell me you were going to take a personal day? At least I could've called out, too."

Ione: "TRAITOR!!!"

Ione: "Carl is pretty pissed. This is your second personal day this month."

Ione: "I'm going to touch all the stuff on your desk and borrow everything you never let me borrow. In fact, I might break some stuff."

Ione: "Carl is having me go out with a newbie. Seriously can't believe you subjected me to this."

Ione: "YOU OWE ME!"

Greg rolled his eyes. For a guy, Ione was certainly dramatic. And he really hoped Ione didn't break his stapler again. It was the main reason he wasn't allowed to borrow Greg's things. Oh well, if Ione broke it, Greg would just perpetually ask to use his, which would annoy Ione to no end.

Without replying to the texts, Greg pulled the information pamphlet regarding the complex from the file and began to look it over as he walked towards the gates.

The apartment complex was large, with portions of duplexes as well as traditional high rises. The pamphlet boasted two pools, a gym, and even a tennis court. The smiling woman on the back page said he could come for a tour any time. Greg glanced up from the pamphlet in his hands to the wide gates in front of him. It was obvious the pamphlet had been printed years before, as the color of the buildings was no longer a vibrant blue, and the gates were no longer colored at all. There were remnants of paint here and there but, for the most part, the iron had rusted.

"Hey!"

Greg spun around to see a tall black man approaching him from a small building that was probably a guard hut on his right. He must be on duty to man the gates.

"Can I help you, sir?" The black man stopped about six feet from where Greg was standing, obviously afraid too get to close. Greg understood. There were real crazies in this world. Greg pulled out his badge.

"I'm officer Sanders. Can I talk to you for a minute?" The black man looked surprised, and maybe slightly fearful for a moment, before he motioned back to his guard hut.

"Sure, but I'm on duty."

"No problem. Lead the way." Greg motioned that he would follow the man back to the hut. Once they were inside, the man pulled out a chair for Greg before sitting in his own chair which faced two computer monitors as well as a television screen. The TV was muted but it was playing a popular comedy that Greg had seen before but couldn't name. There were multiple keyboards and a keypad, which Greg assumed controlled the gate.

"How can I help you?" The black man seemed a little more comfortable now that he had returned to his realm, but Greg could tell he was still nervous.

"How about we start with your name." Greg knew cops made most people nervous, especially minorities. This man looked to be about twenty-five to thirty-years-old. If he had been here five years ago, he would have probably just been new to the job.

"I'm Terrence Green. Can I ask what this is about before we go any further?" Greg smiled, trying to reassure the man.

"Of course. I'm investigating the disappearance of a resident that occurred about five years ago." Terrence visibly relaxed.

"I started working here about three years ago." Greg nodded.

"I figured. But I think maybe you can still help me. Do you know anyone who was working here around that time?"

Terrence thought for a moment, opening his mouth to answer just as a car pulled into the gate. Greg pushed his chair back to allow Terrence to be able to speak to the driver through the window.

Terrence asked for the woman's ID, which she happily handed over, and then he took it to his computer where he began to type in a name. He compared the ID with something on file, printed a ticket, and handed both back to the woman as he pressed the button to open the gate. When he was finished he turned back to Greg. "You should check with Travis. He's been here the longest, as far as I know." Greg added the name to the notes section of his phone.

"Can you tell me a little about the process of checking people in here, like what you just did." Greg motioned to the window and the empty spot on the pavement that the woman's car had previously occupied.

"Sure. When someone comes through who is a resident, they have a remote device for the gate and it opens when they push the button. Just like a garage door that you open from your car. However, when someone is a guest, I have to see their ID and look up the person they are going to go see." Terrence turned back to the computer and pulled up the screen where he had previously checked the woman's ID.

"Each resident here has a guest list of people who visit them frequently. If the person is on there, I just print the ticket and send them on their way. However, if they aren't on the list, or they're a one-time visitor like pizza delivery, I have to call the resident and get verbal permission to send them up."

"Seems pretty intensive." Terrence nodded.

"It is. Personally, I don't understand it. I've never had anyone sketchy try to come in. But I know a lot of wealthy people live here and I suppose some of them don't want visitors or to be bothered in general." Greg stood up.

"Thanks, Terrence. Any idea where I can find Travis?"

"Well, he does a little of everything around here. He's a gate guard, like me, most week days during the day. But he picks up any and all overtime, so, you can find him working valet, front desk, and even security." This information was not useful to Greg.

"Any idea where he is today?" The young man shook his head.

"No, but the front desk will know." Greg smiled.

"Thanks, Terrence. Now, do I need one of those papers to get in?" Greg motioned to the machine he had seen print the ticket.

"Nah, your badge is all you need. I'll open the gate for you, though." Terrence smiled at Greg and reached over to push the button for the gate.

Greg said thank you one more time as he stepped back outside and began to walk through the gate. He took in the sight of the complex in front of him, mentally dialing the clock back seven years. He wondered just what had drawn Ava to this place and the picture in his mind did nothing to answer his questions. With a huff, he turned to his right and headed into the nearest high rise, hoping the front desk was inside.

Greg stepped into a wide lobby furnished with white leather couches and wooden accent tables. The ceilings were at least two stories high. And off to the side was a large front desk outfitted with multiple computer screens. Behind the desk was a middle-aged woman who obviously had her hair done in the '80s and hadn't bothered to update it since. Greg stepped forward and showed her his badge.

"I'm looking for Travis. Is he nearby?" The woman didn't have quite the same reaction as Terrence. Instead, she just looked bored.

"What do you need him for?" She continued to type something on one of the keyboards that occupied the desk in front of her.

"Just a few questions. Can you call him and ask him to come here, please?"

"No need. There he is. Right outside."

Greg spun around to see a middle-aged black man pulling up in a golf cart. He was well groomed and wearing what looked to be an expensive suit. He must be some sort of manager. Greg stepped away from the desk without bothering to say goodbye to the woman who was manning it. As he stepped back through the automatic sliding doors, he called out to Travis.

"I'm Travis. How can I help you, sir?" It was the most polite greeting Greg had heard all day and it seemed much more appropriate for this caliber of a complex. He pulled out his badge once again.

"Greg Sanders. I have a few questions for you if you have a minute." Travis surprised him by smiling.

"Sure, officer, shall we go back inside?" Travis pointed at the doors Greg had just emerged from. Greg nodded and followed Travis back in. Travis took a seat on one of the plush white couches and Greg did the same.

"So, what can I do for you?" Greg pulled out a picture of Ava from five years ago when she disappeared.

"I heard you've been here for quite a few years and I was wondering if you remember her." Travis smiled immediately at the sight of the photo.

"Yes. Ms. Ava Miller. Of course I remember her." Greg hoped this was the break he had been waiting for.

"Can you tell me about how you met?"

"Of course. I was manning the gate one day and here comes this girl. She pulls up and gets out her ID just like everyone else who comes through. But it was weird. She was really nice to me." Greg looked at Travis incredulously.

"She was *nice* to you?" Travis nodded.

"In this sort of complex, pretty much everyone who comes through here is either a prissy princess, annoyed she has to stop at the gate, or some rude asshole who can't believe you don't recognize him even though he's only been here once before." Travis took a deep breath.

"Ms. Ava was different. She asked permission. She didn't demand it. And when Mr. Lund didn't answer the phone right away, she waited patiently instead of chewing me out. Then one day, to my surprise, she calls me by name. I asked how she knew my name and she tells me she got it from the passes I'd been giving her." Seeing the confusion in Greg's eyes, Travis elaborated.

"Back then, they were handwritten passes and we had to write our names on a corner. She'd actually taken the time to read it. I'd never had anyone do that before." Travis paused for a moment and smiled.

"And that was just the beginning. She would always bring me cookies and candy, and she always bought me a Christmas gift. She was the sweetest girl I know." As he said that, his smile disappeared, and Greg could sense something was wrong.

"But?" Greg prodded.

"Mr. Lund, He treated her like trash." This was news to Greg. He had always assumed everything had been great between Kyle and Ava.

"How so?" Travis shook his head.

"I don't think she was the only girl he was seeing. I mean, everyone has to check in at the gate if they don't have a key fob. I sent many girls who weren't Ms. Miller up to that apartment on various occasions."

"Could they have been Ava's friends?" Greg remembered the multitude of girlfriends who had swarmed around Ava ever since high school. Travis looked even more distressed.

"No. Ms. Ava went on work trips. And she often told me about them. The girls, they only came when she was out of town." Greg could feel the pang in his heart at the thought of someone hurting Ava.

"Did you tell her?" Travis shook his head.

"I tried. I really did. I dropped hints all the time. But . . . I . . . I just couldn't."

"What kind of hints?"

"I told her one day that a girl had come to see Mr. Lund earlier that day and I asked if it was one of her friends." Travis took a deep breath.

"She looked crestfallen. She asked who it was. I didn't know the name. And, even if I did, we sign a confidentiality agreement. I wouldn't be able to give it to her."

"When was this?" Greg had pulled out his phone and was making notes.

"About three weeks before she disappeared." Greg was taken aback.

"Did you tell the cops about all of this?" Travis shook his head.

"I tried. I even went to the police station to tell them to stop looking. But they wouldn't listen to me. Probably, because I'm black, they assumed I was lying."

"Wait. Back up. What do you mean, stop looking for her?" Travis shrugged. "The day she disappeared, I was on security rounds. I was walking around the building and I saw her standing across the street." Travis motioned to the north side of the building. Greg was having trouble picturing it.

"Can you show me?"

"Of course." Travis stood up and walked out of a door on the east side of the lobby. There was a second door right in front of that one and, when that one was opened, they found themselves in front of a pool. Travis turned to his left and walked around the pool through an area of duplex-type homes until he reached the back gate. Using his key, he opened the gate and motioned for Greg to step out. They were on some sort of side street but, about half a block to the left, was a busy four lane road on which traffic was zooming by.

"I was walking out here. Doing a perimeter check. Making sure all the gates worked and that no one unsavory was hanging around." Travis and Greg walked until they came to the corner of the busy road. Travis pointed to an area across the street, just before a bridge that crossed the main highway.

"That's where I saw her. Right there. She was standing and leaning on the wall."

"You weren't alarmed by that?" Greg stared at the spot Travis had pointed to and willed it to tell him what had happened to Ava.

"Nah, Mr. Lund and Ms. Miller were always walking places. I think they both had a small fear of driving. If you walk along this street, you come to a shopping mall with plenty of restaurants as well as some stand-alone restaurants outside the mall."

"So tell me, again, why you thought they should stop looking." Greg was still confused.

"Well, Ms. Ava was standing there, and a large cab with some men pulled up. There was a man sitting in the front seat and he leaned out to talk to her. She spoke back. She was smiling. I just can't imagine, if she didn't know them, why she would be smiling. They spoke for a few more moments. Then they opened the back door of the cab and she climbed in."

"She went willingly? Are you sure they didn't pull her in?"

"Yeah, she was smiling the whole time. And I don't think Ms. Ava would smile if she didn't want to do something." Travis turned and began walking back towards the gate. Greg knew it was a long shot but he had to try.

"Do you remember anything about the cab? A number? A brand?" Travis laughed.

"Man, it's been five years. Of course I don't remember the cab." Greg sighed. "You should've told the cops."

"I'm telling you, man, I did," Travis said defensively.

"They didn't want to hear it. Besides, I would've tried harder but Ava didn't seem to be in distress, so, when they dismissed me, I didn't push." Greg ran a hand through his hair and they walked back around the pool and stepped back into the lobby.

"Well, thanks, Travis. Here's my card if you think of anything else."

"Well, there is one thing you should know." Greg's ears perked up.

"When I saw her get in the cab, they were in the right turn lane." Greg wrinkled his brow.

"What does that have to do with anything?" Travis shrugged.

"I can't be sure, but a cab full of men in that right turn lane usually only means one thing. They were headed to a strip club. There's a whole lot of them right around that corner and, honestly, not much else."

This confused Greg even more. Ava definitely wasn't the type to go with a bunch of random men in a cab, much less if they were headed to a strip club. But he thanked Travis none the less and then headed back outside towards his car.

As the iron gates slid shut with a clank behind him, Greg couldn't help but feel skeptical of Travis's recollection. He knew this classified him with the other officers who had turned Travis away five years before but he couldn't help it.

Because, if Travis was telling the truth, he had just created more questions than he answered.

8

NOVEMBER 10, 2010

The shrill ring of Greg's alarm woke him from a deep slumber. He tried to reach over as quickly as possible to silence it before it woke Ava. After he shut it off, he looked over to find Ava's side of the bed empty once again. With a sigh, he rose and began to dress.

Greg headed into the bathroom, flicking on the light to observe his mop of hair in the mirror. He really needed to get it cut but work had been busier than usual these days. He felt bad leaving for work early and then also staying late, but he didn't have much choice in the matter.

After he finished brushing his teeth and attempting to tame his mane, Greg headed into the living room to be greeted by the familiar sight of Ava asleep on the couch in a sitting position.

Ava hadn't slept in the bed for months. At first, she would start out there, then end up on the couch. But recently, she'd given up trying, claiming that her heartburn began the moment she laid down. Greg urged her several times to see a doctor, and Ava said she had, but nothing seemed to be improving.

Greg walked into the kitchen towards the fridge where a lunch packed by Ava would be waiting. As he passed the island, he noticed an open, and almost empty, bottle of red wine sitting by the sink.

With a sigh, he dumped what remained down the sink and tossed the bottle quietly in the trash. Ava had begun to drink lately. Not to the point of being an alcoholic, but to where it worried Greg. She would open bottles of wine two or three nights a week and almost finish the bottle every time. He couldn't imagine that it was good for her heartburn, much less her liver.

Grabbing his lunch from the fridge and a banana from the counter, Greg headed back to the living room to give his girlfriend a kiss goodbye. He pulled her favorite blanket over her shoulders and placed a chaste kiss on her wine-stained lips. And, as he did so, he noticed Ava's jawline had become more pronounced. She must be losing weight. This only worried him more but Ava was so self-conscious right now and he knew, if he brought it up, it would only worry her. Greg looked at his watch one last time and headed out the door.

It was a Wednesday. Ava was supposed to go to class this morning and then work starting at two in the afternoon. Recently, Ava had taken to ditching classes, which also worried Greg, but she insisted the term was almost over and the teachers were mostly in review mode anyway. She also seemed to be working later which might explain why she seemed to be losing weight. In the past, she had rushed home at ten every night to see him. Now, it seemed as if she always came in sometime after Greg had gone to bed.

Greg was unsure about what to make of all this. Ava had explained to him that, by volunteering to stay late, she would make more money which he understood she needed right now. But he also didn't understand why she wouldn't just accept help from him. After all, he was making more money than he needed to pay his bills.

There was no reasoning with Ava, though. He would have to find someone to give her money in a way that she would think she had earned it. With that, a plan began to form in Greg's mind.

9

PRESENT

The next day, Greg walked into the office early, knowing there would be hell to pay if he was late after taking a personal day. Even though he was early, Ione was still there before him, sitting at his desk with his arms across his chest, watching Greg approach.

"Do you even go home, Ione?" Greg tossed his jacket over the back of his chair and sank down to begin the pile of paperwork that awaited him.

"Yeah, but I don't feel the need to spend whole days there like some people." Ione glared in his direction. Greg rolled his eyes.

"Why'd you take a personal day, anyway?" Ione began to click the pen in his hand over and over, knowing it would drive Greg crazy.

"It's personal. That's why they call it a personal day."

"Please tell me you weren't binge-watching Chicago PD."

"Ione, when have I ever watched Chicago PD?" Greg swiveled his chair to face his partner who was still clicking the pen relentlessly.

"On your last personal day." Ione tilted his head to the side in an accusatory manner.

"No, Ione. I think you're thinking of *your* last personal day." Greg rolled his eyes and turned back to his dinosaur of a computer.

"Oh, right." Ione's face broke into a smile.

"At least I had the decency to invite my partner." Greg huffed. He should've known this would be a problem.

"Next time, I will. This one was last minute, okay?"

"Sure. Last minute. Got it." Ione obviously didn't believe him but he stopped clicking his pen and turned back to his computer to resume his work.

As soon as Greg's computer had booted up, he opened the program they used to file traffic tickets. But before even imputing a single one, he opened the internet window and began researching more information on the strip clubs in the area. They were legal in the state and often funded their own security. In fact, he couldn't remember the last time he'd been called to one. He was so engrossed in his research that he didn't notice Ione had stopped his work and was looking over Greg's shoulder.

"So, when are we going to a strip club?" Greg jumped halfway out of his chair, startled.

"Uh, never, this was just research for a . . . a ticket," Greg stammered and quickly closed the window. He could feel the blush creeping up his neck.

"And what ticket would that be? I certainly don't remember any of our traffic stops involving strip club research." Ione rolled his chair back over to his desk.

"It was a special thing Carl wanted me to look into. One of the cars we pulled over was registered to one of these places." He hoped his partner wouldn't see right through his lie.

"Are you sure? Because I don't remember anything of the sort." Ione began to rifle through the stack of papers on his desk.

"By we, I meant the Department. Not you and I. I think he's trying to get back at me for yesterday." Greg clenched his teeth. Ione shrugged and turned back to his work.

"Oh, okay." Greg let out a breath of relief as he realized his partner was accepting the excuse. He knew he would have to tell Ione he was investigating Ava's disappearance again at some point, but he wasn't ready to do so just yet.

"THAT'LL BE TWENTY DOLLARS, PLEASE."

Greg pulled out his wallet and shelled out his third twenty of the evening to the young woman laced up in a corset. He had never been one for strip clubs and now this was his third one in a night.

The first two clubs had been a bust. No one remembered or even recognized Ava. Greg knew strippers came and went at jobs like a revolving door but he couldn't help but hope that there was one out there who would remember a beautiful female patron like Ava.

After Greg received his ticket from the young corseted woman, he stopped at the change booth to cash another twenty dollar bill for ones. It turned out that strippers didn't want to talk to him unless he was willing to shell out a few bucks. As the man counted out his change, Greg took a look around the room that was shrouded in darkness. All the strip clubs looked the same to him. They were all just rooms with no windows, outfitted with plush chairs and small tables barely big enough for drinks. This club was much busier than the other two he had visited, but he had no idea why. All the women looked the same to him. They were all young, with fake tits, wearing lingerie that barely fit.

Greg collected his change and headed to the bar. He wasn't usually a drinker, but he still had another strip club to go to after this, and he didn't think he could take it without a little alcohol to dull the edge.

"Hi. What can I get you?" The bartender was a beautiful blonde with legs that went on for days—which her outfit made sure to highlight.

"Gin and tonic, please." He pulled out yet another twenty dollar bill and placed it on the counter as the blonde began to make his drink. He also pulled out the photo of Ava and placed it on top of the cash. The woman was back with his drink within a few seconds. She reached for the twenty, pausing as she noticed the picture.

"Where did you get this?" She slowly reached for the picture, picking it up gently. Greg's ears perked up.

"Do you know her?" This could be the break he was waiting for. She nodded sadly as she looked at the picture.

"Yeah. Tyra. She worked here for a couple years. Last I heard, she moved to another state."

"Tyra?" Had Ava really changed her name? Had she really been a stripper? Greg had a hard time believing it.

"You're sure?" The woman did not like Greg second-guessing her and her demeanor quickly lost some of its warmth and friendliness.

"Yes, Tyra. She was blonde, though. Could've been a wig." She snatched up the twenty and turned to make change. Greg realized he had upset perhaps his one link to Ava.

"Listen, you can keep the change if you tell me more about this Tyra girl." Eager to earn a 300 percent tip, the bartender quickly turned back to Greg, a suspicious smile on her face.

"What and why do you need to know?"

"I'm looking for her."

"Why, she in trouble?"

"Nope, I just want to find her."

"Are you lying?"

"I swear, I'm not looking to bring her any trouble." This seemed to somewhat satisfy the bartender and she grabbed a towel to wipe down the counter as she leaned towards him and began to speak.

"Tyra worked here for about three years. That was two years ago. I only remember her because she was here for much longer than most of the other girls. And, unlike the other girls, she wasn't rude. She always asked nicely for everything and was never demanding. It was great."

"Do you remember when she got hired?" Greg wanted to pull out his phone to make notes but he knew the bartender would be suspicious and wouldn't continue to be honest with him. She gave him an incredulous look.

"Now, I don't pay that much attention. A lot of these girls just come here for the weekend. She was here every day. That's all I know."

"She talk about her life outside of here at all?" The bartender shook her head. "None of us do. Now, I have work to do." And with that she turned to another man who was walking up to the bar.

So Ava had been here. Working. As a stripper. This thought pained Greg but, for some reason, it didn't shock him as much as he thought it would. Pulling the one dollar bills from his pocket, Greg headed to the dance floor. It was time to talk to some strippers.

10

DECEMBER 25, 2010

Greg awoke early to finish wrapping the gifts he had purchased for Ava. She had told him he didn't need to get her anything, but he'd seen the pile of gifts she'd been slowly adding to under the tree. There were at least ten, and he could only assume they were all for him.

He'd selected some simple gifts for Ava. A new cooking pot he'd seen her looking at online a few times, a few seasons of her favorite show on DVD, and a dress from her favorite website. He'd been nervous about purchasing clothes for her, but Ava had assured him she was not picky and would wear anything. He could only hope that was still true.

He exited the bedroom and headed down the hall to the sitting room. It was still dark outside, but Greg could see Ava's form illuminated on the couch from the light of the TV. As he passed the TV on his way to Ava, he switched it off, leaving the room barely illuminated from the multi-color lights surrounding their three foot tall Christmas tree. He gave Ava a light peck on the lips and then quickly slid his six packages plus a white envelope under the tree. Greg hoped that someday, when and if Ava agreed to marry him, there would be children to spend the holiday with as well.

Growing up as an only child had been tough. Greg would say it had been "the worst" but he didn't have anything to compare it with. His mother had often expressed wanting to have other children and, now that Greg was older, he knew it was her anatomy that forbade her from doing so. Greg was Maria Sanders' first, and would forever be, her only child.

Becoming a cop had nearly broken his mother's heart. She was terrified something would happen to him. Greg had assured his mother that he would be careful and that he would do his best to progress so that he wouldn't be on the streets for too long. So far, he hadn't progressed as quickly as he had hoped, but he also had never been in a standoff of any sort, much to his mother's delight.

Greg headed to the kitchen to begin cooking up some breakfast for Ava. The poor thing had been working more and more lately and had been doing things she previously seemed to enjoy, such as cooking, much less. Greg didn't mind. He'd been learning to cook well enough on his own and Ava swore she loved most of the limited meals he prepared.

He was in the middle of chopping onions to toss in some scrambled eggs (making an omelet was beyond his abilities) when he felt slender arms encircle his waist. Pausing and setting the knife down, he turned around and took Ava into his arms, kissing her on the forehead.

"Merry Christmas," she whispered into his chest.

"Merry Christmas, Babe." He rubbed her back slowly as she leaned her weight into him. She had been much more serious and a lot less happy-go-lucky lately and it was really starting to concern him.

"I was cooking breakfast but do you want to open presents first?"

Ava leaned back so he could see the wide smile on her face. He knew it, presents first. He removed her arms from his waist and led her back towards the tree.

With a bounce in her step that Greg hadn't seen for months, Ava headed to the tree and began stacking her arms with all the gifts she had bought for him. Pulling off a balancing act that would have impressed the circus, she carried all of the presents she had selected to the couch and sat down patiently waiting for him. Greg grabbed his small stack of gifts and followed suit. No sooner had his behind touched the couch than Ava was thrusting a wrapped package in his face.

"This one first." The smile on her face was practically lighting up the entire room. That is what Greg had missed the past couple of months.

Taking the package from her outstretched hand, Greg removed the wrapping carefully, finding a T-shirt on the inside. With an inquisitive look on his face, he unfolded it so he could see the front.

"Oh, Ava, thank you, I love it!" It was a T-shirt with characters from his favorite TV show. She always knew the perfect presents for him. He started to hand her a gift, but she pushed it away.

"I want you to open all of yours first, then I'll open mine." Greg smiled. "Whatever you want," as she pressed another package into his hand. The next gift was a box set of his favorite TV show to go with the shirt. He couldn't help but smile even wider than he had before, if that was even possible. The DVDs were followed by new headphones he had been eyeing for a while, as well as a decorative phone case that had their picture on it. How Ava had accomplished that, he had no idea. The next gift was a pair of Abraham Lincoln socks which made him laugh out loud. Seriously, where had she gotten all these personalized things? Or do they seriously make Abraham Lincoln socks? Finally, they were down to his last gift. As a joke, he lifted it to his ear and shook it lightly.

"Hmm . . . let me guess . . . bowling ball?" Ava laughed.

"Just open it, silly!"

Greg tore at the paper at snail speed. First, he undid one piece of tape, sliding his finger slowly under the paper, then he went to work on the second piece of tape. Ava became impatient, grabbing the gift and removing all the remaining wrapping in one motion, and handing the box back to him. Greg gave her a look.

"What? You were going too slow." She crossed her arms and a smirk appeared on her face. Greg laughed.

"Well, aren't you Miss Impatient. You know, usually people don't get so eager to watch other people open presents."

"I've been waiting all month for you to open these. I could hardly restrain myself from telling you." Leave it to Ava to be unique. Greg removed the lid to the box to find tickets on the inside. When he flipped them over, he gasped.

"How did you get these?" Ava smiled.

"It's a secret."

In his hands, he held two tickets to Les Misérables on Broadway. As a French enthusiast, it was his favorite show of all time. He was in shock. The show had been sold out for weeks. Ava must of bought these from a resale agent or someone who didn't want them anymore.

"Thank you so much, Babe. I can't wait to go see this with you." Ava didn't say anything more, she simply grinned. Remembering he still had gifts for her, which now seemed lame compared to all she bought for him, Greg handed over the first of the movie sets.

"These all kind of go together," he said as she opened the package.

When Ava saw what it was, she muttered a quick thank you, flashing him a brief smile before quickly opening the other two box sets. Greg couldn't help but notice her attitude had done a complete 180-degree turn and suddenly the room seemed devoid of excitement.

After she was done opening the DVDs, he handed her the pot which was received in much the same manner as the two previous gifts. Then he handed her the box with the dress.

Ava opened the box just as quickly as she did the other presents. And, when she lifted the dress out of the box, she held it up silently, inspecting it. Greg feared the worst.

"You don't like it." It wasn't a question.

"No Greg, it's great, I love it," she assured him, but her voice was strained and Greg could tell she was trying to force it.

"No you hate it. Put it back in the box, I'll return it tomorrow."

"No," Ava said picking up the dress and turning towards the bathroom.

"I'll go put it on now." The smile was gone from her face. Greg looked down, as she headed into the bathroom, and saw the white envelope on his lap.

"Wait, Ava, there's one more present." Ava poked her head back around the corner, her face expressionless.

"Hm?" Greg handed her the white envelope.

"This is from my coworkers."

"Your coworkers? But Greg, I've never met them, why would they get me a gift?" Uh oh, Ava was about to catch him in his lie. His words tumbled over one another while he tried to find an explanation.

"Well, you see, I talk about you so much that they feel like they know you, and I told them how much you work, and they wanted to help."

Ava opened the envelope and pulled out the typed letter that Greg had typed himself and had his coworkers sign. The signatures were real but the gift in the envelope wasn't really from them. As Ava unfolded the letter, her eyes went wide as the hundred dollar bills fell in her hand. She quickly skimmed the letter, then dropped it to the floor, counting the bills.

"This is a thousand dollars, Greg. I can't keep this!"

"You can and you will. Trust me, they wanted to give it to you." By 'they' he meant that he wanted to. He knew there was no way Ava would take money from him but he figured she wouldn't refuse if the money seemed to come from another source. Ava shook her head.

"But, Greg—"

"No buts. You put that towards your bills and don't look a gift horse in the mouth, okay?" Ava smiled a half smile.

"All right, if you're sure." Greg nodded.

"I am. Now, what do you want in your scrambled eggs for breakfast?"

"Uhhh, mushrooms, onions, and spinach, please," Ava said as she turned to once again head for the bedroom.

"No cheese?"

"No cheese. I'm trying a no-dairy diet for my heartburn." Greg nodded in understanding.

"Coming right up." He smiled at her retreating figure. She didn't turn around or say anything more.

11

PRESENT

Greg frowned and looked down at the two remaining twenty dollar bills and the smattering of one dollar bills that remained in his hand. It was his second night at Island of Treasure, the strip club where the bartender had recognized the picture of Ava, and, so far, the second night had been as much of a bust as the first. He had spent over two hundred dollars last night paying for lap dances from various women who knew nothing about the picture he had shown them. As much as it dismayed him, when they would shake their head in confusion, he was glad they at least weren't lying to him.

Tonight hadn't been much different. Greg had looked for the bartender from the night before to see if she had remembered anything else in the meantime, but it turned out that today she seemed to have disappeared as well.

After two more below-par lap dances, after which the women were much too eager to take his twenty, Greg headed to the bar. He was exhausted. He'd had to work today, his normal ten-hour shift and, as it turned out, staying out late at the strip club and working a long day just didn't mix.

It was Monday night, so, there were fewer people in the strip club than had been there the night before. In fact, the bar was only occupied by a single, stooped-over, possibly drunk, young gentleman who was flanked on either side by strippers who were all too happy to hang off his arms for the promise of free drinks.

Against his better judgment, Greg sat on a bar stool and ordered a gin and tonic from the bored young bartender. As she brought it over, he pulled out his picture of Ava once again.

"You ever see this girl around here?" he asked hopefully.

"Nope." She popped the 'p' in the snarky way that drove Greg crazy.

"And, even if I did, I wouldn't tell no cop."

Taken aback, Greg glanced down to double-check he hadn't forgotten to take off his uniform.

"You don't need to be wearing a uniform for me to tell you're a cop. My radar is just that good." The young blonde turned back to the side counter and began to flirt with one of the busboys there.

Greg, who was still in shock, tried to recover as he reached for his wallet in his back pocket. As he pulled out a crisp ten, he looked up to see one of the strippers next to the other bar patron staring straight into his eyes. Clearing his throat nervously, Greg slipped his wallet back in his pocket, looking up once again to signal the bartender, only to find the stripper was still staring straight at him.

She had long black hair that came almost to her waist. Whether it was real or extensions, Greg had no idea, but it complimented her light skin nicely. Her nose was smeared with a smattering of freckles and her skin showed little age, but enough that Greg could tell she was no longer in her twenties. She had the same body as all the other strippers, but her dark eyes seemed to have much more intelligence compared to the empty looks he'd been getting all night.

Without breaking eye contact, she leaned in and whispered something in the male patron's ear as she slid off the barstool next to him. The man was too far gone and didn't even make a motion to acknowledge that he'd heard what she said. Before Greg knew what was happening, the dark haired woman slid onto the stool next to him, touching the picture that remained on the bar.

"Want a dance?" She leaned in close to Greg, setting the hand that wasn't on the picture on his shoulder. She stretched her neck to where her lips were almost touching his ear.

"I'm Vanessa."

Greg gulped. There was something much more sultry about this woman than the others he had dealt with and he found himself leaning into her touch.

"Come with me," she whispered.

Greg was about to protest but then he noticed Vanessa had slid the picture into her hand and was holding it by her side. She either knew something or was going through a lot of trouble just to get his money. She led him through a maze of half-dressed women and closed curtains. He could hear hushed conversations occurring, both between the women and behind the curtains, but he couldn't make out anything that was being said. Finally, Vanessa pulled him into a booth in the corner and pulled the curtain. She put Ava's picture on the table.

"She said you would come." Greg was confused for a moment. Was Vanessa referring to the bartender or Ava?

"Who?" Vanessa rolled her eyes.

"Her." She pushed the picture towards Greg.

"Tyra. I don't know her real name. I don't think she ever told anyone. But I knew her as Tyra and she told me a man would come looking for her."

"Did this man have a name?" Vanessa shook her head.

"She just said, a man, and you're the first one who's ever asked, so, I assume it was you." They weren't getting anywhere with this, so, Greg decided to change the direction of the conversation.

"How did you meet Tyra?" A smile spread across Vanessa's face.

"She came in one night with a group of guys. I could tell she didn't belong. I went up and asked her if she wanted a lap dance and the men begin to cheer. Before I knew it, one of them had shelled out a twenty so I went to work." She spun the picture around under her finger while she was speaking.

"After the dance, the men began to holler for an encore. But she wanted to go to the bathroom. I offered to show her." Vanessa paused and Greg waited patiently for her to continue.

"And that's how it all started." He was lost again.

"What started?"

"Our relationship." Greg felt his jaw drop open. Ava had been dating a girl? "Wh . . . what?" Vanessa shrugged.

"I think she was a little tipsy, but I took her to the bathroom, and she started making out with me. I asked if she wanted to leave and she said, sure. I told her we could tell her friends goodbye and she said there was no need."

Greg was finally over his shock and was able to finally snap back into police mode.

"How long were you guys together?" It was really hard to get out the words without choking.

"Two years. Then, one day, she said she had to leave. And I understood."

"You understood?" Vanessa wrinkled her eyebrows as if Greg were the weird one.

"Yeah, that's how our relationship was. We loved each other but we both knew it was only temporary. After all, we both still slept with men, and often we just went home with each other every night." Greg put two and two together.

"She worked here." It wasn't a question.

"Yeah, I got her the job. No problem. We rode to work together every day, did our own thing here, and then, unless she told me that she had someone, we rode home together."

"Had someone?" Vanessa nodded.

"A guy to sleep with. If that was the case, she would take a uber home when she was done. Same went for me in the opposite situation."

"Interesting." Greg really didn't know what to say, so, he looped back to something he wanted to cover once more.

"So, when she left, did she take anything with her?"

"Just her purse and the clothes on her back. Same way I found her three years before."

This was so odd to Greg because Ava had loved clothes when they'd been together and he couldn't imagine her leaving with nothing but the contents of a purse.

"What about all her things?" Vanessa shook her head.

"She didn't have much. A few outfits, I suppose, but we basically shared our wardrobe, being the same size and all, and it was always easy. Car was mine. She could use it if she asked, but she didn't." Vanessa shrugged, as if your girlfriend walking out with nothing was absolutely normal.

"Didn't she have a phone?" Ava had been so attached to her phone when they had been together.

"Yeah, a prepaid one. My number was the only one in it. She took it with her but I doubt she kept it for long. That's how she was, off the grid." That definitely didn't sound like Ava.

"And you're sure she was the girl in this picture?" Greg motioned once again to the photograph.

"Positive. Dyed her hair after that first night, and wore colored contacts, but it's her." Realizing that this conversation maybe wasn't as fun as she thought it was going to be, Vanessa rose from the table.

"I have to get back to work. It was nice seeing you," she lied as she pulled open the curtain. Greg stood and brushed himself off. Physically, there was nothing on him, but strip clubs always made him feel dirty.

"Thanks, Vanessa." The woman was already walking away and didn't seem to hear him. But just as she was about to leave the hallway, she turned back around.

"Just so you know, I think she's happy."

"Happy?" This puzzled Greg.

"Wherever she is, she's happy." And with that, she turned and disappeared into the smattering of half-dressed women, leaving Greg standing there to stare at the picture in his hand.

12

JANUARY 12, 2011

"Ava?" Greg called, as he walked into the apartment. It was dark, but that didn't mean Ava was out. She'd been getting migraines lately, bad ones, which usually required that she retire to a dark room to sleep immediately. Greg had told her she should see a doctor, but Ava insisted they would only tell her to do what she had already been doing.

Greg called her name once more as he circled around the island in the kitchen, just to be sure, before he flicked on the light. The couch across the room, Ava's usual habitat, was empty. He glanced at the clock, noting it was ten in the evening and he reasoned that Ava must still be at work. Opening the fridge to forage for dinner, Greg noticed it had recently been stocked. So, she had been here at one point during the day.

Snagging the open jar of pesto sauce from a shelf in the door, Greg decided to make himself a quick pot of gnocchi, with leftovers for Ava if she so desired. As he headed over to the cabinet to grab the box of pasta, a scrap of paper on the floor caught his eye. He leaned down and scooped it up, only to notice it was a piece of what must've been a whole check at one point. Stepping on the pedal to flip open the garbage can lid, some of the rest of the check pieces were sitting right on top. Greg was curious, but not curious enough to dig through the garbage, so, he grabbed the few pieces that were right on top and inspected them.

The name pieces were missing but there were sections of an illegible signature, a date, and the amount the check was written for, which was almost seven hundred dollars. Greg didn't know what to think. It was only Ava and him in the apartment, and he knew the paychecks for both her jobs were direct deposit to her bank account, so what was she doing with a check for that amount? Realizing how accusing he was sounding, Greg tossed all the pieces back in the trash and resolved to talk to Ava later. He was overreacting, she was probably going to tell him all about the check tomorrow, which was her day off.

As he renewed his path towards the cabinet, Greg thought about how his work had been going lately. They were expanding, which was great, but it had meant longer and later hours for him on most days. Not that Ava seemed to mind. In fact, she seemed to be working even longer and even later herself these days. Greg wondered sometimes how much money she was really making. He knew she was a college student and paying for it all on her own, but she also lived very frugally and he couldn't imagine all of it was going towards school. He quickly shook the thoughts from his head and tried, once again, to focus on the task on hand.

That's when he heard a key in the door.

He felt a smile spread across his face automatically, as it always did, when Ava was near. There was no doubt she was the woman for him.

"Hey." Her soft voice broke through his thoughts as she came around the corner into his view. She was wearing her all-black serving outfit.

"You're home early." She smiled sadly.

"Yeah, it's the slow season. It's been bad since school started back up. I only made fifty dollars tonight."

Greg wanted to ask about the check but held his tongue. He didn't want her to accuse him of being nosy. Ava set down her purse on the island and headed into the bedroom to change just as she always did when she arrived home from work.

"How was your day besides that?" Greg shouted after her as he started a boiling pot of water on the stove.

"Great, seems like a fun school semester ahead of me." Her voice was muffled, but not too badly to obscure comprehension, so, Greg assumed she was just in the bedroom and not their giant walk-in closet.

"How was your day?"

"Good!" Greg shouted back, wondering just how much he should tell her about his work. She seemed to not care when he went into too much depth about it so he decided to keep it short.

"Well, the office secretary—"

"Ooh, is that gnocchi?" Ava had popped her head back into the kitchen and was staring at the box in Greg's hand. Greg was caught off guard.

"Er . . . yes, would you like some?"

"You bet." A rare happy smile overtook Ava's features as she headed to the couch and flipped on her new favorite TV show, Law and Order Special Victims Unit. This was the first time she had been interested in anything he was making in a long time.

"I thought you'd been eating at work lately." Ava's eyes didn't leave the episode list she was scrolling through on the TV.

"Yeah, I usually do, but tonight I decided to come straight home instead of waiting for food."

Greg had been to the restaurant where Ava worked fairly often, and she always ordered massive portions of food—some for him to eat there, the rest for her to put in a box and eat on her break. But Greg really didn't mind. Beyond rent, food was the only thing Ava let him pay for.

"Did you get that pasta dish that you always order for me when I'm there?"

"Nah." Ava pushed play on the remote and got up to go to the fridge and grab an Izzy soda.

"That's too expensive. Even after my half-off discount, its six dollars." Greg was taken aback that six dollars was too much for her, but he didn't want to interrupt. This is the most they had talked together since New Year's Day, with their competing hectic schedules.

"When you're not there, I usually order something off the happy hour menu for four dollars, get a side salad for a dollar fifty, or wait until the cooks aren't looking and steal a baked potato." She chuckled. Greg was a little worried that she felt the need to resort to stealing food but he forced a chuckle right along with her. He knew, if he offered her money, she would only decline. Which he didn't understand because he made plenty.

As the Law and Order theme song filled the room, Ava fell silent, drinking her drink and watching the TV. Greg drained the gnocchi and added olive oil and garlic along with the pesto sauce he had picked out earlier, and stirred it all together. Ava hadn't seemed to notice, but Greg felt his cooking was getting slightly better. Pulling down two of the rainbow bowls from the cupboard, Greg split the pasta into two somewhat equal portions but then, remembering Ava's eating habits, removed some of hers and put it into his bowl. She was always concerned about her weight.

Greg walked over to the couch handing one bowl to Ava as he passed her lounging in her favorite corner spot. The corner spot was also now Ava's permanent bed. Even after months of different types of diets, her heartburn was still unbearable and she had to sleep sitting up on the couch. They hadn't been sexually intimate in months. Not that it bothered Greg, he was willing to wait forever for Ava. And he understood that work and school were her main priorities right now and that coming home and being unable to sleep due to heartburn wasn't helping. She would come around, she always had when they'd had dry spells in the past.

Ava was vigorously texting and seemed to have yet to touch her gnocchi. "The food okay, Babe?" Greg asked cautiously. Seeming to remember it was there, Ava put her phone down and picked up her fork, popping a couple of gnocchi in her mouth.

"Yeah, Babe, it's great," she said with her mouth still full. Then she picked up the phone and began texting again.

Greg had always known Ava had a bustling social life but, for some reason, her texting was bothering him tonight. She had come home early from work just to be on her phone it seemed. But rather than start an argument, Greg decided to once again keep quiet. Instead, he focused on watching what was going on in Law and Order. He would never admit it to Ava, but he also thoroughly enjoyed this show. So much so, that when he turned back to Ava thirty minutes later, she was sound asleep with her practically untouched bowl of gnocchi beside her. With a sigh, Greg picked up her bowl and covered her with a blanket.

Walking back into the kitchen, he stopped by the drawer containing the plastic wrap and placed a sheet over Ava's food. He hoped she would eat it for breakfast, but knew it would more than likely end up being his dinner tomorrow.

After he washed the dishes, he took one more look at his beautiful girlfriend sleeping on the couch as he set the sleep timer on the TV and turned down the lights. As he headed down the hall to his room, Greg wished things were easier, like back when they first started dating. Before Ava was constantly stressed about money, school, and her health. Back before Greg had to work long hours and couldn't spend a lot of time every week visiting her at work. Back when Ava used to tell him everything.

13

PRESENT

Greg sat at his desk, staring at the picture of Ava in his hand once again. The trail had gone cold. Ice cold. Unlike before, where he had some leads and ideas of people to speak to, this time he had absolutely nothing. It had been two long days since Greg had spoken to Vanessa. And, although she had given him more information than anyone else, it had honestly led nowhere. After all, Vanessa herself seemed unconcerned with Ava's future.

"Sanders, got that report on the driver with no license yet?" Carl asked as he passed Greg's desk.

"Sure, boss, coming right up," Greg responded as he pretended to search through the pile of papers on his desk. In reality, he had yet to start, but a traffic report would take him thirty minutes at most to write. And, honestly, it would probably be at least that long before Carl passed his desk again.

Greg flipped on his dinosaur of a computer and waited as patiently as possible for it to start up. The station needed new computers, and badly, but the budget had been so low lately that they hadn't been able to look into it. Hopefully, they would find the money soon, though, or it would be back to handwritten reports for them.

As he pulled up the report document and began to fill in the blanks, Greg began to think for the first time about moving on. Maybe it really was time for him to let go of Ava, maybe their love really was in the past. In reality, their last few months together had been anything but heaven. Greg was deep in his thoughts when Marie, the new secretary for the department, passed by his desk.

"Hey Greg."

"Marie," Greg answered back without even looking up from his monitor.

"Nice day, isn't it?"

"Sure thing." Greg really wasn't one for small talk and didn't really understand what Marie could possibly want.

"Um, well, I was wondering if you had time—" Ah, so she needed a favor. Her and everyone else, apparently. He cut her off.

"Sorry, Marie, I'm really busy with work and I have a side project going right now."

"But—" Marie struggled to finish her sentence which Greg had rudely interrupted. Greg didn't give her the chance.

"I'll talk to you later, Marie."

"Uh, okay, uh, bye then." Marie had a dejected look on her face as she left Greg's desk but he didn't seem to notice. Ione, who was only a desk away, most certainly did.

"If a cute girl like that came to my desk, I definitely wouldn't turn her away." Greg rolled his eyes at the comment.

"I'm sure you see plenty of women, Ione."

"Plenty of women doesn't mean pretty little Marie stops by my desk," Ione smirked.

Greg chose to ignore his partner and began putting the final touches on his report. He and Ione definitely saw the world differently, like night and day.

"We getting some post-work beers tonight?" Ione was always ready to go out. Greg didn't really want to but he agreed, anyway. He knew, if he went home, he would just sit and stew over Ava and wonder what he could possibly be missing.

"How about The Martini? It's close and they've got dollar-off beers tonight." Ione could definitely drink quite a few beers.

"Sure Ione, whatever is fine," Greg snapped.

"With that jerk attitude, you're never gonna get a girl." Ione stood up from his desk and walked across the room to the printer.

Ione's comment didn't even phase Greg. Ione had always been critical of Greg's tendency to look for a relationship instead of another notch for his bedpost. Pushing the print button, and heading over to the printer to grab his hard copy of the report, Greg almost collided with Marie.

"Sorry," he muttered. Grabbing his paper, he turned to start the trek back to his desk. But to his surprise, there was a wide chest in his way. Greg looked up to roll his eyes at Ione. Ione didn't seem to notice and obviously had planned this.

"Hey, Marie, Greg and I are headed to The Martini tonight, want to come?" A smile spread across Marie's face.

"Sure! I'll see you guys there!" She tried to meet Greg's eye but he was too busy trying to step around the bear of a man in his way. Ione was satisfied with Marie's answer and let Greg pass, turning to follow right behind him.

"See? Was that so hard?"

"Brutal," Greg said sarcastically, grabbing his jacket from the back of his chair.

"I have to head home and change. I'll see you in an hour."

"Later, Bro." Ione waved as Greg stepped out of the office. Greg couldn't believe the nerve of him sometimes. Not that Greg was against Marie, he was just more of a fan of guy's night. Girls tend to invite too much drama for him. That's why Greg had loved Ava. She had been so drama free. When people made her mad, she cut them out of her life. When Greg had done the wrong thing, she had been so quick to forgive and forget. She had been so different.

Greg mentally smacked himself at the use of the word had. Ava was alive, she just had to be. If she was dead, he would feel different. And that's when he realized that, no matter how much he felt like giving up, he just couldn't. Not until he found his answer.

He was climbing in his truck when a snippet of a memory passed through his mind. He squinted, closed his eyes, and dared the memory to complete itself. It was about the day Ava had come home early from work. There had been that check he had found torn up in the trash can. There had been a bank logo in the corner. And it wasn't Ava's usual US bank. Greg tried to recall the picture of the logo, to no avail. After all, it had been years but he knew, if he saw it again, he would recognize it. Maybe he wasn't at such a dead end after all. With a smile, he started his truck and looked over his shoulder to back out of the space. He wasn't throwing in the towel just yet.

IT WAS ALMOST two hours later when Greg stepped into the door of The Martini and began searching the decent Friday night crowd for Ione and Marie. Ione was an easy one to spot and Greg quickly located him at a table in the bar area across the room. Greg began weaving in and out of the crowd of men in collared shirts and women in short skirts. He didn't know why, but bars like this had never been his thing.

"Gregory!" Ione called as he arrived at the table, simultaneously giving him a huge pat on the shoulder.

"It's just Greg," he corrected and began to survey the people at the table. Besides Marie, two other co-workers had decided to join them. Or at least Greg assumed they were co-workers. Ione made the introductions.

"Well, 'it's just Greg,' this is Andy from Fingerprinting and his girl, Leila."

"Nice to meet you guys." Greg shook both of their hands and pulled up an empty barstool.

"So, what conversation was I interrupting?"

"We were just talking about how much of a killjoy you are." Ione smirked. "Oh really, now?"

"Yup, you really should work on that." Ione took a sip of his beer which, to him, was half a beer.

"Sure, I'll work on that." Greg rolled his eyes as the server arrived at the table. Ione ordered two more beers for himself plus one for

Marie, Greg stuck to his gin and tonic, and Andy and Leila claimed they were good with what they had.

"So, Marie," Ione asked as he drained the remainder of his beer. "How's the love life?" Leave it to his partner to not beat around the bush. Marie was taken aback.

"I, uh, I mean, well, my ex has been out of the picture for a while now. So I guess . . . nonexistent?"

"Stop embarrassing her," Greg defended and then turned to Andy.

"How's life in Fingerprinting these days?" Marie visibly relaxed at the change in subject.

"Great, well, not that great. I'd rather be in CSI but they don't have any openings in this state. Right now, I'm signed up to be notified when they do but who knows when that will be."

"Why not move?" Greg asked as the server placed a gin and tonic in front of him. Andy looked at Leila with a look that Greg knew well. They couldn't move because he loved Leila and she didn't want to move for whatever reason.

"It isn't really an option right now. But, if I'm still waiting in a few years, I'll reevaluate if it would be worth it then."

"Do you know what state you would consider?" Greg picked up the lone food menu on the table which was quickly snatched from his hands by Ione.

"We've considered California. But the cost of living there would be tough if Leila didn't have a job awaiting her there as well." Greg nodded in understanding and turned to Ione.

"Is there a reason you snatched that from me?" A wide grin was occupying Ione's face.

"I already ordered one of every appetizer right before you got here." Greg felt his eyes go wide.

"But doesn't this place have twenty-some appetizers?"

If possible, Ione's smile grew even wider, giving Greg his answer. And right on cue, a server approached their table, her arms laden with plates. She was followed by three other servers who were also heavily weighed down by plates of food. Greg shook his head and groaned.

When they were done, the table was completely filled with a variety of mozzarella sticks, soft pretzels, wings, veggie plates, chips, flatbreads, and sliders. Greg didn't know where to start. Ione had already dug into the wings and his face was a mess with buffalo sauce.

"So Marie, what are your hobbies?" Ione asked with his mouth full. Greg realized Ione would never let this go, and he picked up some sort of egg-roll-like creation as he turned his attention to Marie.

"Well, I'm really big on hiking and—" Ione cut her off.

"Do you know who likes hiking? My friend, Greg, here!" He put his arm around Greg, trying his best to keep his wing sauce fingers off of his collared shirt. Marie brightened.

"Really? What's your favorite hike in the area?"

"The Valley Loop. You?" Greg knew he would get an elbow in the ribs if he tried to brush her off now. He really wished Ione would stop trying to set him up though.

"I like The Staircase. Challenging but rewarding."

"Leila loves to hike!" Andy added in from across the table.

"We should plan a hiking day one of these days. If we can ever find another day when we are all off." They all chuckled, as they all worked in the industry and knew police work was neither regular nor predictable. Ione, tiring of the wings, picked up four slices of the flatbread, stacked them on top of each other, and began navigating them to his mouth.

"Really Ione?" Greg shook his head.

"Eating one slice at a time takes too long." Ione finally figured out how to fit the four slices in his mouth and shoved them in.

"Oh, my God," Marie gasped. "That's disgusting."

Ione grinned, with his mouth full of food and his cheeks puffed out like a chipmunk. He chewed, then swallowed, a visible lump going down his throat.

"I know." Ione replied. Marie grimaced.

"That's why he's single," Andy added, making everyone laugh.

Greg had to admit this was the most fun he had ever had at The Martini. His relief was short-lived, however, when Ione rose and began to drag Marie and Greg to the dance floor.

"Ione, it's early, no one is dancing yet," Marie protested. Greg looked and saw that she was right. The dance floor was populated by only a few couples, most of them awkwardly grinding, while people stood on the sidelines and watched.

"That's why you guys have to start the trend!" Ione placed Marie's hand in Greg's and pushed them both towards the dance floor. Greg looked over in embarrassment but didn't withdraw his hand. When he turned to tell Ione to stop, he found the burly man had already disappeared. Probably back to the table with the mountain of food.

"So . . . " Marie turned to face him, biting her bottom lip.

For the first time, Greg looked at Marie. Not like he did at work, but really looked. She was a slender girl with a somewhat athletic figure. Her skin was light and unmarred, complimenting the purple dress she had chosen to wear perfectly. Her eyes were a light blue, somewhat unusual with her dark hair. Ione had been right, Marie was beautiful. Suddenly, Greg realized he had just been standing and staring and, as quickly as it had come over him, he snapped out of it.

"Sorry . . . I guess . . . do you want to dance?" He looked down at her hand that he was still holding. She nodded.

"Sure." And she turned around as if she were going to start grinding on him like the other couples on the floor. Greg stopped her and turned her back around.

"I prefer to dance like this." And, with utmost confidence, he stepped easily into the West Coast Swing, spinning Marie every which way. She picked it up quickly, a huge smile on her face even when her steps faltered compared to Greg's precise ones.

They danced for one song, then another, and another. Before he knew it, the dance floor had filled with couples and it had gotten too difficult to swing dance. Without missing a beat, Greg spun Marie into a close hold, starting the steps for a simple waltz. The smile had yet to leave Marie's face.

"Wherever did you learn to dance?"

"That's classified," Greg whispered as he worked Marie towards the edge of the dance floor. As much as he loved dancing, he hadn't had a chance to eat much of the mountain of food that Ione had ordered before he had been dragged out here. Marie giggled, noticing they were moving towards the edge of the dance floor. "Tired?"

"More like hungry," Greg responded, as Marie broke the dance hold, instead opting to follow behind him as Greg weaved through the crowd. When they reached the table, they found Ione surrounded by a group of giggling girls, and no sign of Andy and Leila, and no food in sight. Greg turned to Marie.

"Looks as if we will have to scavenge for our own food." She was staring at the table.

"Is he always like this?"

"If you mean, does he always harass me out of his way and then find himself surrounded by a group of girls all too happy to hang off his arm, the answer is yes." Greg looked at Marie out of the corner of his eye, wondering once again how he could have missed how pretty she was.

"I really wanted to finish that beer." Marie sighed. Greg glanced at his watch. "Tell you what. It's only ten. I think Ben's Tavern is open down the street. Their food is nothing compared to here but we can get a beer and a burger at least."

"Sounds great." Marie flashed her smile once again as they turned and left The Martini.

Ben's Tavern was not near as busy as The Martini, but it was still populated with a decent Friday night crowd. There was no dance floor, so, there was a much higher ratio of men to women and Greg could see the men sizing him up as he walked in. Marie didn't seem to notice the numerous eyes following her around as she slid into a table in a corner. Greg slid in next to her and pulled out the menu, although he already knew this place by heart. He had come here quite a few times back in the day.

The server came over to their table within minutes and Greg ordered another gin and tonic and asked for the house burger. Marie ordered the same but a beer instead of a mixed drink. As the server walked away, Greg turned to look at Marie, not really sure what to say. Luckily for him, she noticed his predicament.

"So, you've obviously been here a couple times." Greg winced internally. That was not a part of his life he wanted to discuss, but at least she had broken the awkward silence.

"I used to come here a lot back in the day." He knew he was being cryptic, but he was having such a fun night, and he didn't want to ruin it. Marie seemed to sense she'd picked the wrong topic.

"Ah, okay. Well, I've been here a couple times but usually only very late at night after The Martini closes."

"So you're a fan of The Martini?" Greg raised an eyebrow.

"Of course, what woman isn't? It's got appetizers, drinks and, of course, dancing. However, I've never danced as much as I did tonight. Really, you're a great dancer. Any other talents you're hiding?" Greg had never been good at flirting and it had been so long since he'd tried that he wasn't exactly sure what to say.

"Well, I can cook. Nothing else I can think of at the moment."

"Wait, you can cook and dance? Oh my God, where have you been my whole life?" Marie joked. Their drinks arrived at that moment, saving Greg from responding.

"So, you're a beer girl, eh?" Greg dropped the lime wedge into his gin and tonic.

"Not really. I'm actually usually your cliché sex-on-the-beach girl. However, when I'm having a burger, I almost always crave a beer." Marie brushed her long hair over her shoulder. Greg realized this was the first time he had ever seen it down. She always wore it pulled up at work.

"You're a gin and tonic guy?"

"Yeah. This is it, too. Don't think I've had anything but gin and tonic in years."

"Why?" Marie looked up at him through her dark eye lashes. Another topic Greg didn't want to dive too deep into.

"I honestly never liked alcohol much. Gin, I guess, is the least offensive." He shrugged.

"Least offensive? Oh God, gin tastes like rubbing alcohol to me."

For a minute, Greg's mind stopped. His vision flashed back to another place. Another time. And another woman.

"Ugh, I can't even stomach the thought of gin." Ava. Greg had no idea how long he sat like that, staring at Marie, but he was snapped back to the present by her apologizing.

"Sorry if I offended you. I mean, I don't like it but you're welcome to it."

"It's nothing I—" Greg was cut off as their burgers arrived. Both of them were so hungry they dug in without a word. When they finished, they began to talk about work, mainly Ione, laughing at all the dumb things he was always doing. When the bill came, Greg pulled out his wallet.

"I got this." He pushed Marie's hand with her card away.

"Are you sure?"

"Very," he said as he placed two twenties down and stood up. Marie stood up as well.

"This has been really fun." She nodded. This time it was her turn to look at the clock on her cell phone.

"It's only half-past eleven. Want to head back to my place for some wine? Or we can pick some gin up for you on the way." Greg's heart came to a halt. Could he do this? Go home with a woman, a co-worker, none the less? Greg hadn't been in a relationship since . . .

"Marie, I really did have a great time tonight but I can't. I mean, I'm not ready. I mean . . ." Oh, God, now she was going to think he was a dweeb. To his surprise, she smiled, but it didn't reach her eyes.

"It's okay. I understand. How about we do this again sometime?"

"That I can promise. Let me walk you to your car." Greg held the door of Ben's Tavern open for her.

"No need. I called a Uber. Thanks for the offer, though."

"So, you were planning to get drunk tonight?" Greg asked as they walked towards the parking lot.

"Not planning, hoping," she answered. Greg was just about to ask her what she meant when a black Toyota pulled up and rolled down the window.

"Marie?"

"This is me." Marie turned and gave Greg a quick hug.

"Thanks again. See you at work." She slid quickly into the car and closed the door.

"See you," Greg said to no one in particular as he watched the car drive away.

14

FEBRUARY 14, 2011

Greg pulled a bag of microwave popcorn out of the cupboard, unwrapped it, and stuck it in the microwave. After pushing the popcorn button, he headed over to the TV and began to flip through the channels, trying to find something, anything, that wasn't a romantic movie.

It was Valentine's Day and Ava had to work. Turns out that in the restaurant industry they don't even consider letting you have the day off. Greg wasn't upset, though. He had made reservations for Ava and himself at her favorite restaurant the following Monday. It didn't matter to him what day they celebrated, as long as they did.

Finally, Greg found a channel that was running reruns of Bonanza. Definitely not his first choice, but at least it wasn't Harry Met Sally, or Friends With Benefits, or some other bullshit movie that channels only play on February the fourteenth. He heard the microwave ding and headed over to pull out his half-popped bag of popcorn. For some reason, he was never good at timing these things. Microwave popcorn was Ava's department. At least he didn't burn it this time.

Returning to the couch, Greg pulled out his phone and sent Ava a quick Happy Valentine's Day text. This year, she had insisted he not get her anything, which seemed odd to Greg. Didn't women always appreciate presents? Either way, he hadn't found a gift waiting for him, either, so, maybe she was just trying to save money. After all, she had just paid college tuition.

He sank back into the couch and let the TV melt his brain a little bit. It was nice to have an evening off for once. About halfway through the episode, Greg's phone buzzed telling him he had a text. Thinking it was probably Ava, Greg set down his popcorn to pick up the phone, only to find it was one of Ava's friends, Samantha.

SAMANTHA: "Hey, Greg, I'm worried about Ava".

Greg scrunched his eyebrows. Ava had been hanging out with Samantha every weekend since they graduated from high school. If something was wrong, she would know. Greg fired back a quick question mark and waiting eagerly for the reply. Samantha replied within seconds.

Samantha: "She hasn't come out with me in over a month. And, when I text her, she barely speaks to me. It's one-word answers at best."

Something wasn't right.

Greg: "What do you mean, she hasn't gone out with you? She told me she saw you just last week?"

Greg was really worried now. Why would Ava lie about where she was last week? And, if something was wrong, why wouldn't she tell him? Greg lost interest in the TV and the popcorn, choosing instead to stare straight at his phone and will Samantha to respond. But minutes passed without the screen lighting up. Greg sent another text with two question marks and continued to wait, but Samantha seemed to have gone dark on him.

He pinched the bridge of his nose and leaned forward to set his elbows on his knees. What was going on? Deciding not to wait, Greg pressed the speed dial on his phone for Ava and waited as the phone rang. At least she would get the voicemail right when she got off work. To his surprise, after only four rings, Ava answered with a breathy, "Hey." It took a minute for Greg to get over his shock and to get his lips to move.

"Hey, Babe, what are you doing? I thought you were working?"

"I am." She was keeping her voice low and it was difficult for him to hear her. "I'm in the coat closet at the restaurant. You never call so I figured it must be important." Now he felt bad for accusing her.

"Oh, well, it sort of is. I just got a text from Samantha saying she's worried about you. And she said she hasn't seen you in weeks," he explained.

"Huh?" She seemed genuinely surprised and Greg could just picture her lifting her eyebrows in her signature way he had come to know only as 'the look.' "Well, she's lying, Greg, I just saw her on Tuesday. We went to the Greek restaurant down the street. I swear." Her tone was stern and Greg knew better than to second-guess her.

"It's okay, Babe. I believe you, but I wonder why Samantha would lie like that."

"Probably because she's jealous or something." Now it was Greg's turn to be confused.

"What?"

"I'll explain later. Listen, I have to go. I've been in here too long already."

"It's okay. I understand. But while I have you on the phone, Happy Valentine's Day, Babe." Greg smiled as he said the words.

"Same to you. Talk to you later. Bye." The words came out in a rush and then the line went dead. Greg hung up the phone and picked up his popcorn, satisfied that he had heard his girlfriend's voice. He was still confused as to why Samantha would text him like that, but decided not to question it. Ava would explain when she got home.

He must've fallen asleep on the couch because he awoke hours later to Roseanne reruns and a lap full of popcorn kernels.

"Uh," he grunted to no one in particular as he began to gather the kernels in his lap and try to get them all back in the bowl. He glanced at the clock on the microwave only to reconcile in horror. It was almost four in the morning and Ava hadn't come in.

Telling himself to calm down, he placed a hand over his racing heart and began to walk down the hall to check the bedroom just to make sure he wasn't making a big deal out of nothing. When he got to the bedroom, he flicked on the lights only to be greeted by the familiar sight of the empty bed.

Oh God, where was Ava?

Rushing back into the living room, he picked up his phone only to find the battery was almost dead. He quickly plugged it into the charger Ava kept by the couch while simultaneously dialing her number. It rang for what seemed like forever, until finally a voice came on telling him to leave a message.

"Ava, it's Greg. Where are you? I'm worried. Call me when you get this, please." Greg ended the call, only to dial her number again.

Once more, he only reached the voicemail. He hung up before leaving a message this time and sent Ava a text identical to his message. Hopefully, she would answer at least one. Greg began to pace back and forth across the living room in front of the TV which was still illuminated with the old sitcom. He'd never been religious, but he began to pray, telling God he would go to church every week from now on as long as Ava was okay.

After pacing for a long time, Greg decided to call Ava at work. Maybe they really had been busy and maybe she had gotten stuck there. He quickly googled the restaurant, found the number, and pressed the digits into his phone. Again, he reached nothing but a voicemail reminding him that the restaurant's regular hours were ten a.m. to two a.m. Where could she be? Had she gotten in a car wreck? Was she lying bleeding by the side of the road? Was she dying in a hospital somewhere alone?

He brushed the thoughts out of his head. She had an I.D. on her and they would contact him if she was in trouble. That's when Greg realized he didn't know what address was on Ava's I.D. Had she ever changed it to his? Or was it the apartment she lived in before? Or what if it was still her address from high school?

Telling himself to calm down, Greg sat on the couch and began to reason with himself. Ava was only an hour late. She could have stopped by the twenty-four-hour supermarket, or to get gas, and maybe she was driving home now and couldn't answer the phone. Yes, that was it. Ava often ran errands in the middle of the night. She claimed it was the best time to shop because the stores were empty. She would be home soon. Flipping the Channel over to a different late night sitcom, Greg sat on the couch right by his phone resolving to wait up until she got back.

He must've drifted off again, because he awoke to the sound of a key in the front door lock. Not even waiting for her to unlock it fully, Greg rushed over and threw open the front door. Ava stood on the mat, disheveled, and slightly shocked looking.

"Oh ,thank God you're okay." Greg quickly and roughly embraced Ava, noticing the sunlight streaming in the stairwell from behind her. What time was it? Pulling Ava into the apartment, Greg shut the door behind her, all without letting her go.

"Where the hell were you?" Ava's face was impassive.

"Sorry, Babe. I went out with co-workers for drinks and got a little drunk, so, I slept it off at a co-worker's place before driving home." Greg glanced at the clock. It was nine a.m.

"And you couldn't call?" Greg tried to stay calm but he was furious. Here he was, up half the night worried, and his girlfriend had been out drinking?

"You couldn't text? Email? Facebook? Something to tell me you would be late?" When he looked back at her, there were tears streaming down her face.

"I'm sorry," she sniffled as she turned and ran to bury her face in her favorite blanket on the couch.

Great. Now what had he done? Ava had always been very sensitive to being yelled at and he knew that. With a sigh, he walked over to where she was curled up on the couch and began to rub her back as she cried.

"I'm sorry, Babe. I didn't mean to yell. I was just worried sick, okay?" Ava nodded but didn't look up from the blanket to meet his eyes.

"Can you look at me, Babe? Please?" he begged. She shook her head no.

"I'm really sorry." Greg continued to rub her back as he let her cry. Ava was rarely upset and this time it was definitely his fault. He wasn't sure how much time had passed but, awhile later, he felt Ava's breathing become deeper and even beneath his hand. She was asleep.

With a sigh, he covered his girlfriend with the second blanket they kept on the couch, going into the bedroom to get another for himself. He returned to the couch, curling up in the corner opposite to Ava. They would talk about this when they both had more sleep.

15

PRESENT

Greg slipped into his seat at the precinct quietly the next morning. Even though it was Saturday, and he had every right to work, he knew someone was bound to notice his presence. And his goal was to stay as undetected as possible. As he waited for his old as dirt computer to power up, he began to make a list of everything he knew so far. He listed Ava's steps as far as he had traced them, ending with a question mark after her stint at Island of Treasure.

Turning back to the computer, which had finally reached the Department login screen, Greg quickly typed in his passcode and watched as the case database loaded. He was only supposed to have access to the database for traffic case purposes, but he'd been into the case database once before to print off a background check on Kyle, and he figured one more time wouldn't hurt.

Shifting through all the officer reports and interviews, Greg finally reached the part he had been looking for, the section which mentioned what banks they had checked and what accounts they had frozen. Greg opened a second window and placed it directly next to the first on his monitor.

Ava had maintained multiple bank accounts, which didn't

surprise Greg. Even before he found that check in the trash, he had known she had at least two accounts. The police report listed three banks, with a savings and checking account associated with each one, as well as a credit card that had been frozen the day of her disappearance years before. As far as Greg could tell, no activity had occurred, nor had the banks sent any alerts of someone trying to access the accounts. And across all three banks, there was almost thirteen thousand dollars that hadn't been touched.

Greg began to type the bank names into his search engine on the other screen, clicking on images to see each bank's logo. None of the three matched the check Greg had found years before. He leaned back in his chair and rubbed the unshaved stubble on his chin. Any bank that Ava would have opened an account at, even if she used a fake name, would have required her social security number or driver's license number, which would have shown up in the system.

Unless it was a credit union. Greg quickly typed in the search bar for a list of all the credit unions in the area. There were over fifty results. He clicked on the first, looked at the logo in the corner, only to immediately press the back button. He did the same with the second, and then the third. He was about to click on the fourth when a shadow came over his desk.

"Sanders?" It was Carl.

"Oh, hey, Carl, what are you doing here on a Saturday?" Greg quickly minimized the case file screen so his boss wouldn't be able to see it.

"I could ask you the same question. I don't remember approving any overtime for you this week."

"Don't worry. I didn't clock in." Greg ran a hand through his hair, hoping that would placate his boss. It didn't.

"So, again, why are you here?" Greg scrambled for an excuse.

"Uh, the Wi-Fi is out at my house and I, uh, had some stuff to research."

"Such as?"

"Oh, just personal stuff." Greg noticed his boss's eyes flit towards the screen. "Looking for a new credit union. You know, personal stuff." Carl didn't quite seem to believe him.

"All right, Greg, but I swear, this better not be about that girl again. You need to let her go. We discussed this at your last performance meeting." Greg mentally winced.

"I promise, it's not. Just using the internet."

"All right. Well, since you're here this Saturday, I suppose you'd be willing to cover one of the new guys next Saturday? He has a wedding to attend." Obviously, Greg couldn't say no now.

"Sure."

"Perfect. I'm only here to grab paperwork, but I'll see you at the regular time on Monday."

"Thanks, Chief." Greg returned to his work of clicking on credit unions, looking at the logo, and clicking back to the original screen. He reached the last one on the list, holding his breath as he clicked on the link, only to let out his breath as it wasn't the logo he was looking for. He had been so sure about the credit union idea. What was he missing?

Greg leaned back in his chair once again, pinching his eyes closed. He'd looked at all the credit unions in the state. *In the state.* What if Ava had driven to another state to open an account? He quickly did the calculations in his head. California was only about an hour and a half to the west. Utah, maybe two hours to the East. The Arizona border was an hour to the south. His search had just multiplied.

Like a madman, Greg began pulling up lists of credit unions within a four-hour drive. He couldn't see Ava being able to go much further than that but, then again, she had been gone for twelve to sixteen hours a day back in the day. Greg shook his head. He would start with the four-hour drive and widen his search later. He started with California, which returned the same results as his initial search. However, as he was clicking through the Arizona credit unions, he stopped and did a double-take.

That was the logo. It belonged to a credit union located in a small town in Arizona, about a four-hour drive to the south. He took a shot of the screen with his phone and magnified the image—to be sure it matched the one in his memory. It had to be it. Clicking back over to the website, he pulled over the pad he had made notes on earlier and began to scribble down every piece of information about the credit union he could. After he was finished, he glanced at the clock in the corner of his computer screen as he powered it down. There was still time for a trip to Arizona.

Grabbing his keys and notes, Greg practically ran out of the office.

16

MARCH 10, 2011

Ava hadn't been home in days. Greg didn't even know when the last time he saw her was. She'd been pet sitting for her grandparents, which had taken her away for the weekend, and now she had just sent him a text saying she was too tired to drive home and she would sleep in her car. Greg had been appalled and had offered to pick her up, but Ava insisted it wasn't worth the drive home since she would just be driving back to work in under six hours. Still, Greg didn't like the idea of his girlfriend sleeping in her car in a dark parking lot.

With a sigh, Greg opened the door that obscured his stacked washer and dryer combo and began emptying Ava's clothes into a basket on the ground. She barely had time to do anything anymore and laundry never seemed to make the list of things she could accomplish. But Greg didn't mind. In fact, he enjoyed laundry. Kicking the basket over to the couch where he could watch TV as he folded laundry, Greg reminisced about the good old days. Back when Ava was carefree and her life seemed to revolve around him. Hard to believe that was only nine months ago.

What had happened to Ava? She was no longer the happy-go-lucky girl he had met in high school but, rather, some overstressed, overworked, exhausted version of herself who never seemed happy. Greg wondered briefly if it was his fault.

Pushing the thought from his head, he abandoned the laundry and headed over to his laptop computer situated on a desk behind the couch. He flipped it open and typed in amazon.com. It seemed like a good time to get a small gift for Ava just to help perk her up a bit.

Greg didn't know how long he spent on the computer but, before he knew it, the sun was rising and he had a shopping cart full of gifts that were not quite perfect for her. He had a season of her favorite TV show, which he quickly trashed, knowing she would have no time to watch it. There was a set of scented lotions but none were the juniper breeze scent that he knew was her favorite. He had found some bath bombs that were supposedly 'all the rage' among girlfriends according to guys in the comments, but a nagging feeling told him that if Ava was allergic to bubble bath, which she was, these bath bombs probably wouldn't agree with her either.

He'd also put a pair of slipper socks in his basket which he quickly deleted as well. What a lame gift that would be.

Leaning back in his chair, Greg rubbed his bloodshot eyes and looked around the room. The TV had long ago flicked off due to the built-in inactivity timer. The pile of laundry lay abandoned on the couch. Honestly, he didn't want to face anyone today. He leaned back in his office chair and an idea suddenly zinged through his mind. A massage! That's what his girlfriend needed!

Opening a new search engine window, Greg typed in the name of a local massage chain. He quickly scanned the website, realized how reasonable their prices were, and ordered an E-gift card that he could print from his work printer.

With a smile, he patted himself on the back. He had found the perfect gift! After emailing himself the e-gift card, Greg pulled out his phone and dialed the number for work. They could get along without him for one day. Greg quickly informed his supervisor he would be working from home as he shut his laptop and headed towards the bedroom. He barely had time to listen to his supervisor agree before he fell on the bed and dropped into an immediate deep sleep.

17

PRESENT

Greg slammed his fist on the steering wheel. How could he have forgotten it was Saturday? The credit union in small town Arizona he had just driven four hours to was closed. As was almost every business in the vicinity. What a waste. He quickly calculated when he would be able to drive back down and he wasn't liking his odds. It would be over a week before he would be able to make it down during normal business hours.

A small voice in Greg's subconscious began to nag him. What if she really was dead? What if this was all in vain? Why was he doing this, anyway? Because Ava was the only girl he'd ever loved. But wait, was she really? Or was she the only girl he'd let himself love? Greg thought back to the previous night and dancing with Marie. He hadn't been that happy in a long time. Maybe everyone was right. Maybe he needed to move on.

But, then, Greg remembered all the information he had uncovered over the past week. He was the only one who knew that Ava hadn't been kidnapped that night five years ago. And he needed to see this through until the end. He needed to know.

Greg started the truck and pulled back out onto the street, and headed towards the highway. He would just have to come back on his next weekday off. His phone began to buzz in the center console. He glanced down quickly to see Ione's name on the screen. With a groan, he pressed the 'speaker' button.

"Yes?"

"Greg! Buddy! What happened to you last night?" The background on the call was filled with noise. In fact, it sounded like Ione was at some sort of sports game.

"I went home." Greg pulled onto the highway and accelerated his speed to match that of traffic.

"With Marie?" Greg rolled his eyes.

"By myself. Now, what's this about, Ione?"

"Just wanted to see if you'd like to come over and watch the game and drink some beers." Greg glanced at the clock on his dash. Why not?

"Sure. But I'm in Arizona so it'll take me a couple hours."

"Why are you in . . . seriously, Greg? The girl again?"

"Her name is Ava."

"She's dead, Greg. Let her go." Greg shook his head even though he knew Ione couldn't see him do so.

"I'm not so sure, man. I've found new evidence . . ." Ione cut him off.

"Don't you think, even if she was alive, if she wanted you to find her, you would have done so by now? Have you ever thought that? If, and this is a big if, she is alive and in hiding, maybe there is something she's hiding from?" Silence filled the truck as Greg didn't know quite what to say. Finally, he broke the quiet.

"I just have to know."

"I know," Ione responded understandingly before snapping back to his usual banter.

"So, get us a six-pack while you're out? Scratch that, I'm thirsty, make it two."

"Sure thing." Greg reached over to press the button to hang up the phone.

"And get something nice, none of that cheap stuff, you hear me?" Ione's voice caused Greg to pause.

"Got it, Ione."

"And . . ." Greg didn't wait to see what else Ione had to say. He disconnected the call.

Surveying the land on either side of the highway, Greg noticed how desolate it was. Miles would go by without a house or a business in sight. Every now and then, there would be a dirt road that branched off the highway and this made Greg think. All those roads were built for a reason, right? Glancing off to his left, Greg noticed the rise of hills in the distance. Arizona was a very unforgiving climate but, if he was going to live here, he would do so in the mountains.

Or, if he were to bury a dead body, he would do the same. With a shudder, Greg shook the thoughts from his head. He would have to follow this idea later. In fact, he made a mental note to see if he could use Google Earth to trace any of the roads without actually having to drive them.

Greg pulled up in front of Ione's house hours later with the two six-packs in tow. Ringing the doorbell, he could already hear loud voices inside. He should've known that Ione would make an event out of this. Ione's large figure filled the space as the door swung inward.

"Greg! My man!" He quickly slapped Greg on the back and snatched the beer. He gave it a once over, grunting in satisfaction as it met his approval.

"Hey, guys! Greg is here with beer!" he shouted over his shoulder. Greg heard a shout from the other room as he stepped into the front hall.

"Who's here?" He would never have agreed to come if he knew it was a party.

"Just Andy and my brother, Dan." Ione didn't even wait for Greg to remove his shoes before heading back into the other room. Greg took a quick look around the foyer of Ione's house. It was an obvious bachelor pad as it lacked decoration and only contained a shelf for shoes. Ione's shoes were so big that his shoes didn't even fit on the shelf and hung off the end. The majority of Ione's shoes were in a pile on the floor.

The house was moderately sized. It was a single story but Greg knew it had at least two bedrooms. And he suspected there was a third he hadn't been in. There were hardwood floors, which spanned the entire house, and the walls were all painted the basic white. There was a single potted tree in one corner that hadn't been there the only other time Greg had come to visit. He touched one of the leaves on his way into the living room. Just as he thought, it was fake.

Greg walked into the living room, which was filled with a massive TV on one wall, and a huge black leather couch directly opposite. Game consoles and controls were strewn about the floor. Nothing had changed much since his last visit.

There was an already opened six-pack on the ottoman next to various bags of popcorn and Doritos. The typical guy fare. Andy and Ione both sat on the couch with their feet up. A man, who Greg could only assume was Dan, stood in the kitchen off to the left microwaving what could only be a bowl of nacho cheese dip.

"Hey, I'm Dan. Nice to meet you." He raised his beer in greeting to Greg.

"Greg, if Ione didn't already tell you."

"He didn't but he forgets to tell me a lot of things." The microwave dinged and Dan turned to pull out the bowl of steaming dip.

"I can hear you guys, you know," Ione called from the couch as he simultaneously popped open another beer.

"That's the point, Ione. It's called sarcasm." Greg rolled his eyes and sat on the corner of the couch. He had to admit that the cheese dip smelled pretty good and he hadn't eaten all day . . .

"SCCOOOOORRREE," Ione yelled, jumping off the couch and sloshing beer everywhere. Greg rolled his eyes and leaned forward to grab a handful of popcorn. Andy, on the other side of Ione, had also been showered in beer.

"Ione, seriously, man, you have to watch it. I can't go home smelling like beer."

"Sorry, bro." Ione polished off his bottle of beer, letting out a large belch as he did so. Dan set down the bowl of nacho cheese dip, opting instead to pick up the popcorn as the screen switched from the game to a commercial.

"So, Greg, Ione said you work with him but didn't tell me much else."

"Well, that's probably because I don't do much else," Greg answered honestly. Ione jabbed him in the ribs.

"What Greg means to say is that he's a traffic cop for now but excited to work his way up the ranks to detective."

"Really?" Dan asked, intrigued.

"Well . . . yes, but Ione makes it sound a lot closer than it is for me."

"Have you ever considered private investigating? There's tons of demand for it these days." Dan began to reach in his pocket.

"Are you a private investigator?" Greg raised an eyebrow. Dan shook his head, handing a card that he had fished out of his pocket over to Greg.

"No, I work in information technology, though a lot of grey market stuff. Companies hire us to investigate people they think are cheating them, etc. But . . ." His phone began to vibrate and he quickly silenced it and slid it into his pocket.

"I've always wanted to start my own investigations company, but I've never found someone to partner with. Most detectives are very anti-personal investigator." Greg nodded in understanding.

"Yeah, they pretty much drill it into us that personal investigators are worthless compared to them."

"Do you feel that way?" Greg shook his head.

"Not necessarily but I guess I've never considered becoming a PI."

"Well, if you decide to, please give me a call. You seem like a great guy and I'm sure we could work something out . . ." Ione cut in.

"Greg would be GREAT! You should ask him about the investigation of his ex-girlfriend. He's . . ." Greg groaned.

"Please, Ione. We don't need to bring that up."

"Why not? You are still investigating, right?" Greg had obviously underestimated Ione's ability to read him.

"Yeah, I am," he admitted begrudgingly.

The game illuminated the television and Ione and Andy turned their attention back to the screen. Dan stood and motioned for Greg to follow him into the kitchen where it was a bit quieter.

"So, tell me about this investigation of yours," Dan asked the moment Greg sat at a barstool situated at the island in the middle of the kitchen. Greg really didn't feel like getting in depth with an absolute stranger, but something told him that talking to this guy was something he couldn't pass up.

"Well, you're going to think I'm nuts, but my first girlfriend, the girl I thought I was going to marry, disappeared five years ago. Everyone thinks she's dead, but I knew this girl. She's not dead." Dan studied Greg for a moment, probably trying to decide if he should take him seriously or discount him as a crazy person.

"Why do you say that?"

"Like I said, I knew this girl like the back of my hand. She wouldn't go down without a fight. She used to joke about disappearing and, the more I look into this, the more I think she did exactly as she said." Dan rubbed the stubble on his chin.

"I think you've pretty much already become a PI."

"I guess, in a way, I have." Greg shrugged feeling like this conversation was going nowhere.

"Hear me out. You don't have to quit the police force. I just want you to give this idea a shot, even if it's just a side job for you. I really want to get this company off the ground and I think you're just the guy for the job."

"But you just met me, how do you even know?" Greg was skeptical.

"I have a confession." Dan took a deep breath.

"I don't even like football. Ione invited me here just to talk to you. For weeks, he's been discussing your investigating abilities and he doesn't think you'll be with the police force much longer."

Greg sat there stunned. What did Ione mean, he wouldn't be with the police force much longer?

"I can tell I've shocked you, so, I'll give you time to think it over. But, please do. Ione is just looking out for your best interests as your friend. And listen, if you take the job, your girlfriend's disappearance will be our first case. After all, if we do solve it, it'll be great publicity for an up-and-coming investigations firm." Dan stood up from his barstool and returned to the couch.

Greg looked down at the card in his hand. He didn't know what to say or think. But, suddenly, he had a nagging feeling in his head he couldn't place. He stood up and glanced over at the couch, decided that Ione wouldn't care, and headed for the door. He turned the knob and slipped silently into the night. After all, he had a lot to think about.

18

APRIL 11, 2011

Greg was sitting on the couch alone, watching another sitcom rerun when his phone vibrated. He picked it up and smiled when he saw Ava's name displayed on the screen with a text message notification.

Ava: "Greg, I'm sorry."

His heart stopped as he read the message. His fingers shook as he typed his reply.

Greg: "Sorry for what, Babe? Everything okay?"

His breathing was shallow and he moved to sit on the edge of the couch. His heart was pounding in his chest as the little speech bubble indicated she was typing her reply.

Ava: "I can't do this anymore. It's not you, I promise, as cliché as that sounds. It's me. I'm stressed to the max and I'm unhappy."

What? No!

Greg: "Don't say that, Babe. I'll help you. We will get through this together."

Ava: "That's just it, Greg. I need to do this on my own. It's the only way I know how."

Greg didn't even realize he had stopped breathing until his vision began to fade. He quickly gasped in a large breath before he passed out. He sat there staring at the phone for what felt like forever.

Ava: "I'm really sorry. I just can't be on the pedestal that you put me on anymore. Please bag up my stuff. I'll send someone to get it."

THE PHONE SLID from his sweaty fingers. He couldn't even breathe deeply enough to reply. He felt as if his world was crashing around him. Shock began to fade to anger and the outstretched hand that had been holding the phone began to shake. How could she do this to him? How?

Phone forgotten, he stormed into the bedroom and over to his dresser. Opening his underwear drawer, he withdrew the small black box he had hidden in a sock. He slipped it into his left pocket and then headed into the bathroom. Without thinking straight, he slid open Ava's jewelry box drawer and withdrew her favorite necklace he had given her a year before. It was a sapphire encrusted with diamonds and had cost him almost two thousand dollars. Ava had known the price tag and had been too afraid to wear the necklace for anything other than special occasions. He added it to the pocket with the black box and grabbed his keys as he headed out the door. It was barely spring, but the cold didn't even seem to affect him as he walked down the stairs to his car.

19

PRESENT

Greg sat at his desk, repeatedly lifting his pencil and letting it slide from his fingers, to land with a clink on the desk, only to lift it once more. He must've been on repetition number two hundred when Ione finally broke.

"STOP, MAN. I CAN'T THINK WHILE YOU'RE DOING THAT!" Ione yelled while banging his fists on the desk. Greg couldn't help but crack a smile.

"So, are you going to tell me what you apparently told Dan? Or am I going for the Indy 500?" Ione shook his head.

"Fine, dude. Just please stop, that is so fucking annoying I can't take it."

"So?"

"So, what?" Ione wouldn't make eye contact. Greg lifted and dropped the pencil.

"Ugh, fine. I told Dan the truth." Ione pushed his swivel chair back from the computer and leaned back crossing his arms across his chest.

"And what exactly is 'the truth?'" Greg turned his chair to face Ione. He hadn't been able to get any work done all morning with these thoughts weighing on his mind. It had gotten so bad he had decided to finally confront Ione.

"You're not happy here, man. I mean, look at you." He motioned to Greg's desk.

"You say you couldn't get any work done this morning but, Greg, I haven't seen you do any actual work in weeks." Ione took a deep breath and leaned forward, resting his elbows on his knees.

"I know you won't stop looking for this girl, Greg, and honestly at this point you need help. Whether that's help chasing this ghost, or a shrink, I'm not sure. But please, just get help." Ione stood up from his desk and grabbed his jacket heading for the door. It was probably time for lunch.

Greg leaned back in his chair and let out a deep breath. He hated to admit it, but Ione was right. What was he doing here? He always said he was here because he wanted to be a detective but, obviously, waiting for someone to retire wasn't the way to go. Maybe he should take Dan's offer. As he stood up to grab his jacket and follow in Ione's footsteps, he came face to face with Marie.

"Hi, Greg. Headed out for lunch?" She had a hopeful look in her eyes.

"Marie, hey." Greg glanced at his jacket in his hand and then back at Marie, trying to think of an escape route, but then changed his mind.

"Sure, want to come? I'm probably just going to get a sandwich at the deli down the street."

"Sure, sounds great!" Marie walked back over to her desk to grab her sweater, then headed for the door, checking behind her to make sure Greg was following. Realizing he was still standing by his desk, he quickly began to walk towards the door. Once they were outside, Marie tried to start a conversation.

"So, how's your day going?" she asked sweetly.

"Great." Greg kept running over Ione's words in his head. Had it really been weeks since he filed a report? He had started that one report, did he really never submit it? Now that he thought of it . . .

"Any big plans for the evening?" she tried again.

"Just another Monday." Had he sent that report in? Or was it still sitting on his desk? Marie didn't try to say anything more. They slipped into the deli line which was only about ten people for once. Greg suddenly realized that maybe he had come across as a jerk and that he should say something to clear the air, but he just couldn't bring himself to.

As they ordered their sandwiches, to go, he couldn't help but bring the job debate back to the front of his mind. Should he really leave the police force? While the pimple-faced teen behind the counter made their sandwiches, Greg decided to apologize.

"Sorry."

Marie looked and him and smiled softly. "It's okay. I know what you said Friday. I was just hoping we could be friends, or even just better co-workers. Sorry if I pushed it too soon."

Greg nodded. "No, really, I'm sorry I was so rude on the way over here. I guess I've just got a lot on my mind these days and I'm not myself."

"Oh, really?" She cocked an eyebrow.

"What do you mean, 'Oh really?'" Now he was confused. Marie reached out to grab her sandwich as the boy handed it to her, not looking at Greg as she answered. "Greg, I don't want to tell you about yourself, because you're right, I don't really know you. But I've been with the Department for a few years now and, let me tell you . . . pensive, reclusive, jerk, describes you to a tee and I've never seen anything but that from you. So, if you're 'not yourself lately' I don't know what your 'self' is because you've always been the same to me." With a huff, she turned for the door. "I'll walk myself back."

Greg was stunned.

"Sir?" The boy was still trying to hand him his sandwich, even as he stood there like a statue.

Quickly regaining his composure, Greg mumbled a quick 'thank you' and he took the sandwich and headed for the door. Without another thought, he walked back into the station, pointedly avoiding looking at Marie's desk, went over to his desk, logged out of his computer, and grabbed his laptop. He then proceeded to walk into

Carl's office and he laid his badge, handcuffs, gun, and credentials on Carl's desk. Carl, who had been on a phone call, looked up in shock.

"What's this?"

"I need to take a leave." Carl looked at Greg and the phone and mumbled a quick, "I'll call you back," before hanging up, and leaning back in his chair. He let out a deep breath.

"Greg."

"Carl," Greg replied sarcastically.

"Close the door. Have a seat for a minute." Greg did as he asked.

"Listen Greg. I like you. And I can't deny you leave. But I have to tell you this, your performance here has been nothing but subpar, and there may not be a job when you come back. I've given you lots of leeway over the years and I can't just leave Ione hanging without a partner indefinitely."

Greg scrunched his eyebrows. "I didn't even tell you how long the leave was going to be for." Carl shook his head.

"It doesn't matter, Greg. A week or a year, when you walk out that door, I have to put in a request for a replacement for you. Now, the position may not fill before you return but I cannot promise you anything."

Greg thought long and hard for a moment, contemplating if this is what he really wanted to do. When he realized the only thing he would miss about this job was Ione, he realized his decision was already made for him.

"I understand." With that, he stood up and left the office, carrying nothing but his personal laptop in his hands. And as he walked out the door without a second glance behind him, he knew he had made the right decision.

Greg sat in the coffee shop spinning his full coffee cup around on its saucer. His mind was so much clearer, but why did he feel he made the wrong decision?

"Greg." A man's voice interrupted his thoughts.

"Hey, Dan." Greg stood up to shake the man's hand before sinking back into his seat.

"When I said to think about it, I didn't think you would make a decision so soon." Dan rested his elbows on the table, clasping his hands together.

"Coffee?" Greg motioned to the coffee bar spanning the length of the shop. Dan shook his head.

"Could never drink the stuff, myself." An awkward pause came between the two men.

"So . . ." Greg broke it a few moments later.

"Oh, sorry, I forget you don't know much about this." Dan pulled out his phone.

"We will have to meet with an accountant to work out the business side of this. And, I'm not going to lie, I already have one in mind. It won't cost much to open a PI business. I'm thinking we just start with a separate phone line and printing some business cards. You'll need to get a PI license, of course. They require firearms training, but I'm sure you can get that waived since you've completed the police firearms training in the last couple of years. But, overall, we are only looking at a few hundred dollars to start up." Greg could feel his eyebrows rising.

"I guess I didn't realize it was that easy."

Dan shrugged. "Well, usually you would have to hire someone with my training but, since I'm already here, we are golden. If we get a few cases, we can later look at investing in an office but, for now, I think we really don't need one. We can just meet clients in public places like this." He motioned to the area around the table.

"And you have all the computers and stuff you need at your place?" Greg thought this sounded too good to be true.

"Yep. Been working in tech for long enough I have quite the set up. How about you?"

"I've got a laptop and personal firearm if that's what you're asking."

"Perfect." Dan pulled out his phone, his fingers flying over the keys. "How do you feel about taking the PI course next Tuesday? Or, too soon?" Greg realized he had no income, so, the sooner the better.

"Sure, sounds good. So, how are you thinking we will make money for this?"

"Easy, I'll put an ad out later next week and build us a website. You should work on getting the second phone line up and running. I'll order the business cards. Then start talking to people, handing out the cards. Ione already said he knows a few people who could use a PI." Dan was still typing on the phone.

"You're all registered for the class." Greg sat in silence for a moment, listening to the sound of Dan's fingers hitting the glass screen of the phone.

"About what you said . . ." Dan looked up, waiting for him to continue.

"About my ex-girlfriend being our first case? Well, I've been thinking, and I think, if I solve it, we can advertise but for now I want to keep it quiet."

Dan nodded. "Understood. That's an unpaid case, anyway, so probably better we have at least one paying one going simultaneously." Greg agreed.

"How many cases will you accept at once?"

"Ha, you're optimistic. I doubt people will be breaking down the door to get a PI but it also depends on the cases. Some might be tech-based only, so, those will go to me. And I can take on a lot more cases than you because you'll be doing all the footwork and face-to-face work."

Greg was confused. "What do you mean by tech based?"

"Some people might hire me to investigate a hack or security breach and that wouldn't involve anything on your end."

"Makes sense."

Dan glanced back down at his phone. "Okay, we are meeting the accountant I want to use Friday at three. Can you get a separate phone line by then?" Greg glanced at his watch. It was late in the afternoon but he could stop by the phone company in the morning.

"Sure. I'll get it in the morning."

"Perfect. I'll see you then." Dan stood up to leave but, right before he reached the door, he turned around.

"And Greg, bring any info you have about your girlfriend. I'd like to at least look over what you've got." Greg was about to correct his use of the term 'girlfriend' but Dan was already gone.

20

APRIL 11, 2011

G reg sat in his car outside of the jewelry shop, looking down at the box in his hands. When he had picked out this ring almost a month ago, he never dreamed he'd be returning it. He had been so sure. Ava was the one for him.

He pulled the necklace out of his pocket, turning it over in his hand. He knew he couldn't return it, it'd been worn too many times. But he didn't want Ava to have it either.

With a sigh, he got out of the car and walked into the store, the bell jingling on the handle, alerting the sole sales rep to his presence. Greg winced when he realized it was the same guy who sold him the ring.

"Hello, sir, how can I help you?" The man smiled in a way that seemed almost annoying to Greg. He obviously didn't remember him. Greg set the ring on the counter.

"It didn't fit?" The salesman picked up the ring.

"She didn't want it." The man's demeanor changed almost immediately, his face becoming much softer.

"I'm sorry, let me process a refund for you." He quickly moved over to the register positioned below the glass counter.

Greg could barely move. He could feel his heart breaking. How could she do this to him? His anger quickly faded to concern. Where was she staying? Was she going to be able to afford to rent a place on her own? He shook the thoughts from his head, the anger creeping back in. Ava didn't want him, and he needed to not care about what happened to her.

"Sir, can I see the card you used to pay? I need it to process the refund."

Greg nodded mutely and handed the man his card, feeling the necklace in his pocket as he slipped his wallet back in. A thought came to his mind. He pulled the necklace out of his pocket as the man handed him his card back. Greg pushed the necklace across the counter toward him.

"Sir, I don't think I can process a return on this." He shook his head at the necklace.

"You don't have to. I just don't want it. Please just take it back." Greg felt the tears brimming in his eyes as he raised them to look at the man. Realizing that Greg was about to fall apart, but also not quite knowing what to do, the man took the necklace, stuttering his response.

"Uh, su ... sure."

Without another word, Greg turned and left the store. Once he got back to his apartment, he couldn't control it anymore. He flew up the stairs in a rage and began pulling out all of Ava's belongings and tossing them in a pile in the living room. When he was finished, his anger once again flashed to sadness and he sank on the floor to begin putting her things in garbage bags.

This is what the love of his life had come down to. Three garbage bags.

PART II

21

PRESENT-2018-THREE WEEKS LATER

"D and G Investigations, this is Greg, how may I help you?"

"Um, yes. I think my husband is cheating on me. Can you find out for sure if he is?" a female voice said. Greg reached into his desk drawer and pulled out a small notepad, grabbing a pen from his university emblem cup on the corner of his work space.

"Sure, but I'll need more information. If you provide me with a full name, work place, and home address, I can do some preliminary checks and then meet up to discuss prices with you." The woman sighed.

"Well, I can give you all the info, but do you have a ballpark for cost now? I don't want to waste your time."

"Yes, ma'am, these cases usually range around one thousand dollars for basic checks of email, phone records, and similar things. Usually, they're cut and dry. If your husband, however, has lots of security procedures in place, we may have to follow him. And that's where it gets expensive." The other side of the phone was silent for a moment, then he heard an intake of breath.

"All right, let's do it. I just hope he isn't too crafty."

Greg rolled his eyes at this. They had officially opened their private investigations company a week ago, after Greg had completed his PI badge training, and, so far, this was the third call they got for a cheating husband. In fact, they hadn't gotten any other sort of call. The woman rattled off the information, and Greg copied it down on his notepad. The husband worked at an investing firm, typical. From the sound of it, this would probably be too easy.

"All right, ma'am, I will get right on this and give you a call when I have a cost estimate. What is your name and a good number to reach you at?"

Greg wrote down that information, as well, stifling a yawn as he wished the woman a good day and hung up the phone. He let his forehead come to rest on the desk. This was not what he had in mind when he thought of opening a PI firm with Dan. With a sigh, he lifted his head and typed the husband's name into his background-check website. Each background check did cost them $35 but it was worth it if the client ended up purchasing their services.

After running the background check, Greg opened a window to Facebook, and another to Twitter. He quickly logged into his fake account, which featured a beautiful woman as the profile picture, and requested the husband as a friend and to follow him on twitter. Most wives didn't realize they could easily find out what their husband was up to just by making fake accounts. But then, again, if they did, Greg would be out of a job.

Now it was just a waiting game. Within forty-eight hours he would hear back with the background check and the speed at which the guy either accepted or declined his friendship request would tell him quite a bit of information, all on its own. As it was, Greg jotted down some of the public information available on the guy's profile. Never know when you might need to know what high school he went to.

While Greg was in the middle of writing, the phone rang with the ring tone assigned to Dan. Greg looked at the screen, debated whether he actually had to pick it up, and then pushed talk.

"Hey."

"Hey, Greg, my man, how's it going?"

"Decent. I got a call from a potential client about another cheating husband. Getting the prelim info now." He put his pen down and switched his phone to the other ear.

"Great. How about that other lady, uh . . ." You could hear papers rifling in the background.

"Phyllis? Did she agree to pay for us to follow her husband?" Greg flipped a page forward in his notebook.

"Yes, she paid the first thousand up front, two thousand more if we can find out the name of the mistress. Says that she doesn't want to spend more than that, though. So cut off the tailing at two thousand." Dan was quiet for a moment

"Am I going to follow the bastard or do you want this one?"

Greg looked around the dark room of his apartment, which he had barely left in over a week. Curse the person who invented Postmates. "Uh, I need to get out, I'll take it. Plus, aren't you still working on that first case we got?"

"Hannah hasn't committed yet. I don't think she really has the money for the tail. But there are lots of suspicious phone calls and texts, so, I told her we could probably cut the tail and just look at phone records. She hasn't called me back."

Typical. At least they were lucky to be working on one case within their first week.

"And, Greg?"

"Hm?" Greg was flipping through his notes on Phyllis's husband to get ready for the tail.

"I've been reading your notes about Ava and I think you were on to something when you went to that credit union in Arizona." Greg dropped his pen. "Really? You really think so?"

"Yeah, I mean, it's an account that hasn't been closed due to her death. At least, I'm assuming it's still open based on the police report of her closed bank accounts that you gave me." Greg felt his spirits lift. But, for some reason, he didn't feel the usual pull at his heartstrings that he had always felt before. And it was a weird feeling.

"Now, here's the tough thing. We can't just walk in there demanding information. But I think maybe, if I go in there looking all official with a PI badge and maybe her death certificate, maybe I can get some information." Dan didn't sound too sure but, then again, it was worth a shot.

"Maybe I should go?" Greg suggested.

"Actually . . . I don't think that's a good idea, Greg."

"What? Why?" Greg was taken aback. After all, he was the former cop. If anyone could look official, it was him.

"Well, besides the fact that I need you here for the tail, I also think that, although you are on to something, Greg, and honestly, I believe you are, I think you're too emotionally involved. From just reading your notes, I think you need an outsider to start looking at these things for you."

Greg thought for a moment. Dan was right. He had been so emotionally invested in this for so long that it had caused him to quit his job. That wasn't something that a halfway sane man would do.

"You're right, Dan, you go to the credit union." Greg felt, as he said those words, that a piece of his heart went with them. After all, the case had been his secret child for years.

"Great. But let's switch cars. I want you to use mine with the dark tinted windows for the tail. Plus, I took the front license plate off just in case he notices you in his rearview mirror. Plus a red truck doesn't blend in all that well." Leave it to Dan, Greg hadn't even thought of those things.

"Okay, I'll come switch them at your place first thing tomorrow."

"Actually, I'm stopping by the accountant's office, so I'll come do the switch at your place."

"Roger."

"See you then." And with that, the phone line went dead.

Greg looked down at his notes about Phyllis's husband. He felt bad for the woman, he really did. She and Harvey had met almost twenty years ago when they had both been twenty-one-years-old. Now, after all these years and six children later, she was reporting that her husband never came home and, when he did, he wanted nothing to do with her.

Greg had tried to look at the guy's social media, only to find it a barren wasteland. The last post was almost four years old. He did add Greg's female profile as a friend, though, and that did mean something. The wife had only reported Facebook but, during preliminary investigations, Greg had found an Instagram, as well, though it hadn't helped much. It was just as vacant as the Facebook.

When Dan and Greg had met Phyllis in person, they had asked her to get copies of their joint account statements. Most men were too bright to purchase things for the mistress on the joint account, but you could never be too sure. Most men slipped up somewhere.

Greg pulled his copies out of the folder and began going over the purchases line by line. Phyllis had highlighted all her purchases in pink, and the ones of her husband, or "un-sure" in yellow. The card statement was mostly pink, but the few yellow lines did tell Greg quite a bit.

First of all, there was a once a week visit to a restaurant for lunch. At least, he assumed it was lunch based on the price. But perhaps it could be dinner, as well. He jotted that restaurant down as a place to scope out. There were vending machine purchases, which Greg assumed were made in the office. He also noticed gas purchases, but at an alarming rate. It seemed as if the guy was filling up his tank twice a week. Greg decided to check out his commute and how much gas it should take.

After looking at the accounts, Greg checked the folder to see what else they had on Harvey. There was a picture of the guy, notes about his car, and a business card for his job. Greg picked up the business card and flipped it over, jotting down the address to check it out on Google Earth. He would need to find a good place to hide his car. The guy was a CPA for a large firm of lawyers and that could get dicey— and fast.

Turning back to his computer, Greg thought about sending an email to the wife, but then he had a better idea. He picked up his phone instead.

The line only rang for a moment before an auto-answering machine picked it up and asked for his extension. He waited on the line.

"Hello, this is Ranger, Grove, and Ralley, how may I direct your call?" It was a young female voice on the other end.

"Hi, my name is Paul and I'm looking to hire a lawyer. I guess I'm wondering who I need to speak to and how much a consultation is?" Greg made sure to keep his voice even and unassuming.

"No problem, both Grove and Ralley are taking on new clients at this time. Can I ask what your case is about?" Greg hadn't prepared for this question. He looked down at the card. It just said "full service." Here went nothing.

"I'm getting a divorce and the wife is trying to bleed me dry," he lied.

"Ah, that sounds like a case for Mr. Ralley. He doesn't charge any fees for a consultation. I could get you in on Thursday. Does that work for you?" Greg glanced at the calendar on his computer. It was Monday. Thursday was perfect.

"That works great. Can I come in the afternoon?"

"Let me look at his calendar. He has a 2:00 p.m. Does that work?"

"Perfect. See you then."

"Do you need our address or anything, Mr. . . . ?"

"Smith. And, no, I have your card right here." Greg smiled. One thing he learned in police work is that the people with common last names were the hardest to track.

"Okay. We will see you Thursday, Mr. Smith."

Greg hung up without saying goodbye. Now, he would plan his visit to the lawyers. He sat back in his chair. As much as he hated to admit it, he was really right for this job. Ione had definitely known what he was talking about.

22

TUESDAY

BANG! BANG! BANG!

Greg eased open his left eye only to fix it on the clock and saw that it was barely five in the morning. He must've been dreaming. He closed his eyes again.

BANG! BANG! BANG!

Greg scrunched his forehead. Someone was definitely banging on his door. He barely had any friends. Who could it be?

BANG! BANG! BANG!

"I know you're in there! You have nowhere better to go these days!"

Ahh. Ione. Greg rolled out of bed, not bothering to put on any clothes. Ione would be able to handle seeing him in just his boxers. He opened the door slowly, blinking as the light in the hallway of his apartment complex tried to blind him. "Yes?" Ione didn't even wait for an invitation. Instead, he pushed past Greg and headed to the kitchen, snapping on the lights.

"I'm starving. What you got?" Ione opened the fridge without waiting for Greg's consent. Greg sank down on the couch, half asleep once more.

"I don't know, Ione. Don't you have food at your place?"

"Ha-ha, no." Ione began rummaging through Greg's meager supply of groceries. Granted, it had gotten better over the past few weeks since Greg was home more, but it still wasn't much.

Ione found Greg's egg carton and a pan, immediately cracking all ten eggs that remained into the pan. From his position on the couch, Greg could practically hear the mess Ione was making.

"Please tell me you aren't eating all my eggs."

"I am."

Great. Greg thought, now he would have to go to the store if he wanted breakfast. He could hear the sizzle of the eggs as the pan began to heat up on the stove.

"Please tell me you didn't just come here for food."

"'Course not," his partner replied, his mouth full of something, hopefully not half-cooked eggs.

"I came to check on you. I miss my partner."

"So . . . Carl hired someone else, didn't he?" It was a stab in the dark but Greg wasn't stupid.

"Yeah."

"Who?" Greg stood and headed for the table as he heard the stove switching off. He rested his head in his hands.

"Marie." There was nothing in his mouth but that didn't keep Greg from almost choking.

"What?" Ione shrugged as he sat next to Greg with a plate full of eggs. He began shoveling them into his mouth at an alarming rate.

"I guess she's been to the academy and has a degree in criminal justice. She was just waiting for a position to open up. You left and she took it."

"That bitch."

"Now, now, Greg, you gave up the job." The plate of eggs was already empty. Ione's eating habits would never cease to amaze Greg.

"I know. But—" He didn't even know how to finish the sentence. Ione was right. There was silence for a moment.

"She misses you." Greg's head snapped up.

"Really?" Ione nodded, pulling out his phone.

"She wants me to give you her number."

"Can't she just look my number up?" Ione rolled his eyes.

"That is so unromantic, Greg, and you know it."

Greg looked at the ceiling. Last he had seen Marie, she had been mad at him. What woman gave a man her number when she was mad? Women didn't do that, Greg knew it.

"You liar. You want to give me Marie's number."

"Fine, fine, you're right. Please, just take it, and call her. Seriously, Greg, this hermit lifestyle doesn't suite you." Ione had taken the time to scribble her number down on a paper towel he had torn from the roll on the counter. He placed it on the table in front of Greg and walked towards the door.

"I've been a bachelor as long as you've known me, Ione." Greg glanced over his shoulder as his partner opened the door.

"I know. And it doesn't suit you. Call Marie. Seriously." The door slammed behind him as the behemoth left, his steps ringing off the walls as he headed down the hall.

Greg glanced at the paper towel and thought about what he had to do with his day. A whole lot of nothing. Well, besides seeing if the new subject had accepted his friend request. He supposed he could send Marie a quick apology text.

He headed back to his bedroom to grab his phone from the bedside table. He opened his contacts and began to enter the number on the paper towel as he headed back to the kitchen. After adding the number, he began to scroll through his limited contacts to make sure it saved. He saw that it had, and he began to click it to select it to send her a message. As he did, his eyes were drawn to a number at the bottom of the screen that he hadn't seen in a while. Samantha. She had been Ava's best friend. Greg's mind flashed back to the day she had texted him, accusing Ava of not being where she said she was.

Suddenly, warning bells went off in his mind. That had been the last time he had spoken to Samantha. What had happened? What had she meant? Surely, she knew Ava had disappeared? He felt he had to talk to her.

All his thoughts of Marie forgotten, he began to type out a text to Samantha, asking if it was still her number, and if she remembered him. He hit send, then glanced at the clock in the background of his phone and grimaced. It was a little early. Hopefully her phone was on silent. He was shocked when a message beeped back a few seconds later.

Samantha: "Yes, it's me, and yes, I remember you, Greg. What's up?" Greg immediately answered back.

Greg: "Can I call you now?"

Samantha: "Are we that old now? LOL. Sure."

Greg's hands were practically shaking as he dialed the phone. He couldn't believe he hadn't thought to call her sooner. She answered on the third ring.

"Hello, Greg."

"Samantha, hey." God, he hated how awkward he sounded.

"Please tell me this isn't a 6:00 a.m. social call." Ah, she was still the same easily-annoyed girl he remembered.

"No, listen, I'm investigating Ava's disappearance and I . . ."

She cut him off. "I thought I read in the paper that she was declared dead."

"Um, well, listen," he rephrased, "I'm a private detective now and I'm looking into the case on my own." Samantha made a clicking sound with her tongue.

"Ah, Greg. Some things never do change, do they?"

Now Greg was confused. "What do you mean?"

"You really don't know?" she asked, but then didn't wait for him to answer before she continued. "Even back in high school you only had eyes for Ava. Scratch that, you only had tunnel vision for her. It made you incapable of seeing or caring about anything else." Greg was quiet as her words sunk in. They weren't untrue.

"I loved Ava a lot," he responded pathetically.

"Trust me, me of all people, I knew." She sighed.

"Greg, that day I texted you . . . well, I wasn't lying. Ava hadn't come to lunch in a month. But she told me why . . . and I was stuck in a hard place. After all, Ava was my best friend but you . . . you were my first real crush. I couldn't believe she got you first." His mouth hung open.

"Your . . . first crush?" He was in shock.

"Yes, Greg! I had a crush on you all through high school! First, you were too oblivious to notice, then you found Ava, and, well, after she dumped you, it didn't seem quite right and well . . . I moved on." She let out a breath.

"I guess it doesn't matter if I tell you now, though, does it? Now that she's gone . . ." Greg felt as if he couldn't breathe. He opened his mouth to encourage her to continue but there was no need.

"She, well, needed out, Greg. Not just of your relationship, but of her life. She met this new group of friends, and she knew you wouldn't approve, but they really made her feel free. But then, again, that could've just been because they always drank together but . . ."

"Group of friends? Who?" Samantha sighed again.

"Listen, Greg, she would never have cheated on you, but it was Kyle's group of friends from the restaurant they worked at. She broke it off with you before it got serious with him, but they definitely met one of those nights while you were still dating."

Greg felt his heart shatter into a million pieces. How had he not seen? Samantha sensed his shock.

"You wouldn't have noticed if a semi hit you, Greg, that's how in love with her you were. I tried to hint that night, but you, well, you called her. She got mad at me for tattling and, well, that was the end of our friendship. I should have tried hard to fix it, I really should have, but I didn't, and now . . . now, it's too late."

Silence hung between them on the phone. Greg had no words. Suddenly, a loud, "Mommy!" could be heard in the background of the call.

"Listen," Greg heard her sniffle and imagined her wiping away a stray tear, "I gotta go. And Greg, although it was nice talking to you, I have a life to live. And my life involves moving forward. So, until you can get out of wherever your love for Ava has trapped you, don't call me again." And the line went dead.

Greg wasn't sure how long he sat there, the phone pressed silently to his ear. But by the time he came to, the sun had already risen. He just couldn't process it. His angel, Ava, had been hanging out with new people, even seeing a new guy, behind his back? How could she have done that to him?

The same way she dumped you, you idiot, his inner voice replied.

Tossing the phone on the table, Greg stood and made his way over to his computer, pulling up his old email list from when he worked at the Department. Marie's name, as secretary, was at the top. Before he could lose his nerve, he quickly typed out a message with his phone number and hit send. Hopefully, this would be less creepy than him suddenly having her number.

Ione was right. The bachelor life had never suited him.

23

WEDNESDAY

I t wasn't until the next morning that Greg finally received a text from Marie. It was a quick hello, and asking how he was doing, but not much more. Greg responded and invited her out to dinner later that week. She said yes.

He didn't have much time to dwell on the outcome of the texts, as he had a tail to start. He pulled on a button-down shirt, making sure it was sufficiently wrinkled, and a pair of slightly rumpled slacks. With a glance in the mirror, he knew he could play the part of ruffled divorce well. He used his comb to slick over his hair, and put a pair of readers he had purchased at the grocery store on his nose. They were wide rim and would hopefully sufficiently distort his face. He had also let his beard grow out the last week. Although it was only about an inch long, it still changed his look considerably.

He went to grab his keys, panicking for a moment when they weren't on his hook by the door. Then he remembered he had switched cars with Dan and breathed a sigh of relief. Losing the car keys would not be the correct way to start his official work as a PI.

The drive to the lawyer's office was quick, and Greg made sure to park in the next lot over between two cars larger than his. That way if anyone did watch, they couldn't be quite sure which car he emerged from. Walking up the stairs to the fourth floor where the offices were located, he took a moment to observe his surroundings. The office building was nothing special, and it was shared, telling him that although the lawyers made money, it was not enough to afford their own building. That might seem trivial but, to Greg, it definitely gave him an idea of the type of mistress he would be looking for.

Opening the door to the front portion of the lawyers' office, Greg was greeted by the woman he assumed he had spoken to on the phone earlier that week. The room was white and barren except for the secretary's desk and two waiting chairs. There was also a potted plant, probably fake, in the corner. The only way out was through the door he had just emerged from and a second wooden door alongside the desk.

"Hello, how can I help you today, sir?" The pretty brunette secretary looked up from her computer. Greg feigned wiping the sweat from his brow.

"Yes, I'm Paul, I have an appointment at three." The girl turned towards the computer, brushing a strand of her long hair behind her ear. She was a very beautiful woman.

"Paul . . . Paul . . . I'm not seeing you here. Do you remember who you were seeing?"

"Uhhh . . . I think it was Ralley." Greg scratched his head and pretended to search his pocket for his phone, which he had deliberately left in the car.

"Ahh, I found you. You are supposed to come tomorrow at two, not today."

"Oh, shoot!" Greg pretended to be embarrassed.

"I'm so sorry. This whole divorce has my life turned upside down! Is there any way I can see Ralley today? I did just drive a long way . . ." The secretary smiled, showing off her perfectly straight teeth.

"Let me go and ask him about his afternoon schedule. Do you mind waiting a moment?"

"Of course not," Greg smiled back. "But I'd like to use your restroom if there's one close . . ."

"Certainly!" The secretary came around the desk, using her key to open the wooden door into the inner offices for him.

"Just go down this hall and it's the last door to your left." She pointed it out to him with her perfectly manicured left hand, then made her way into the first door, shutting it behind her.

Greg quickly looked up. No cameras. Perfect. He slowly made his way down the hall, trying not to be too suspicious, but also trying to read each name plate as he passed each door. The first two doors belonged to the lawyers, the third and fourth doors were unlabeled. The last door on the left was the bathroom, as the secretary had described. The door directly across from it simply had a label that said 'Finance.' Greg turned around to make sure no one had poked their head out of a door to see what he was doing. Luckily, he was unobserved.

He turned and opened the door that was marked 'Finance'. Inside was a room very similar to the one he had just come from with a secretary sitting at her desk. Behind her there was a window with a single partition. The only other difference was this room had two doors leading out of it, both were open, and both had name placards. Bingo.

"Can I help you?" The blonde secretary looked at him suspiciously. She was clearly older than the woman who was manning the front office, but she was still good looking. She wore suit jacket that one would expect of a lawyer, but it made her look very trim and professional. Greg also sensed she wore it to appear younger.

"Oh, uh, sorry. I came out of the bathroom and guess I got turned around." He pulled at his collar to feign nervousness.

"I was supposed to see . . . Ralley . . . I think?" She smiled sweetly.

"Ah, well, he's two doors down! Just go back out and turn to your right. Last door on the right before the end of the hall."

"Thanks." Greg smiled, looking at the two nameplates briefly as he left the room. He made his way back to the waiting room just moments before the first secretary reappeared.

"I'm so sorry, Mr. Smith, but Mr. Ralley has meetings this entire afternoon. Can you make it back tomorrow?"

"Um, I'll try. I'm not sure I can get off work another day. Can I call you and let you know?"

"Sure thing, sorry about the confusion. Hopefully, we can see you tomorrow." She smiled sweetly and opened the exit door for him.

Greg acted as if he was going to walk down the stairs until the door closed behind him. Then he stopped, glanced around, and began to count the windows for each floor. Then he quickly returned to his car. Once there, he pulled out his notepad and a pencil and began to sketch the layout of the entire office to his knowledge. He was bummed that most of the doors were closed but, based on the amount of footsteps it took him to get to the bathroom, and upon seeing the size of the window in the finance offices, he believed he had enough information.

After Greg finished his map, he quickly drove to the side of the building where the finance offices had been, parking his car safely across the street. Then, he pulled out his notes and his binoculars. He zoomed in on the office he figured belonged to Phyllis's husband and was glad to see there was a man sitting at the desk with his back to the window. No blinds. Greg pulled out his bottle of water and a snack and leaned back. This was going to be a long afternoon.

It was nearly five in the evening when Greg's phone finally rang. He saw it was Dan and quickly picked up.

"Dan, what'd you find out?" he asked eagerly.

"Well, hello to you, too," Dan laughed.

"Sorry, I just—" Greg caught himself. For some reason he didn't quite feel the usual pull he did when he started that sentence. There was still an ache in his chest, but it wasn't the same, something had changed.

"No worries, man, I got you." There was the sound of papers flipping in the background.

"Well, the credit union was a little more tight lipped than I had hoped but, get this, the account, the one you think belonged to Ava, it's still open. And get this, there's still an authorized user." Greg felt all the words leave his mouth. He couldn't speak.

"I asked who the authorized user is, and they wouldn't tell me.

They said I need a court order. So, hear me out. You hold down the fort there and I'll case out things here and, hopefully, I can get a picture of our authorized user."

"And just how are you going to know which is her?" This didn't sound clean-cut to Greg.

"I won't. I'm just going to hang out for a week and take pictures of everyone who goes in and out. It's a small town down here, there can't be that many people who use this credit union. And Greg, I'll ask around town, maybe they'll know something."

"Thanks, man."

"No problem. I really hope we can solve this, both for your sanity, and for the fame I'm going to get." He broke out in laughter. Greg chuckled in return.

"I started the tail today here. Nothing really to report. Honestly, the guy spent most of the day in his office. I'll observe his lunch break tomorrow and we can go from there." Greg jotted down a few notes on his notepad.

"Good. Also, don't rule out a co-worker romance. Definitely possible, if the guy never leaves his office."

Greg had already thought of that. "I know. I checked out the secretary today in the main office. She has a ring but we all know that means nothing. Didn't get a complete look at the second female co-worker who I saw, but she was a little older. I know that doesn't rule her out, but there wasn't an obvious mistress that I could see."

"Well, keep on it. Anything on that new case? Uh, Ms. Williams?"

"Not yet, still combing the social media. Nothing stands out so far. I'll keep at it tonight. Did Hannah ever decide on her next move?" Dan let out a breath.

"Yeah, she doesn't have the money for a tail. She's going to pay us to look over the phone records. It's not much, but it's some business." Greg could practically hear Dan running his hands through his hair. Greg had sufficient savings to last him a few months to get this business rolling, but he knew Dan hadn't had quite the job security he had enjoyed over the past few years.

"Want me to look through the phone records?" Greg asked.

"Nah, I'll have them printed here. I can comb them while I'm sitting on this credit union. You have your hands full with those two cases."

"No problem. And Dan?"

"Yeah?"

"After this week, I really think regardless of what you see, I need to go down there." Greg couldn't help it but something Ava had once said was suddenly nagging at his mind. He willed the thought to fully form, but instead it drifted away. Dan let out a breath.

"All right, Greg. We can work that out. I'll keep you posted." And with that, the line went dead.

"Someday I'd like to live away from society. Way away, where no one could find me." Ava's voice came like a whisper through his head.

And, suddenly, Greg remembered.

24

THURSDAY

Greg stood nervously outside the restaurant adjusting his collar for about the fiftieth time. He checked his cell phone clock. Five twenty nine, she should be here any minute.

"Hey, Greg." Marie. Right on cue.

"Marie." Greg leaned over and gave her what could only be classified as an awkward side hug.

"It's been lonely at work without you." Marie turned towards the door as Greg pulled it open for her.

"Really?" For some reason, he had a hard time believing he was missed. She smiled.

"Okay, what I really meant is that Ione is lonely without you."

"Ahh, the truth is revealed." They approached the host stand and checked in for their reservation. Marie looked around the restaurant.

"Interesting place." Greg nodded.

"Yeah, I know it's a bit cliché, and not the fanciest, but for apps and drinks this really is the place."

They were both silent as they were lead to their table. As soon as they sat down, Greg figured he just had to go for it.

"Listen, Marie, I'm really so—" She held up her hand to stop him.

"I understand. Everyone has their mountains and valleys in life. You've been in a massive valley for the last few years, but I think you're approaching a mountain." Greg cocked his eyebrow in confusion. Marie rolled her eyes and then explained.

"You're having a tough time and I get it, okay? Everyone has tough times. Just don't drag us all down with you, okay?" He nodded and then thought of something. "Marie, why are you still single? Seems like some guy would have snatched you up long ago."

Whether she was aware of it or not, when Greg said the word single, Marie reached down and fingered her ring finger on her left hand. That was a telltale sign to Greg that something had happened. Marie noticed Greg's eyes becoming fixed on her hand, and she looked down and noticed she had been touching the spot she'd always thought a ring would be. Well, there was no hiding anything from him now.

"I was almost engaged once."

"Almost engaged? Is that even a thing?" Greg opened the menu, just so he would have somewhere to look and make her feel like she was less on the spot. She sighed.

"Yes. My boyfriend of two-and-a-half-years bought a ring, and he planned to propose. I found out because he showed the ring to my best friend, and I flipped out."

Greg found his breath had left him. He looked up to see Marie was also looking down at the menu. In his mind's eye, he saw the jeweler and the look on his face when Greg had returned the ring he bought all those years ago.

"I loved him. I really did. But, he wasn't right for me. We wanted different things. I knew, if I said yes to him, I would never have the career I wanted. So, I broke it off, and we went our separate ways."

"Do you regret it?" She shook her head.

"I never have."

"Then it was the right decision." She looked up from the menu and smiled a sad half-smile.

"I know."

"How long ago was this?" Greg asked.

"Almost eight years." Greg could feel his eyes widen in shock. Marie must have noticed because she quickly added.

"I've been on dates since then, but nothing serious. Most guys don't like to hear that my career comes first."

Silence once again came over them for a short period of time as they looked over the menu. The server approached not long after.

"I'll take the Balsamic Steak Salad, please." Marie ordered first.

"The Rainbow Trout for me." Greg handed the waiter his menu as he repeated the order and walked away. It was quiet once again.

"So . . . ordering a salad, huh? Isn't that the female date cliché?" Greg knew it was kind of a rude remark, but the silence was getting to him. He shouldn't have brought up a serious topic so soon. It worked, she laughed.

"I guess you're right. I didn't even think about that, it just looked so good!" Greg found her laughter contagious and joined in.

"I guess I shouldn't be talking. Ordering the trout isn't that manly."

"I don't know what you're talking about. Trout is the manliest fish there is."

"As opposed to?"

Marie laughed again. "You know, the more girly fishes, like salmon and tilapia."

"Salmon is girly? That's not fair. You women can't claim the best fish for yourself!"

And just like that, they were bantering like old friends. Greg hadn't laughed this much in a long time. Not since . . . well . . . And just like that, it was silent again. Their food arrived and they both dug in. Marie broke the silence this time.

"Why don't you tell me about her?" she asked as she drizzled dressing on her salad. Greg knew immediately who she was referring to, but decided to clarify it just in case.

"Her who?"

"The woman who controls your life. I don't know her name, or much about her, because Ione wouldn't let me squeeze him for information, but I know she's got a ball and chain on you, whoever and wherever she is." Marie looked down and took a large bite of her salad. Greg really didn't know where to start. Scratch that, he didn't even know how to start. Screw it, here went nothing.

"We met in high school. Her name was Ava."

"High school, wow, and Ava, that's a pretty name," Marie commented politely.

"And she was a beautiful girl. She was so beyond my league, to this day I don't even know how I landed her but we went to senior prom together and, well, she was basically a gift from God." Greg took a bite of his food, chewing before he continued.

"I loved her more than, than, well, anything on this earth. I would have done anything for her. Even died. That's how much I loved her." Greg stopped again, staring quietly at his food. It was so weird to hear this all out loud.

"I sense there's more," Marie prodded. He took a deep breath.

"Yeah, there's a lot more but, well, I don't want to get too deep into it. Basically, I bought a ring, planned to propose, and she dumped me. Just like that. Tossed to the side." Greg subconsciously began to angrily stab at his trout. Marie placed her hand over his to calm him.

"So . . . you've never gotten over her?" She asked hesitantly. He shook his head.

"That's just it. I think I would have, if I had been given the chance. After she dumped me, she dated another guy for a while, and then she just disappeared."

"What do you mean, disappeared?" Marie took another bite of her salad, patiently waiting for Greg to continue.

"Literally, that's what happened. She vanished into thin air. Everyone thinks she's dead now. But I know better. I know this girl. And I think this was it."

"It, it what?" Greg ran a hand through his hair, food forgotten. He had never considered this out loud before.

"Her plan, this was her plan," he whispered, forgetting Marie was still sitting at the table. She seemed to notice that Greg was no longer mentally present, and decided to change the subject to snap him out of it.

"So, your family, are they in town?" It worked. Greg quickly realized where he was and resumed munching on his trout, though he had partially lost his appetite. "Uh, well, it's just me and my mom. And she's around . . . sorta. She's retired now, so she just travels and goes to see friends. She comes to visit me every so often. But her home is in Carson City, so not an every weekend sort of deal. How about you? Big Family?" She moved her head from side to side.

"Not really. I mean it depends on what you consider big. I have two sisters and both parents are still in the picture. But that's it for my close family. My extended family is another story . . ." She trailed off and Greg got the sense she didn't want to discuss it all now.

"So . . . sisters . . . older? Younger?" he prodded.

"One of each. Being the middle child can be tough. But I'm the only one who went to college, and the only one who's not living off of a man right now, so, I guess you can say I'm the one who stands out for being accomplished?" Greg smiled. "Living off a man . . . as in a stay-at-home-mom?" She shook her head.

"Not even. To me, that's acceptable. If you stay at home and take care of kids while the man pays the bills, well, then it's an equal split. What I mean is that my older sister lives with her husband, they don't have kids, and she just sits at home and shops online all day every day."

"How does her husband afford that?" Greg placed his silverware on his plate and pushed it away. He was finished. Marie shrugged.

"I'm not really sure. I think she returns a lot of what she buys, because he's not rich or anything."

"And your other sister does the same thing?"

"Nope. She still lives at home with my parents." Marie pushed her dish to the side, she was finished as well. The server noticed and began to make his way over. "And before you ask, she's twenty-seven and definitely old enough to not be mooching off mom and dad." He laughed at the expression as the server collected their plates and asked about dessert.

"Do you want anything?" Greg asked politely. Marie shook her head.

"I know you're just gonna laugh but that salad really did fill me up."

He smiled, realizing all at once how relaxed he was and how much fun he was having. He hadn't done something like this is a long time. He looked at the server and requested the check.

"Soo . . ." Marie looked at him.

"So what?" He was perplexed.

"Want to go somewhere else? Get a drink? My place?" She winked at him.

Greg thought for a moment. He really was having fun with her. But it was getting late, and tomorrow was a big day for the tail because it was Saturday, and Phyllis reported that her husband always went to work on Saturday. Greg definitely wasn't buying it.

"Marie, I'm having so much fun and normally I would love to get a drink. But tomorrow I have to work and it's not the type of work where I can slack off."

"Like you did at the station?" Marie interjected, a smile still present on her face.

"Exactly. Since I'm self-employed now, if I slack off, I don't get paid." Marie placed her hands on top of his.

"No worries, I get it. Just promise me a second date? None of this 'I'll call you' stuff, please."

It was Greg's turn to smile. "No problem. How about Monday?" He figured the tail would be mostly done by then and he and Dan were planning to switch out on Tuesday if it wasn't.

"It's a date," Marie answered and they both laughed once again as Greg pulled out the necessary cash to cover the tab. They both rose from the table and walked together over towards the door. Greg held it open just as before and then proceeded to follow Marie to her car. Before he could chicken out, Greg leaned in and placed a quick kiss on Marie's lips. As he pulled away, he noticed a smile on her lips before she grabbed his shoulder and leaned in for another kiss. They kissed a third time before Greg pulled back nervously.

"I better go, have a good night."

"You too. See you Monday," she replied as she slid into her car.

Greg's smile occupied his face the entire way home.

25

SATURDAY

Greg spent all of Saturday sitting on Harvey, but something definitely wasn't adding up. The guy really did go to work on Saturday and, from what Greg could tell through the binoculars, he spent most of the day sitting in his office, well, working. He thought maybe his break had come when Harvey left his office for lunch. Greg followed him only to find that he headed to a modest Italian restaurant and, when he walked in, a man at another table waived him over. Was this it? Was the guy gay? Greg thought about it as he told the waitress he was headed for the bar. The bar was only a table away from the two men and a lot less conspicuous than asking for the table right next to them.

He quickly ordered a water and an order of ravioli's from the bartender and opened his phone and pretended to scroll so she would leave him alone. He needed to listen. The men were talking in hushed voices, but Greg was able to hear the general gist of their conversation.

"Have you told Phyllis yet?" The mystery man took a sip of what appeared to be plain old water. Harvey shook his head.

"I just don't know how. We have six kids. What is she going to do?" Greg's mind began to go wild but he kept silent and jotted notes in his phone.

"I know it's going to be hard, but she needs to know. I think not telling her is contributing to your depression." Harvey seemed pensive for a moment.

"I know. I'm working all I can now. I hoped to have some money saved up for her. I only wish I had picked out a better life insurance policy back in the day." He leaned over and placed his head in his hands.

Greg felt his eyes go wide. This was not what he was expecting. Their food arrived and both men paused their conversation to take a few bites. Greg's food also arrived, but he didn't dare put down his phone.

"I just want to protect her a little longer before I send her world crashing down, you know?" Harvey appeared to wipe a tear from the corner of his eye.

"As your psychiatrist, I can only listen and give you advice I feel is best but, as your friend, Harvey, you need to tell her, and soon." The mystery man continued to eat his meal. Harvey no longer appeared hungry and, instead, became distracted by wiping the condensation off his water glass.

"I know. I just wish the treatments had worked. Then I wouldn't have ever had to tell her."

"I know, Harvey, but you can't go back now, only forward." The man glanced at his watch.

"Listen, I don't feel right billing you for this, so, how about you just get my lunch and we will call it even?" Harvey sighed.

"Jack, I haven't paid you in months, I've only been buying you lunch." The pieces suddenly clicked into place for Greg. Everything made sense. The mystery man, who Greg now knew as Jack, smiled.

"I know, man. But you're my friend and you need help and, well, I don't feel right charging you for it. Beyond you paying for my lunch, that is."

"All right, if you're sure," Harvey replied, motioning to the waiter that they wanted the check.

"I am sure, and Harvey, please, tell Phyllis. It will help, I promise." With that the man called Jack got up and left the restaurant.

Greg thought for a moment. He knew it wasn't protocol, but he realized what he needed to do. He motioned to the bartender, telling her he would be right back, and he headed over and sat right next to Harvey in the spot recently vacated by Jack. Harvey looked up, startled. Greg smiled, trying to lessen his alarm.

"Sorry to scare you, I just need to talk to you real quick." Harvey glanced around, confused.

"Me?"

"Yes." Greg could feel the sweat on his forehead. Dan would eat him alive for this.

"Listen. You don't know me, but your wife hired me to follow you." Harvey's eyes grew wide and his mouth dropped open.

"Wha . . . what?" Greg held up his hand, sensing the man was about to flee. "Hear me out." He took a deep breath. "She was worried. You're never home, you were spending more than one guy should on lunch," he motioned to the plates on the table, "and there was some money missing from your joint account. She thought you were seeing someone else." This seemed to break the guy. He slumped over, his head in his hands.

"I feel so terrible," he whispered. Greg touched the guy's shoulder.

"I know, now, you're not cheating. But I don't want to be the one to report all of this to your wife. Please go home and tell her, because I promised her an update on Monday, and I'll be forced to tell her then because she paid up front." Harvey nodded, not meeting Greg's eye.

"I will, I promise. I didn't mean to make this into such a mess but it appears I did."

"No worries, man to man, I understand." With that, Greg stood up and headed back to the bar. The waitress had taken the liberty of packing his untouched meal into a to-go box and bringing his bill. Greg quickly pulled out twenty dollars and left it on the bill, grabbed his food, and headed for the door. He needed to call Dan. He knew the guy was going to be pissed that he wanted to give a discount on their first real job, but Greg didn't feel right taking another thousand from Phyllis. The money she paid up front would be plenty.

When he arrived back at his apartment, he began to clean out Dan's car, which had remnants of a long trail strewn everywhere. There were fast-food wrappers, coffee cups, and little pieces of paper which Greg had doodled on to keep himself awake during the slow moments. After cleaning the car, Greg went to his desk and began filling out the case notes in the file Dan and he shared. He was midway through his report when his phone rang. It was Dan, of course.

"What's up?" Greg answered and placed the phone on speaker so he could continue typing with ease.

"Not much. Got a bunch of pictures that I just finished uploading from my week of sitting outside the credit union." Greg minimized his report to look in the folder.

"I don't see them on my end yet."

"I'm uploading them now, give me a minute . . . are you still on the tail?" Greg realized Dan could hear the keyboard in the background.

"No . . . the case is closed."

"Closed?" Dan seemed shocked.

"Man, you must be amazing! What did you find out?" Greg pinched the bridge of his nose before he continued.

"I'm writing up the report right now but listen, Dan, I don't want to charge Phyllis any more money and we can't talk to her until Monday."

"What? Why?" Greg could hear the anger brewing in Dan's voice.

"Listen, Harvey, her husband, is sick. I don't know with what, but its terminal. All that extra gas was to see specialists, all those lunches were for him and his psychiatrist, and all those extra bills were treatments." Greg took a deep breath.

"He was working Saturdays and long hours to try to put more money away because I guess he doesn't have a large life insurance policy." Dan let out a low whistle on the other side of the phone.

"Now, I don't like you giving out discounts on our first major case but, you're right, I can't charge her any more money."

"And Dan?" Greg continued.

"I approached the guy. I know it wasn't kosher. I didn't say my name or anything. I just told him he needed to tell his wife because she thought he was cheating. I told him I had to report to her on Monday so he had until then."

"Now, I wouldn't advise any of what you did in future cases, Greg, but in these circumstances, I think you did the right thing. I'll edit Phyllis's bill to paid in full. Since she paid a thousand for the digital digging, and a thousand for the tail, we at least broke even, maybe made a small profit . . ." Dan trailed off.

"You can reduce my hourly for the tail. I'll take half-pay and that way you can take what's left as your paycheck," Greg volunteered.

"Nah, man, you take your full hourly. I'll take the two hundred that's left over. But I'm taking all of the pay for this digital digging I'm doing for Hannah Williams."

"No problem, sounds fair to me," Greg agreed.

They talked a few more minutes about what time Dan would be by to exchange the cars the next day and then they hung up. Greg quickly finished typing his report and then pulled up Google Maps. He entered in the name of the small town where the credit union was located and began to zoom out, inspecting the surrounding area. It was a small town of only about twenty thousand people, and many lived on the outskirts. In turn, Greg began to trace each of the small roads, seeing where they led.

Many of the roads led to what looked like active farms, and he immediately eliminated those. Ava liked to garden but she definitely wouldn't be farming. Some of the roads led to neighborhoods, which Greg considered, but again eliminated. Ava had always mentioned being alone. A few of the roads led to what looked like abandoned farm houses, or small cabins. Greg dropped pins at each of these. These were exactly the types of places Ava would stay.

By the end of his search, Greg had dropped five pins. There were five locations that fit what he believed Ava would like. Now, he had only searched in the immediate vicinity of the small town, and he knew that she could be somewhere on the long drive between

Nevada and the town, but something in the back of his mind told him that she wouldn't have wanted to be without the modern conveniences of grocery stores, restaurants, and a job. *If she was even working a job.*

He pushed that last pesky thought to the back of his mind. Ava would never be without a job, she liked working way too much. As he exited his internet browser, he noticed the photos from Dan had been uploaded to their folder. He quickly opened them and began clicking through.

Over two hundred people had come in and out of the credit union that week. Lots of men, some women, and quite a few women with children. But none of them looked anything like Ava. Greg didn't let this thought discourage him though. He was going to Arizona next week regardless of what this turned up. Maybe Ava hadn't needed to visit her credit union last week.

Re-opening his browser, Greg quickly booked a three star motel for Tuesday to Friday of the coming week. After entering his credit card information, he clicked over to his bank website to see what his funds looked like. Not dating over the last several years had certainly saved Greg a lot of money, as did having a consistent government paycheck. His hourly rate for the tail was twenty an hour, so, a nice paycheck would be coming his way from Dan. Greg estimated he could afford to take next week off and continue to pursue this PI business for at least three more months. If they didn't have regular cases by then, well, Greg would have to look into finding another job.

Dan had said it would pan out though and, so far, it had. Greg trusted that the cases would continue to come in. He closed his laptop and headed for the kitchen, thinking about his date with Marie Monday night. Enough of this cliché dinner bullshit. He was going to take her on a real date, now he just needed to figure out what that was going to be. He realized for the first time in a long time that he was looking forward to seeing someone. Something in him had changed.

26

MONDAY

Greg stood outside the video arcade and checked his watch. It was six o'clock, the time he and Marie had agreed to meet. Maybe she was just running a few minutes late, he thought to himself.

Six fifteen came and went. in fact, six thirty came and went. Marie didn't show. Finally, at seven o'clock, Greg decided to call it quits and headed to his car to begin the drive home. Well, this one she couldn't put on him.

When he pulled up in front of his apartment building, he sent Marie a quick text, letting her know he hoped everything was okay. Without worrying too much about being stood up, Greg unbuttoned his collared shirt as he walked up the stairs to his apartment. He didn't know why he had put it on, anyway, the date plan had been to hang out at the video arcade and then head to get burgers at the nearby diner. Nothing fancy. Greg's phone buzzed as he unlocked his door. He could hardly pick it up fast enough.

Marie: "Sorry, got held up at work, will call later."

Greg almost smiled as he read the text. How could he forget the life of a fellow police officer? Marie wasn't avoiding him, she was just busy. As he stepped into his apartment, he heard a faint "Greg!" from down the hall. He turned around just in time to see Ione jogging to the door.

"Hey, man, where's the hot date?" Ione asked as he stepped into the apartment looking for Marie. Greg raised an eyebrow.

"I don't remember telling you I had a date tonight." Ione shrugged and headed towards the fridge.

"You didn't." Now Greg was confused.

"So, you know I had a date tonight, how?" Ione popped his head out from behind the fridge door.

"Man, how do you live? There's literally nothing edible in here." Greg walked up behind Ione to see what he was looking at.

"Um, Ione, there's some carrots and salad right there." Ione rolled his eyes. "Man, that stuff is for rabbits." He slammed the door shut and grabbed a pizza delivery menu from where it hung on its magnet.

"I'm ordering in."

"Are you asking for permission?"

"Nope." Ione pulled out his cell phone and began to dial.

"You still didn't tell me how you knew that I had a date tonight." Greg raised his eyebrows at Ione as he slid down on the couch. Ione held up a finger as he spoke to the pizza delivery guy on the other side of the phone. Once his order for two pizzas, wings, and breadsticks was in, he hung up and turned back to Greg.

"Marie told me, duh." Greg should've known word of him and Marie was going around the office.

"She talk a lot about me?" Greg inquired.

"Nope," Ione replied as he headed back over to the fridge and pulled out the only six pack of beers that was currently in it. He opened the first beer using the counter top. Greg cringed. Ione downed the beverage in two gulps and popped open a second one in the same manner.

"Dude, I'm never going to get my security deposit back if you ruin the counter tops."

"Dude," Ione imitated Greg's voice, "like you're ever gonna move anyways."

Greg narrowed his eyes at Ione. Jerk. Ione just smiled, knowing he had won. He then plopped down on the couch next to Greg, grabbed the remote, and switched on the TV.

"Why are you here again?" Greg stared at his friend.

"Why not?" Ione shrugged.

"Because you have your own house, with your own TV, and can order delivery from there." Greg really didn't understand why Ione always felt the need to eat his food.

"Yeah, but I was out of beer." Ione flipped channels.

"Last I checked, my house is definitely not closer than the liquor store." Ione shrugged again.

"Cheaper to come here than buy beer." Greg couldn't keep the shock from his voice.

"I'm the one with a start-up career here." Ione popped another beer, this time on the side table next to the couch.

"So, now you can't afford beer?" he asked. Greg just smiled in annoyance. "Fine, fine, you win, drink all my beers. I don't care."

"Oh, I'm not going to drink them all buddy, here," Ione popped the fourth beer and handed it to Greg.

Greg rolled his eyes and turned towards the TV to see what Ione had put on. It was some sort of sport commentary, of course. They watched TV in silence for a few minutes until the doorbell rang, announcing the arrival of the pizza. Ione didn't make a move to answer it. Greg rose from the couch, grabbed his wallet, and headed for the door. He was almost there when a wallet came flying through the room at his head. Greg dropped his own to grab it.

"Food's on me," Ione said without moving his glance from the screen.

Greg smiled and opened the door, pulling out the amount necessary to cover the order. With his arms full of food, he turned back towards the table, closing the door with his foot. Before he knew it, his friend had moved from the couch to grab a pizza box and quickly sat back down, opening the pizza box and eating off of it like it was his own personal plate.

"So, was work busy today? Marie said she missed our date

because of it." Greg said as he opened the second box to get a slice of pizza for himself.

"I don't really know," his former partner answered, his mouth full of food. "Marie got reassigned, or quit, or something. Saw her in Carl's office today, then she cleared out her desk. Didn't even say goodbye." This was news to Greg. Marie had only had the new job for a couple weeks.

"Huh, well she said she would call later, I'll ask then. You know, maybe you could've started with that instead of heading straight for the fridge."

"Sorry, can't think when I'm starved." Ione had polished off his pizza and returned to the table to grab the breadsticks. He shoved one in his mouth while he peeked into the box of wings.

"Well, do you think you'll get a new partner tomorrow?" Greg pressed his buddy. He felt a little like a parent prying for information.

"Maybe, but probably a transfer and not someone from within."

Greg didn't say anything else as both men finished eating their dinner. After they were done, they ended up playing video games for a couple of hours. Ione won every single game, of course, even Mario Kart when Greg put it in as a last ditch effort to at least win something.

It was almost midnight by the time Ione headed home, and Greg cringed as he realized he had to get up early to start his drive tomorrow. And he had yet to pack anything for his week of travels. Eh, he could pack in the morning. He headed to his bedroom, ignoring the mess dinner had left all over the table. He would deal with that later too.

$$27$$

TUESDAY

The desert landscape rushed by Greg's window as he crossed the border into Arizona and headed south. He rubbed the sleep out of his eyes and took a sip of the double-shot coffee he had picked up on his way out of town. Granted, he could've slept in a little, but he was suddenly very anxious to get to Arizona and check out the spots he had circled on his map. He didn't know why but he had a feeling he was close, really close.

Greg considered what he would do when he found Ava. And under what circumstances he was going to find her. At this point, he was sure she wasn't a prisoner of some sort. And she most likely left of her own free will, which means he would have to convince her to come back on her own free will.

And what—date you again?

His subconscious was right. Even if he did find Ava, what did he expect? It'd been seven years. She'd probably moved on.

She moved on before, idiot. Remember?

Greg groaned and willed his subconscious to shut up. He should turn back and drive back home. But, then again, what was waiting for him there? Like it or not, the search for Ava had given him a purpose. For the past seven years, Greg hadn't really been living, only existing, and this task he had been handed gave him a reason to get up in the morning.

Glancing at his GPS, Greg got off the highway and pulled into a rest stop to refuel. He'd only been on the road an hour, but he knew he was approaching an area with no rest stops. As he filled the tank, he checked the messages on his phone. There was a voicemail from Dan about the closing of their tail case. Harvey told his wife about his illness and she had called to close the case on her own. Everything had worked out this time. There was a text from Ione, asking him to a football game at his house the coming weekend. Greg decided he would respond to that later. There was another voicemail, from Samantha of all people. Greg pressed play.

"Hey Greg, this is Samantha. Listen, I've been thinking about what I said to you and, well, it was a little harsh and I'm sorry. I've been tired and under a bit of stress lately." As if on cue, there was a child yelling in the background of the recording.

"Anyway, let me know if you want to meet up for coffee or something. I'd love to catch up . . ." She continued on to leave her phone number and then hung up.

Greg was unsure what to do. He didn't really want to call Samantha back, but he also didn't want to ignore her message. He decided to make his decision later. There was nothing on his phone from Marie. The old Greg might have called her and asked or texted her even but, for some reason, he couldn't bring himself to care. Guess she wasn't that into him after all. Not that he cared. He climbed back in his car and resumed his drive.

It was almost four hours later when Greg pulled into the parking lot of the credit union. Granted, he had stopped for a quick lunch about fifty miles back. He stepped out of the car and checked his appearance. His clothes were a bit wrinkled, but still professional looking. This would have to do.

He walked up to the door and stepped inside. The credit union was small, a waiting area on one side, a line of teller counters on the other. The corner held a water jug and coffee machine. Behind the teller counter, there were three closed doors. Probably managerial offices, Greg assumed.

"Hello!" A pretty young woman of Asian descent looked up from whatever she was writing at the counter to greet him.

"How can I help you today?" She smiled, her white teeth all perfectly aligned.

"Good afternoon," Greg replied, walking up and leaning on the counter. "I am here to enquire about an account."

"You'd like to open one?"

Greg kept the smile on his face and pulled out his PI license. "Actually, I am here to ask about an account that's already been opened."

The girl raised her eyebrows. "I'm sorry but we can't give out any information about accounts."

Greg had figured this would be the response. He had a plan, though. He pulled out a piece of paper from inside his pocket and laid it on the counter. The woman didn't flinch.

"Who is this?"

"I believe this is the owner of the account in question. Now, I know you can't give me any names, or any information, but can you just tell me if you've seen her in this building before?" The girl stared at the picture for a moment, biting her lip. "Umm . . . I'm new here and I really can't afford to lose my job . . ."

"That's not a breach of security, I promise. And no one will ever know," Greg reassured her.

"Well . . ." She looked up to meet Greg's eyes.

"Yes, I've seen her around . . . er, in this building." She cleared her throat and looked around as if she was being watched. Greg nodded and then pulled a second piece of paper out of his pocket. It was a map of the immediate area. A red star was drawn over the credit union.

"So, when she leaves here, can you tell me which direction she drives?"

The girl seemed to hesitate again, unsure of what she was allowed to say and what was private. Greg looked down at the name tag pinned to her pink top. Her name was Karena.

"Please, Karena? This is my last question, I promise. And this will only be between the two of us." He tried to 'lay on the charm' like they did in movies, but he was pretty sure he just sounded desperate. Karena nodded her head to the left briefly but enough so that Greg knew that was the answer.

"All right. I get it. Thanks again." He gathered up his papers and headed back to his car.

Greg pulled around the corner, out of view of the credit union, and unrolled his map once more. He placed the small section over the bigger map he had printed at FedEx over the weekend. He quickly deduced that three of the five properties were in that direction. Not quite as narrowed as he had hoped, but doable.

The three properties in question were on his way back out of town—from the direction he had just come. He had enough daylight to check out at least one of the properties today.

Greg leaned over and opened the glove compartment. He pulled out his legally registered firearm, put it in the small of his back, and covered it with his shirt. He knew that wasn't the safest, but he didn't want anyone to feel threatened.

It took about twenty minutes to come to the first property. And, honestly, it looked completely deserted when he pulled up. It was a dilapidated old farmhouse, surrounded by broken farming machinery. When he had looked at the place on Google Maps, it hadn't looked like an active farm. Greg quickly looked around and surmised it wasn't. Either the machinery was from a past time or perhaps the owner of the house repaired farm equipment for a living.

Greg stepped out of his car and headed for the door. He knocked politely and waited. He heard some commotion inside, but the door didn't immediately open. He wondered what was going on.

He quickly got his answer as a little old lady opened the door a crack.

"Who's there?" she demanded.

"Hello, ma'am, my name is Greg and I'm an investigator." He figured that sounded more official than private investigator and he mentally crossed his fingers that she wouldn't slam the door in his face.

"Investigator? I haven't done nothing illegal," she scoffed.

"No, ma'am, you haven't. I'm investigating a missing person." The woman seemed to think for a minute, then opened the door fully. She was a short woman, with tanned skin from what was probably years of working the land. Her silvery grey hair was braided in a single thin braid down her back. She wore what looked like a nightgown, obviously not expecting any guests.

"What's that got to do with me?"

"Can I come in? Then we can discuss it. I promise I'm not here to investigate anything regarding you." The woman looked him up and down and then stepped inside to let him in.

"Well, I guess. But I wasn't really expecting no guests today."

"It's all right, ma'am, this will only take a moment."

Greg stepped past her into the dilapidated farm house. It was a brick and wooden structure, a typical mid-1950s build. The walls were coated in wallpaper that had been changed or treated for decades. He could only see the front room due to the traditional closed floor plan of the time. But from what he could see, it was dirty. Although it wasn't in complete disarray, it could use some TLC. The woman motioned to the sunken-in couch that had obviously been in that exact spot since about 1970.

"Want some tea? Or water? Don't have much else."

"I'm okay," Greg answered as he sat down, observing how the ceiling seemed to be caving in. That wasn't a good sign. The woman sat down in the overstuffed chair directly across from him.

"I'm Greg Sanders." Greg leaned across to take the woman's frail hand.

She just looked at him confused.

"You can call me Mrs. Atkinson."

He decided he better just get to the point. "All right, Mrs. Atkinson. I came to ask if a young woman has ever lived here at this address." She cocked an eyebrow at him.

"Well, Greg, once upon a time I was a young woman and lived here."

"But no one else? No children?"

"Just my husband, Elijah, but he died years ago." Mrs. Atkinson crossed her arms across her chest. She obviously wasn't amused. Greg pulled the missing poster from his pocket and handed it to her.

"Have you ever seen her around? Maybe even in town?"

"I never go into town." Mrs. Atkinson shoved the paper back at Greg. He glanced around.

"Never? Not even for groceries or supplies?"

"Nope. I have them delivered." Greg was a little surprised by this. Oftentimes the elderly didn't even know their groceries could be delivered, much less how to set it up.

"Can I ask what service you use? This is the last question, I promise." Her expression didn't change.

"No service. My niece lives across town. Her and her husband take care of me." She then rose and opened the door for him.

"If that's all . . ." she trailed off. She obviously wanted him to leave.

Greg stood and headed for the door. He wondered why she didn't want him around. He'd always assumed old people were lonely but, then again, maybe she liked to be alone and he was interrupting. Greg quickly bid her a polite goodbye which she didn't return. Instead, she just slammed the door in his face. Well, he tried.

Greg walked down the drive to his truck and glanced around the property as he opened the door and stepped inside. The property seemed to go on for miles. And he bet the sunset was beautiful as it set over the hills to the west. He checked the clock on his phone as he started the engine. It was still fairly early but he was tired from driving that morning and decided he better check into his motel and call it a night. He would check the other two properties first thing the next morning.

When he arrived at his motel, it was mostly deserted. The parking lot only had two cars, and Greg assumed that they belonged to employees.

The motel was small, located off the side of the highway just on the outside of town. It was three stories, with a flight of stairs criss-crossing at the end of each row of rooms. There was a Mexican restaurant in the same parking lot, and he could smell the spicy flavors even from fifty feet away. His stomach rumbled. He walked into the motel lobby and was greeted by an overweight, middle-aged man behind the counter.

"Checking in?" the man asked, barely looking up from his magazine.

"Yes, Sanders." Greg pulled out his ID but the clerk waved it away.

"No need, you're our only guest checking in today." He set the magazine down and turned to the only computer that could possibly have been older than the one that had once occupied Greg's desk at the police station. He clicked a few buttons.

"Credit card?" Greg took out his wallet and handed his card to the man, who started typing in all the information on the card. Apparently, they were too archaic to have a credit card swiping device. As if reading his mind, the man spoke up. "Business isn't so good. Have to cut costs where we can."

Greg nodded his head in understanding, not saying anything as the man handed his card back to him and waited for the ancient printer to spit out a document. Once it was done, he slid the two sheets of paper across the counter. The ink was faded and he had to squint to see which line to sign. The man behind the counter offered no directions. Greg slid the paper back across the counter and the man offered a room key in exchange. It was a real key, not one of those card keys most hotels had these days.

"310." Then the man picked up his magazine and resumed reading.

"Thanks," Greg said as he turned and headed out the door.

Greg wondered if the employee was a product of the slow business, or if it was the other way around. No bother, he was able to find 310 easily enough on his own. When he opened the door, the smell of aging carpet reached his nose. It wasn't a bad smell, it just smelled old. The room was small, but held a king-size bed on one side and a couch facing a 1980s box TV on the opposite wall. There was a door across the room, which he assumed was the bathroom. He walked over to the bed and peeled back the sheets. No signs of bedbugs. Well, this would do.

After a quick shower, Greg grabbed his wallet and room key and headed back downstairs to the Mexican restaurant across the parking lot. He was quickly greeted by a friendly young woman who led him to a table. Service was much better at the restaurant than at the motel. His order was quickly taken and the waitress brought him the gin and tonic he ordered within minutes. As he sipped his drink and nibbled on chips and salsa, Greg took a look around the restaurant.

It was mostly empty, no surprise there. The business probably correlated with the business at the motel. In fact, Greg wouldn't be surprised if it was family owned and the woman who took his order had her husband in the kitchen cooking. It would be hard to afford to keep it open any other way.

There was one other table in the restaurant. Seated directly in front of him was a young woman with dark red hair who sat reading a book that was held all the way up to her nose. Greg kept his eyes trained on her, hoping she would move the book so he could see what her face looked like. He must not have been as sly as he thought because within moments he was startled when she spoke.

"Can I help you?" The book didn't move from in front of her face.

"Sorry." Greg scrambled to cover his embarrassment, "You looked familiar."

"Familiar how?" she asked. She pushed the half-eaten plate of food away from her but the book still didn't move.

"I just think I've seen you somewhere before." Finally, she lowered the book to reveal a face covered in light freckles and a delicate mole on her chin. Not Ava. "Where?" she pressed. Greg scratched his head.

"I can't think of it now and, honestly, the more I talk to you, the more I doubt my memory." He chuckled trying to play it off as a joke.

The woman didn't laugh. Instead, she slammed her book shut and flung a twenty on the table. Without another look at Greg, she walked towards the door, speaking quietly with the server on her way out. Well, now the restaurant was empty.

Greg's plate of tacos arrived fairly quickly and, while he was eating, he typed an email on his phone to Dan. He hadn't had a chance to call Dan but he hoped their other currently open case was going well. They hadn't signed on another one yet, but he hoped that would change. He finished his food and asked the woman for his bill.

"You don't have one." She smiled.

"What?" He was confused. "Surely, you can't afford to feed me for free with business like this." He motioned to the empty restaurant.

"No, no, nothing like that. The young woman who left paid for your meal." Greg felt his eyes widen. Why had she paid for his meal? After he had been rudely staring at her? "Really?"

"Yes sir." The woman began to clear his table. Greg pulled out his wallet. "Well, I still need to tip you." The woman laughed.

"I won't say no to an extra tip, but the young woman did cover that as well."

Greg was shocked. He'd never had anyone pay for his meal like that before. Pulling a five-dollar bill out of his wallet, he thanked the woman profusely and walked out of the restaurant back to his room, thinking about the strange woman who had paid for his meal. He must not have realized how tired he was, because the minute he laid on the bed, he found himself falling into a dreamless sleep.

28

WEDNESDAY

The next morning, Greg awoke to find it was dismal outside. Gray. Very unusual for Arizona. He started to slowly get dressed. Today he was in a somber mood, probably due to the weather. Regardless, he was ready to check out the last two of the locations he had picked out. He was beginning to realize that his journey was coming to an end and he could feel it. Soon he would know what had happened to Ava. The ringing of his phone interrupted his thoughts. It was Dan.

"Hey." Greg held the phone between his shoulder and ear as he buttoned up his shirt.

"Greg, my man." Dan sounded a little too excited for eight in the morning.

"What's up?" Greg turned to look at his reflection in the mirror, trying to smooth out his mop of hair.

"You'll never believe this."

Greg wasn't in the mood for guessing games. "I bet I will. Just spit it out already."

Dan chuckled on the other end of the line. "I just booked two more tails."

"Two? Wow, that was fast."

"Yeah, Phyllis has a friend and now the friend wants her husband followed, as well. I doubt it'll be the same sort of ending, but business is business!"

"And the second one?" Greg checked his wallet to make sure all his cards and ID were there and then slipped his gun in its holster at his waist.

"Well, I might have gotten a little ahead of myself, because I have only received a down payment from one, but a second woman wants help finding her son who's gone missing. I figured that would be the perfect case for you. She's going to call me back today with details and, hopefully, I'll secure the down payment then."

"And why would that be the perfect case for me?"

"Because of this thing with your girlfriend!" Dan replied, way too excited about this entire situation. Greg grabbed his backpack and headed out of his room, phone still pressed to his ear.

"Dan, you know I haven't actually found Ava yet. For all we know, I may not even be headed in the right direction."

"I guess I should correct myself, this would be a *good* case for you because of your experience." Greg shook his head as he stepped into his truck.

"All right, all right, send the info over when you get a chance and I'll take a look. I'll be away from my computer most of today, though. I'm going to check out those two addresses I found." Greg started his engine but didn't hang up just yet. "Dan, I'm starting to think I'm chasing a needle in a haystack."

Dan was silent for a moment.

"I know, man. But you made it this far. You've already proved she didn't die the night she disappeared. And, even if you don't find her, at least finish what's in front of you." His serious voice was back.

"You're right," Greg agreed. He needed to at least see this last lead through, then he could give up and focus on something else. Maybe it was time.

"Talk to you later," he said and then hung up the phone.

Greg had a sudden thought that he had never heard from Marie after Monday night. On a whim, he decided he would call her. He hooked his phone up to the Bluetooth system of his truck, dialing Marie's number. It began ringing as he backed out of his parking spot.

The phone rang and rang and rang. In fact, it never gave Greg a chance to leave a message. It just continued to ring. After about ten minutes, he gave up and hung up. Maybe she was working and couldn't talk now. After all, some people still had jobs. He would try again later.

As his truck rattled up the dirt road towards his first address of the day, Greg made an inventory of his surroundings. This place was very similar to the first location, worn down and probably built in the early twentieth century. This one, though, looked much less abandoned. Children's bikes and toys littered the front yard and there were about a dozen patio chairs lying haphazardly around. A lazy dog lifted his head as Greg passed by, but didn't bother to get up or bark. The dog matched the property, tired and worn.

Greg walked up the front steps to the porch, cautious to avoid the broken boards that seemed to be at every other step. There was no denying this place needed work. Before he could even ring the bell, he heard the sound of what had to be a multitude of children pitter-pattering about.

Here went nothing. Ding-Dong.

"MOM! SOMEONE'S AT THE DOOR," came a yell so loud Greg could swear he was already in the house. But the door remained closed.

"CAN YOU GET IT?" a voice yelled back, equally as loud. Apparently it was genetic.

"I'M PLAYING MY GAME," the first voice replied. Greg was so engrossed in the yelling fight that he almost didn't notice when the door opened a crack and a small face peeked out.

"Why, hello there." Greg knelt down on one knee and pulled out his private investigators badge, "I'd like to speak to your mom."

The words weren't even fully out of his mouth when the door was ripped open by a rather large woman wearing a Corona shirt. She cocked one eyebrow.

"What do you want?" she asked, with a sneer, sweeping the child up her in her arms—although it was clear that the child was at the point where she was too big to be carried. Greg thought about how the meeting had gone yesterday and decided that perhaps the people here wanted direct instead of friendly. He pulled the missing poster out of his pocket.

"Just wanted to know if you've seen this girl."

The woman narrowed her eyes, obviously struggling to see. She reached out one hand to grab the poster, jutting out her opposite hip to hold the big child. She pulled the paper close to her face

"I'm not sure. I need to get my glasses." She set the child down and turned around. Then, as if she remembered her manners, she turned back to the door and pushed it open.

"Here, come inside." Greg stepped gingerly over the doorsill and then over a doll on the floor just inside the door.

"Don't mind the mess," the woman said as she pushed aside a pile of hot-wheels cars with the side of her foot.

"Have a seat . . . wherever." She motioned towards a couch but Greg could see it was occupied by a gaggle of children. They all stared at him wide-eyed.

Greg started towards the couch, trying to avoid crushing any toys. He was so worried about stepping on Barbie's arm with his right foot that he didn't notice what his left was doing. He heard a crunch as he walked. He lifted his left foot to see the remains of what looked like a Thomas the Tank Engine train. He picked it up and turned it around. That must've broken whatever spell was held over the children because suddenly they were surrounding him, asking questions, and reaching in his pockets.

"Hi, what's your name?"

"Are you a police officer?"

"Do you have news from my Dad?"

"Are you going to be our new Dad?"

"Come play Barbie with me!"

"He doesn't want to play Barbie, stupid face. He's a guy and he wants to play hot-wheels with me."

The only child who hadn't moved or bombarded Greg was apparently the eldest, and he remained in his seat on the couch and observed Greg questionably. A Game Boy rested in his hands. The smaller children surrounding Greg had begun to drag him towards the couch. He reluctantly moved a stuffed alligator and hippopotamus so he could sit down. They were immediately snatched up by small hands.

"This is Mimi, and this is Coco," the girl explained.

"Those are very nice names," Greg responded.

The kids began looking around the room for their favorite toys to bring to this new stranger. They all had similar facial features, but the skin colors varied widely from white to slightly tan. Greg figured there must've been two dads in the picture.

"Leila, he doesn't want to see your toys. You all go play in the other room," the mother said as she came back into the room, dismissing the young girl who had shown Greg the stuffed animals. The woman took a seat next to Greg.

"Can't find my glasses anywhere in this mess. But I did find a magnifying glass."

"And? Does she look familiar?" Greg waited in anticipation.

"Yes," the mom said with certainty, but then she began to scratch her head. "But I'm not sure when—or where—I'm so busy these days with my kids and my sisters kids . . . I just can't keep track of things, anymore." She looked down at her lap dejectedly. Ah, so, the kids were not all siblings.

"Well," Greg thought out loud, "Do you leave the house often? If so, where do you go?" The woman seemed thoughtful for a minute.

"Well, I don't leave much at all now. There isn't enough room to fit the kids in one car. When my man was around, we would go into town and get the kids ice creams and take them to a park on Friday night." Greg sensed he was getting somewhere.

"What park?" he asked, pulling out his phone to type the name down.

"Aw, c'mon, I used to know this stuff, uh . . . maybe it started with a

C? No, a G . . . ugh . . . maybe Gabler Park? That sounds right, or close to right . . . "

"Gabler Park," Greg repeated as he typed it in. "Anywhere else?"

She shook her head.

"Just the grocery store. The Fry's . . . about three miles down the road. And that's it. Sorry I can't be more help." Greg jotted down the grocery store, as well, barely containing his excitement.

"No, you've helped me a ton, thank you!" He opened his mouth to say something more but was interrupted by a scream.

"And that's my cue to go." The woman rose from the couch and headed towards what she had previously called the other room.

"I assume you can show yourself out." It wasn't a question.

Greg quickly rose and tiptoed his way back through the toy cemetery towards the door. He had almost made it out when the oldest child, who had sat silently on the couch, opened his mouth.

"I've seen her, too, you know." Greg spun back around.

"Really? Where?"

"She came to our door just like you." He didn't look up from his game.

"When? Did she say anything?" Greg had to hold himself from throwing himself back across the room.

"I don't remember. But I think she was looking for someone."

"Who?" Greg asked.

"You," the boy answered.

"She had a picture of you."

"M-me?" Greg stuttered, his resolve and professionalism out the window.

"Yeah. But you were younger. And you looked less tired." Greg stood there, speechless. Had Ava kept a picture of him?

"When was this?" The boy continued to push buttons on his Game Boy, not making eye contact.

"Don't know, a while ago, maybe. Mom doesn't remember."

Greg slowly turned and walked out the door, torn between demanding answers he knew the kid didn't have, or trying to interview the mother again. He decided on neither. He walked briskly over to his truck and stepped in, slumping on the steering wheel and out of breath for no apparent reason.

Ava had been here? Looking for him? But she knew where he was. She was the one who left! And with that thought, Greg's resolve solidified. She was close, and she was alive, and he wasn't going to leave without her. No matter what trouble she had gotten herself into. Maybe she had even gotten amnesia and the picture of Greg was all she had left! He thought manically about how he could tell her they were boyfriend and girlfriend and pick up where they left off! Greg's mind continued down the rabbit hole as he backed out of the driveway.

As if on cue, his phone beeped to let him know he had a voicemail. Without taking his eyes off the road, he pushed play.

"Hi Greg." He almost stepped on the brake as Marie's voice filled his car through the Bluetooth connection. It took him a second to remember this was a voicemail. He willed his heart to slow its rapid pace.

"It's Marie. Sorry about Monday." She paused. "Listen, Ione told me that you were going to Arizona…And he told me why. And look, I think you need to give up this whole finding your missing girlfriend thing, okay? I think you're gonna get yourself in trouble. Anyway, I have to go, but . . . uh, we had a great time the other night, but, uh, don't call me anymore. Thanks. It was nice meeting you. Bye." And with that, the line went dead.

Greg should've felt more shocked, hurt even. After all, on their last date Marie had been ecstatic for another. But, for some reason, nothing, not even being turned down by a girl, could bring him down from the cloud he was currently floating on. Ava had been looking for him!

He remained on cloud nine as he drove to the next address on his list. Honestly, this address thing might be a waste of time. He was proceeding because of things Ava had said to him years before but her desires might have changed. And when he had narrowed it down to the five addresses, well, it had been sort of far-fetched.

It didn't take long to arrive at the next place and, although it looked newer and less lived in than the rest, Greg knew Ava wouldn't have liked it. He sat in the truck for a few minutes, debating whether or not to even bother knocking on the door. His decision was made for him when a young woman stepped outside onto the porch and waived at him. Greg squinted. She didn't look angry. In fact, she was smiling. He stepped out of the car and waved back.

"Are you lost?" she called.

"No, actually." Greg walked forward so he wouldn't have to keep yelling.

"I'm investigating a disappearance and was just coming by to see if you had any information." He pulled out the flyer as he approached her. She took it from his hand delicately. Greg estimated her to be in her early thirties. She was thin and tall. In fact, they pretty much saw eye to eye, something that didn't happen often in Greg's six-foot frame. Her hair was dark, but her skin light. Greg began to wonder what her background was.

"She doesn't look familiar, sorry." The woman handed him the poster back. Greg didn't feel as dejected as he had previously. Instead, he just shrugged.

"Thanks, anyway." He turned towards his truck to leave.

"Want to come in for a lemonade?" the woman asked timidly, biting her lip. Greg considered that for a moment, but then decided he'd rather head back to his motel.

"Thanks, but I've got more work to do." Her face instantly fell and he felt bad. "Rain check?" He hoped that would make it seem like less of a rejection.

"No problem. I'll be here." She motioned to the door. Greg nodded and stepped into his truck. He looked in the rearview mirror and saw her watching him drive away.

Greg arrived back at the motel just as the sun was setting. He realized with dismay that he should have stopped and purchased food while he was in town. Oh well, Mexican food it was. When he walked into the restaurant, he was surprised to see there were more patrons than the last time. It wasn't full by any means, but at least half of the dozen tables were occupied.

The host recognized him and led him to a table by the window. He slid into his seat and realized with a start that the table across from him was occupied by the same redhead as the last time. Just as before, she kept her nose in her book and didn't appear to notice him. He looked around and made a split-second decision. He got up from his table, walked to hers, and slid into the seat across from her. She lowered her book down so it was no longer blocking her face, and she didn't seem surprised at all by his actions.

"Hey." He cleared his throat nervously. "I wanted to thank you for buying my dinner last night." He could feel his leg nervously bouncing beneath the table.

"No problem," she replied coolly. Her voice was cold, but neutral. At least, he didn't note any signs of hostility.

"I'm Greg." He held out his hand. She didn't take it.

"Nice to meet you, Greg." He lowered his unshook hand awkwardly to his side.

"So, uhh, can I buy your dinner tonight?" This conversation was not going as Greg had hoped. She smiled.

"I suppose so."

"So . . . " Greg tried again to dispel the awkward silence. "Do you live in the area?"

"Yes." Her eyes bored straight into his. She sat very rigid, but didn't look uncomfortable.

"Have you, er, lived here long?" Greg reached up to unbutton the top button on his collar. For some reason, the room seemed quite hot. And he was more nervous than he'd been in a long time. Which made no sense, it's not as if he had feelings for this woman.

"Yes. About eight years." She folded the corner on the page of her book and set it on the table in front of her.

"Wow. Do you like it?" he prodded, trying to get her to open up a little bit.

"Of course, that's why I stayed." Her mouth perked up at one end in a partial smile.

"Where were you before?" He felt a small amount of success that her face had at least changed a small amount.

"I moved around a lot before I came here. I can't really think of any place that stands out." Her face returned to the mask it had been before.

"You never told me your name," Greg realized suddenly.

"I didn't," she reaffirmed. "Does it matter?"

This whole conversation was going nowhere. It was clear she didn't want to talk to Greg and would prefer to read her book in solitude. Greg decided it was a good time to excuse himself. Then his mind snapped back to why he was here to begin with and he pulled the flyer of Ava out of his pocket.

"It doesn't matter, I suppose. I'm in town investigating a missing person. Have you ever seen this girl around?"

"Who's asking?" Her voice remained guarded, but now had a note of hostility in it. Greg smiled sadly.

"A friend. I'm not a cop, I promise." She scooted back slightly at the word cop, but didn't seem scared. She pushed her hair behind her ear, using her left hand.

"I know her." Greg nearly shot out of his chair.

"YOU DO?" he yelled. The entire restaurant turned to look at him and he smiled sheepishly. "I mean, you know her? Really?" Greg tried again in a regular voice.

"I know where she lives."

"Where? Do you have the address?" She nodded.

"I have it written down at home somewhere, I'm sure." She seemed lost in thought for a moment.

"How and when did you meet her?" During the exchange, he had pulled out his phone and was now ready to type any information she gave him. She shrugged.

"I don't really remember, it was so many years ago. But she's part of a hiking group I joined when I moved here, so, I'm assuming it was about five years ago. Maybe a little less." Hiking group, interesting.

"When did you last see her?" The woman shook her head.

"It's been about six months."

"So, she hasn't gone with hiking group in six months?"

"No, no, it's not like that," the woman corrected. "We all don't go on every hike. And there's lots of weekend long hikes where they go places like the Grand Canyon and such. We all don't make it to every hike. The moderator, he puts a post on Facebook and then whoever can go RSVP's on there." Greg felt his eyes widen, but the woman knew exactly what he was thinking. "She doesn't have Facebook. I don't know how she hears about the meetings or RSVP's. The moderator must have her number or something." He typed everything rapidly into his phone.

"What's the moderator's name?"

"John something." She shrugged again. "You know, this isn't really a serious thing. He just started a Facebook group and, if you show up, you show up. And other people make events all the time. He's the moderator but I don't see him every time." This all seemed so odd and nonchalant to Greg, but maybe he really was more behind the times than he realized.

"I think you should leave her alone."

Greg was taken aback. "Who, alone?" The woman motioned to the picture. "Ava?"

At the name, the woman furrowed her eyebrows.

"That's not her name. But yeah, leave her alone."

"Then what is her name?" Greg pressed.

"I don't even really know. We all have hiking nicknames. I'm honestly bad with names anyways."

"You said you know where she lives?" Greg tried again. It was clear the woman was getting annoyed at Greg and she rolled her eyes before answering.

"Yes. We hike by her house all the time. I don't have the address on me, but I'm sure I have it written down somewhere. We use it as a meeting spot a lot."

"Can I get your number and maybe you could call me with the address when you get home?" Greg was desperate to get his hands on that address. This was it. Ava was so close. The woman shook her head.

"That's not how I work. I'll bring you the address here tomorrow. Same time." She picked up her book and slid out of her chair. "I really don't know what else to say except that I think she's happy and you should leave her alone." The woman looked at the door.

"And don't try to follow me or I'll call the police." And, with that, she hurried out.

Greg hadn't thought of trying to follow her, but the woman seemed scared. He wondered if she'd had a stalker before this. She had left without giving him her name, or any name, really. He motioned to the server and placed his order, letting her know he would be paying for the woman's check as well as his own. Then he pulled out his phone and opened his Facebook app. Greg had never been one for social media but, with the private investigation firm, he had needed to make a few accounts for investigating purposes. He pulled up his personal account and typed "Hiking Groups Arizona" in the search bar. There were zero results.

Next, he tried every variation he could think of—"Hiking Flagstaff" and "Hiking Kingman"—and in all the surrounding cities. But there were no results. No hiking groups in the surrounding areas. He furrowed his brow in confusion. Had the woman lied to him? And why? Why fabricate such a ridiculous and complicated lie? All she had to say is that she didn't know Ava and Greg would have left her table. No problem. Something wasn't adding up. Now, if he could only figure out what.

His food arrived and he tucked into his plate of chili rellenos with more gusto then he expected. He'd been so busy, there'd been no lunch stop during his day. After he finished, he motioned the server over again and asked for the check. When she returned, he looked over his check with confusion. The server must've noticed.

"Is everything all right, sir?"

"Uh, I said I would pay for the lady's food and it doesn't appear her order is on here." He motioned to the check in his hand. The server shrugged.

"She didn't order anything today, sir. In fact, she only walked in five minutes before you."

Greg's eyes widened in shock. Had she been that mad at their conversation that she left without eating? He pulled out his card and handed it to the server. He had agreed to meet the woman again tomorrow. He would buy her meal then. He signed his bill and then started the short trek back to his motel room. He had come here to find Ava, but something was starting to feel off. He just wished he could put his finger on what it was.

29

THURSDAY

Greg squinted as the morning sun ended his night of restless sleep. He'd spent the entire night plagued by nightmares. Ava was in every single one, but she was always in danger and he could never quite reach her. The nightmare would end just as he was about to get to her and then it would quickly fade into the next. He glanced at his watch, only to realize it was just barely six a.m. He had hours before he needed to meet that mysterious woman in the Mexican restaurant. He debated about what he should do.

Yesterday, Dan had sent him the files on the missing boy. Greg figured this was as good a time as any to look over them. He opened the first folder and found a missing poster, which closely resembled Ava's. He supposed they had a template for these sorts of things. He clicked through and found multiple pictures of a teenaged boy staring back at him. He'd always assumed that he'd chased Ava because he loved her. But, looking at the pictures of another missing individual, Greg found he had same drive to try and find him. Maybe Dan was right, maybe he really had found his calling.

He minimized the pictures folder and opened a document which Dan had also attached. It contained clippings from news articles as well as interviews the parents had given regarding the disappearance. It wasn't quite a police file, but it would get him started.

On January 5, 2018, sixteen-year-old Jeremy Reed was last seen leaving his home wearing a red T-shirt and black basketball shorts. He carried a navy blue duffel bag and told his mother he was meeting friends at the Community Center to play basketball. According to the sign-in desk at the Community Center, young Reed never signed in. The duffel bag he carried was believed to have held a change of clothes, a phone charger, and his basketball shoes.

The newspaper article went on to list a phone number to call if anyone had any information about Jeremy. Greg minimized that document and pulled up a video of a police interview. *How had Dan gotten this?* Then he realized the mother must have asked for her copy and provided it to Dan. A woman, who looked distraught, was frozen and sitting at the metal table on the screen. A cop with a calm demeanor sat directly across from her. Greg pressed play.

Officer: "Did you fight with your son on the day in question?"

Mother: "No, we never fought. Ever. Jeremy was a good kid."

Officer: "Did he ever talk about running away?"

Mother: "I . . . I don't think so . . . no."

Officer: "You don't sound so sure."

Mother: "Well, Jeremy had a hard time making friends. That's why he was a good kid. Didn't get into drugs or trouble because he was home every night."

Officer: "You said he was going to the Community Center to play basketball with friends when he disappeared?"

Mother: "Yes! That's what he told me! I thought he'd made new friends and I was so happy I didn't question it!"

Officer: "Did he go to the Community Center often?"

Mother: "Occasionally. Usually just to shoot hoops. So, it wasn't completely out of his character to say he was going there."

Officer: "Where does he go besides the Community Center?"

Mother: "Nowhere! He stays in and plays video games online most nights!"

Officer: "What games does he play?"

Mother: "No idea."

At this point, there's a break as the officer opens the folder in front of him and shuffles through some papers.

Officer: "According to our technological team, your son's laptop was missing from his room. Why would he take it to the Community Center?"

Mother: "I don't know."

Officer: "Did you know your son was playing games online with other people?"

Mother: "What? Other people? Who?"

Officer: "That's what we are trying to figure out. But we pulled his cell phone records and there are lots of texts and calls between him and unknown numbers."

The officer spread out the papers in front of the mother.

Officer: "And there are texts in reference to an online game called League of Legends. Do you recognize any of these numbers?"

Mother: [aghast] . . . no, sir.

The officer pulls out another paper.

Officer: "Your son's phone last triangulated in this area before it was shut off about four hours after he disappeared. Do you recognize it?"

Mother: "No."

Greg stopped the recording there and scrolled down the list of documents Dan had included in the packet. He didn't see anything mentioning the son's last known location, and he sent a quick text asking Dan to ask the mother for that information. He also sent a second text asking if the mother had sent the down payment yet. He didn't want to get too deep into this case if the woman didn't pay. Dan quickly shot back a text letting Greg know he would ask the mother for the last known location and that, yes, she had indeed paid the down payment.

Greg set his phone down and continued delving through the documents. Finally, he came to the record of the text messages sent between Jeremy and a variety of unknown numbers. The more he read the numbers, the more Greg felt sure that the boy had run away. Many of the texts expressed how depressed and lonely he was with his life. And many of the unknown numbers offered to let Jeremy live with them at various locations.

Greg winced. This boy had no idea who these people were. They could have told him they were anyone. They could be pedophiles looking for an easy victim. Greg made a note to ask the mother if the police had followed up on any of these people. He was sure they had already but it didn't hurt to ask the outcome.

The thing that struck him as odd was that the phone was ditched very soon after his disappearance, but Jeremy had taken his laptop. He could use that to keep in contact with whomever he was talking to—meaning he could have ditched the phone on purpose—intending to disappear. Or whomever he had met up with could have encouraged him to ditch the phone.

Greg's head spun. He wasn't sure if it was Ava's case that was clouding his judgment or if there really was a chance this boy had disappeared on his own. After all, he was only sixteen years old. He opened a browser and typed in Facebook. He quickly found the boy's Facebook and an attached Instagram account. Kids were so much easier to follow than adults, thanks to their social media trails. Greg sent a friend request, figuring it wouldn't be approved, and then began to scroll through what the boy had made public. It wasn't much.

It could be that the guy had no friends, or that he was actually conscious of internet security—but Greg was leaning towards the first. He opened Jeremy's friend list. Jeremy had just under one hundred friends. Definitely quite a few for a boy whose mother claimed he had no friends, but one hundred was also not many for the average teenager in 2018. Greg scrolled through the list, noting most were boys or men, and they were depicted as wearing gamer gear. This kid must've loved his video games.

As he neared the bottom of the friends list, Greg came across a person with just the name of R. No first, no last, just the letter R. Greg clicked to visit the profile. There was no profile picture and no information. The profile was completely private. On a whim, Greg sent a friend request. Something about that profile bothered him.

Greg closed his browser and glanced at his watch. He had about two hours before he had to meet the strange woman at the Mexican restaurant. He decided he would shower and dress and then head over early. He wanted to see what kind of car she arrived in.

HE WALKED into the restaurant just about an hour later, feeling optimistic and skeptical at the same time. He was optimistic that he was getting Ava's address, but he was also skeptical that the woman would show up. She hadn't even given her name and that didn't exactly inspire confidence.

The same woman as the day before greeted Greg with a smile and led him to a table. It was an odd time in the afternoon, quite a bit before the dinner rush, so the restaurant was mostly empty. Greg made sure he sat on the side of the table where he could face the door and also see the parking lot from where he sat.

Once again he had somehow managed to skip lunch, so he decided not to wait and ordered right away. This time he tried the chimichanga, not authentic Mexican food, he was aware, but this was his third time in the restaurant this week and he figured he might as well try a bunch of different things. His food arrived quickly and he dug in ravenously. It was a bit hard to stuff his face while also watching the door but somehow he managed.

Greg wasn't exactly sure what time he had arrived at the restaurant the day before, and the strange woman has just said 'same time,' so, he wasn't surprised when other diners started to file in. This seemed about right. Greg ordered a desert as the dinner hour was in full swing. The sopapilla ended up being to die for and the order was gone before he knew it. Again, he watched the door the entire time he ate.

The other diners were finishing and the tables emptied one by one. Greg looked at his watch. It was definitely past the time they should have met. Had he been fooled? He decided to wait an hour longer and watched the door anxiously.

"Sir, everything okay? You want to order more food?" the kind server asked. Greg shook his head.

"No, I was waiting for someone but I don't think she's coming." The server smiled knowingly.

"The woman with the red hair?" Greg nodded.

"Does she come here a lot?" The server shook her head.

"No, I only saw her the first day I saw you. Then, again, the second time when you came. Then, today, she come by for just a minute." As if suddenly remembering something, the server reached in her pocket and pulled out a folded piece of paper. "She say to give this to the man. I didn't know who the man was, but now I think it's you." She handed Greg the paper.

"I'll bring your check?"

"Please," he answered as he looked at the piece of paper before gently unfolding it.

The paper was mostly blank except for a few typed words in the middle. An address. Greg quickly paid his bill and rushed from the restaurant back to his computer across the parking lot. He typed in the address. Google Maps seemed to think for a second. It then returned and said the address couldn't be located, but it suggested a few places nearby. He zoomed out of the map and surveyed the area. It was far north from him, about an hour, located near the Kaibab National Forest. Near the Nevada border. All this time, he'd been looking in the wrong area. He should've known. Ava had always loved the forest.

Greg began to hurriedly pack up his stuff, only to realize it was already dark and he would have no luck finding an unlisted cabin at this time of night. He would have to try in the morning. He quickly set his alarm for four a.m. and laid in bed trying to sleep. Although he was tired from not enough sleep the night before, adrenaline coursed through his veins, making him restless. He ended up turning on the TV and pacing while watching some sort of sitcom he didn't recognize. It was almost midnight before he had tired himself out enough to lie down again. He glanced at his phone and saw the alarm was only about four hours away. This was going to be a very short night.

30

FRIDAY

Greg awoke early, packed quickly, and checked out of the motel, eager to start his day on the road. On the way out of town, he stopped by a gas station to grab a Red Bull. He still hadn't slept well. Instead of his usual dreams plagued by Ava, he kept dreaming about a young man running off to meet a shadow. Greg would call out and try to stop him, but was never able to. Greg was starting to wonder if detectives always dreamt of their cases or if it was just him.

Dan called early in Greg's drive, and he answered using the Bluetooth system in his car.

"Hey, Dan."

"Greg, my man," Dan said back. He seemed to be his usual cheery self.

"How's it going down there?" Greg smiled before he answered.

"It's going well, really well." He glanced down at the piece of paper sitting in his center cup holder. He hoped this wasn't a fake address.

"I think I have a location. I'm headed there now."

"Uhh . . . " Dan hesitated, "Do you think this is it?"

"It might be." Greg's fingers were crossed tighter than they ever had been before.

"Well, for the sake of your sanity, and our business, I hope so, too." Dan chuckled.

"I take it you looked over the file on Jeremy. I saw your notes, anyway. I want to get your initial thoughts. I mean, I think I've come to the same conclusion as the cops. I think he left home intentionally to meet up with someone, but then maybe it wasn't the person he thought. Or maybe it was the person he thought but that person was older, maybe not as friendly as they seemed online."

Greg's mind briefly flashed to an image of Ava, standing by the road, getting into the first car that had pulled over. Even though he hadn't been there, suddenly he could picture it.

" . . . and I will definitely follow up." Greg had been so lost in his thoughts he had missed the first half of what Dan had said. Rather than admit he had been zoning out, he went with a safe neutral answer.

"Of course, and let me know what you find out."

"Will do. And keep me posted on how today goes."

"No problem." Both men hung up.

Greg surveyed the area around him, taking in the trees and the bareness of the land. It was peaceful, and beautiful in its own way. After another hour of driving, he reached the area where his GPS was no longer helpful. It announced that he 'had arrived' although he was clearly still on the highway and with no pull-off around. *That's modern technology at its finest,* he thought to himself as he glanced in the rearview rear before cutting his speed down to quite a bit below the legal limit. He didn't want to miss what he assumed would be a sort of hidden turnoff.

He held his phone in one hand, the steering wheel in the other. He knew this probably wasn't legal, but he didn't know of another way to compare what he could see on the phone with what he saw on the side of the road.

Greg easily located the first dirt turnoff on his map. It was located just past the point where his phone had stopped giving him directions. He passed it, glancing at his odometer so he would know when he had gone a mile. Based on his phone scale, one mile was where the next "official" turnoff should be.

Looking closely at the side of the road, Greg looked for any signs of a roadway. About half a mile past the first turnoff, he noticed an area where there was grass but it was dead and had tire tracks running through it. Greg hesitated and, subsequently, missed the turn. He decided to keep driving. He could always come back if that was the only area he found of interest.

He continued to closely study the side of the road—trying to find anything and everything that was out of place. Before he knew it, he came to another dirt road and noticed his odometer was about to roll over. He had gone a mile. He pulled a U-turn and headed back to where he had noticed the tire tracks in the grass. Initially, he had hesitated because living somewhere without a road didn't seem like something Ava would do.

Suddenly, it seemed like *exactly* something she would do.

The truck let out a light groan as Greg nosed it off of the road and onto the dirt shoulder, easing it towards the makeshift driveway. As he pulled onto the smashed grass, he looked around for any sort of house number or street name. There was nothing. This place was truly what one could call off the grid. The driveway, if you could call it that, was long and rocky, giving his truck quite the workout. The further he drove in, the more dense the trees became, giving him an odd feeling of being very alone. After about ten minutes, he pulled in front of a small log cabin.

Greg quickly surveyed his surroundings. There were no wires coming from the cabin. There was a chimney, but no smoke, and the cabin was completely dark. No cars and no garage to put one in. Whoever lived here didn't have electricity and probably wasn't home. He stepped out of his truck, grabbing his weapon from the glove compartment and slipping it in his back waistband for reasons he wasn't quite sure of. His subconscious just told him he might need it.

What if you shoot Ava, you dummy?

It might not even be Ava here, he argued with himself. It could be that girl from the restaurant, waiting to rob him or something.

Slowly, he made his way up the walk onto the front porch. The cabin was small, but much newer than any other property he had seen this week. In fact, besides the fact that it was clearly made from wooden logs, the house looked entirely new. He knocked on the wooden door. There was no response. He tried the knob and the door was not locked. He pushed open the small door and it let out a creek as it swung inward. He found himself in a room devoid of furniture, but also without dust, leading him to believe that it had been used recently in some way.

"Hello?" Greg called out. Nothing.

"Ava?" he tried again and walked further into the house.

"Hello?" he called once more.

"Ava's dead."

Greg jumped nearly half a mile out of his skin as the words came from the only completely dark corner in the room. If only he had thought to bring a flashlight. That could have been a fatal mistake. He took a deep breath to try and calm his racing heart before he replied.

"Wha … what?"

"She's dead. Stop searching." The voice was familiar, even slightly feminine. Greg began to approach the dark corner.

"Stop right there. One more step and I shoot." Greg stopped in his tracks, looking down just in time to see the red dot on his chest. He was afraid, but he knew that voice.

"Ava? What's going on?"

"I told you. Ava's dead, Greg."

He raised his eyebrows upon hearing his name.

"Then, how do you know who I am?" he questioned the voice he had no face to match with. His stressed mind frantically searched for a face to go with what he was hearing.

"You think you're so smart. You think you've been following Ava's trail for months. But really, I've been following you. You've seen me at every corner. Dressed as a stripper, a friendly stranger, even a co-worker. But you haven't recognized me, not once."

Greg felt his eyes widen even more if that was possible. Who was this? He looked down only to confirm the red dot was still trained at his chest.

"I tried to deter you at every turn. Assure you that Ava was happy. But you felt the need to keep on coming."

"I need to know," Greg spat out.

"And now you do," the voice replied. "She's dead. Out to pasture somewhere. In a meadow surrounded by yellow flowers. Whatever you want to believe." Greg was having trouble wrapping his mind around what he was hearing.

"What happened? Who killed her?"

"You did. You and everyone else with all your sky-high expectations. Putting her on that stupid pedestal that she couldn't live on. She was done. So she left."

Something here really wasn't adding up. But that voice . . . suddenly, everything clicked.

"Marie?" Greg asked, fear evident in his voice.

The figure finally emerged from the darkened corner. Greg gasped as he recognized the familiar features. He was tense, but less tense as he recognized the woman he had taken on a date just the week before. Well, he was slightly confused, because it was the face of Marie but her dark brown hair had been dyed or replaced with a red colored wig, making her hair the same color as the woman he had seen at the Mexican restaurant.

Greg's relief was short-lived and quickly turned to shock as the woman reached up a hand and peeled off an adhesive skin-toned rubber mask, which had been altering the shape of both her nose and cheeks. The familiar face of Marie quickly morphed into an older version of the face of the Ava he remembered. She kept her gun trained on his chest.

"When I left five years ago, I needed a new life, Greg. I assumed you, of all people, would understand that." She paused, her own breath shaky.

"But you wouldn't quit. You kept at it. For just a minute, I thought maybe I had made a mistake. Maybe I had messed up, maybe you really were the one I loved. I tried to fix it. I really did. But then I realized that I was better off dead."

"Ava—" Greg started.

"How can you say you love someone, Greg, when you didn't recognize me sitting across from you at dinner? When we sat in the same position so many years before? How could you not recognize our own story repeated back to you?"

Greg was speechless.

"You never loved me, Greg. You loved the idea of me."

Greg suddenly noticed the bag over her shoulder and the fact that she was edging towards the door. He backed up, keeping his hands in the air and his eyes on her weapon. He didn't want to piss her off now.

"Ava, I'm so . . . " he started, but she quickly interrupted him.

"Forget you saw me. Forget you found me. Forget I ever existed. For my sake, please." She backed out of the door Greg had conveniently left open.

"Don't follow me. You won't find me. Just remember, all this work, and everything you did to get here. That was all planted by me. This time, there won't be any hints, no bread crumbs for Detective Greg. This time, I'm gone."

At that moment, Greg noticed something from the corner of his eye. It pulled his attention from the woman at the door for just a second. He saw that there were red numbers aglow in the dark corner of the cabin. Red numbers. Oh God, it was a bomb. He quickly glanced back towards Ava, only to find she was gone. There was no longer a red dot trained on his chest. Without another thought, he ran out of the front door of the cabin and ran to his truck. In one fluid motion, he jumped in, jammed the keys in the ignition, and slammed the truck into reverse.

He was halfway down the unpaved road when he heard the explosion.

PART III

31

THE AFTERMATH

Greg sat by the side of the road, leaning back on the tire of his truck, his head in his hands.

"You all right, man?" One of the police officers who had arrived at the scene after the explosion came up to Greg and crouched down.

"I . . . I . . . think I'm in shock," Greg mumbled almost incoherently. The officer placed a hand on Greg's shoulder.

"Not sure why anyone would be exploding something in an area like this, but we've cleared the area and there are no injuries or casualties. You're just lucky you didn't get hurt. Do you want me to call an ambulance for you?"

Greg shook his head. "No, thanks. I'm fine, just in shock."

The officer stood up and walked over to his car, leaning in to type something on his computer between the consoles. Greg remembered those days. He stood and leaned against his truck, observing the wreckage around him. The ground was littered with pieces of cabin and foliage. Smoke rose from just beyond the horizon where the cabin had been.

Greg hadn't been lying, he really was in shock. But, at this point, he was unsure whether it was shock from the bomb or shock at finding out what had really happened to the girl he once loved. The officer interrupted his scattered thoughts. "Do you think you can drive yourself to the station to give a statement?"

"How far is it?" Greg ran a shaking hand through his hair.

"Only about ten miles to the west." Greg nodded.

"I can make it. Just give me another second."

"Take all the time you need."

"Hello, I'm Officer Fletcher Casey, the head and only detective at this precinct." A large hand was held in front of Greg's face, obviously waiting for a handshake. Greg shakily stood up and took the hand that was held out for him.

"Greg Sanders. Used to be a traffic cop up north, but now I'm an independent PI."

Greg observed the man before him, noticing a very similar build to that of Ione. His hair was not nearly as dark, though, and the man had substantially darker skin. Whether from genetics, or years working in the sun, Greg couldn't be sure. The man, Casey, nodded and motioned for Greg to take a seat in a chair on the opposite side of the closest desk. They were in one of the smallest police stations Greg had ever seen. There was a main room with three desks and a couch for waiting, and what looked like a small hall that maybe held two more rooms and a bathroom. This was definitely a small town.

"Do you want water? Coffee?" Casey smiled politely. Greg shook his head.

"I don't think I could drink anything right now."

"Still in shock?"

"Most definitely."

Casey nodded, pulling a pad and paper out of his desk drawer and booting up a laptop. "I do think you should get checked out at a hospital, even though you feel okay, just in case you have hearing damage or anything."

Greg didn't say anything.

"But for now, let me just get your statement so we can get you out of here. So, Greg, what were you doing, or who were you investigating, in our neck of the woods?" Greg pinched his eyes shut, maybe he did have a bit of a headache after all. "I was investigating the disappearance of Ava Miller. She was a Las Vegas resident when she disappeared five years ago. My trail led me to Kingman, then to here." Officer Casey jotted down a few notes.

"What did you find in Kingman that led you here?"

Greg rubbed his eyes, wondering just how much he should tell this cop. The whole story was quite embarrassing, in retrospect. He had just spent months following his ex-girlfriend who he had also been seeing as a co-worker. What a mess. "I found a witness who gave me an address which led me to the cabin which was subsequently blown up."

"You didn't happen to take a picture of the cabin when you arrived, did you?" Casey shuffled through some papers on his desk. Greg shook his head, no.

"Well, we don't have any record of land out there being slated for development. In fact, I'm not even sure I have a record of the land being sold to anyone. I'll have to double-check with the land recording office, though."

"That makes sense." Casey raised his eyebrows, obviously curious for Greg to continue. "The cabin was odd, the road there was uneven, as I'm sure you probably noticed. But anyway, when I got there, there were no wires leading to or from the cabin, meaning no electricity."

"Interesting." Casey scribbled down some notes on his pad.

"I have one of my officers interviewing the neighbors, and it seems odd that someone could build something out there without anyone noticing."

Greg shrugged. "Honestly, it was small and, with no electricity and possibly no official plumbing, well, I think two people could easily complete the level of cabin I observed."

"Was there a car there when you pulled up?"

"Nope. That was another weird thing. When I pulled up, I

thought it was empty." Greg closed his eyes and pictured himself grabbing his gun out of the glove compartment.

"I don't know why, but I did take my gun, not that it did me any good." He took a shaky breath then continued. "Anyway, I walked in, only to find a suspect there—"

"Suspect, who?" Casey interrupted.

"That's just it, I'm not exactly sure yet. I need to do a follow-up investigation to understand who was there."

"I take it they were not happy to see you?" Greg shook his head once again. "Definitely not. They had some sort of sniper rifle trained on my chest the entire time."

Casey raised his eyebrows. "A sniper rifle? In a small cabin?" Casey's voice gave away that he was starting not to believe Greg.

"I didn't get a good look at the weapon. I just know it was long and rifle-like and that there was a red light trained on my chest."

"A lot of people out here modify guns for hunting. The light could've just been a modification." Casey said this more to himself than anyone but Greg felt that he was starting to see his side a bit more.

"Anyway. She was angry."

"Wait, she?"

"Yes, she." Greg sighed.

"Again, I'm not exactly sure of the identity but I'm reasonably confident it was a she. She was mad that I found her and wanted me to leave her alone. And that's about as far as we got before I noticed the bomb in the corner and ran." Casey looked closely at Greg.

"How long after you noticed it, did it detonate?"

"Not long at all." Greg glanced at the ceiling trying to remember. He'd had time to get in his truck and drive a few hundred feet. "Maybe a minute? Maybe slightly longer?"

"Okay." Casey flipped to the next page in his notebook. "Did you see what happened to the woman?"

"No, she disappeared the minute I noticed there was a bomb." Casey looked like he was about to interrupt but Greg didn't let him.

"I was talking to her, saw the bomb out of the corner of my eye, looked over in the corner for a second and, when I looked back, she was gone." Both men were quiet for a minute.

"I normally wouldn't ask a civilian this, but I know you're a former cop and I spoke to your old commander, Carl, while you were waiting and he said you were an upright guy so—how do you think she got away?"

Greg leaned back in his chair, trying to clear his thoughts. The explosion had been his only concern and immediate thought for a while. How did Ava get out of there so fast? He barely managed to get away and he had a truck to take him halfway down the road.

"Honestly, I haven't thought about it in depth until right now, and I guess I'm not really sure." Greg rubbed at his temples trying to clear his thoughts. Casey raised his eyebrows.

"That's my problem, Greg. We combed that area. No signs of a body, nor a person on foot. The neighbors didn't see anything suspicious, other than the explosion . . . so, are you sure someone was with you in the cabin? You said yourself, when you pulled up it looked empty."

"Wait, what? No! I'm . . . " Wait, was he sure? He squeezed his eyes shut, his mind just wouldn't clear, why couldn't he think?

"I spoke to Carl. He said you had an issue with chasing ghosts."

"He meant that figuratively. I like to look at cold cases." Greg tried in vain to save his reputation which he could quickly see was going down the drain in Fletcher Casey's eyes.

"Did he now? He didn't say anything about cold cases. Just ghosts."

Greg began to vigorously rub his temples. Had he just imagined the woman in the cabin? No! It had definitely been Ava, or Marie, or the strange woman at the diner! Oh, great, now he couldn't tell them apart. Maybe he was going crazy. He slumped his head on the desk in defeat. Casey shuffled the stack of papers, lining them up so they were perfectly straight. He placed a clip on the end and slid them into a manila folder.

"I have no reason to hold you, Greg. Setting off fireworks in the woods is not a crime here in Arizona as long as you don't damage any property. But consider this your warning and don't do it again. And, let me be clear, the only reason I'm not ticketing you right now for criminal mischief is because you're a former officer. And despite how dumb I think this whole stunt was, we need to stand together." He stood up from his desk and walked over to the door. "But listen to me, Greg, as a brother officer. Get help. This is a dark path of delinquency you're headed down and the next cop you encounter might not be as understanding as me."

Greg didn't know what to say. He couldn't find the words. Had he really been alone in that cabin? No way! He would never set off a bomb! He didn't even know how to make one. Without saying goodbye to Officer Casey, Greg shuffled towards the door and out to his truck.

Had it been a bomb? Or was Casey right, and had it just been fireworks? How did that explain the numbers he had seen out of the corner of his eye? Dejectedly, Greg started up the truck and began the drive back north to home. His phone beeped, letting him know he had unanswered texts and calls, but he didn't even bother to glance at it. The more he thought about it, he became more concerned that he was actually crazy. He decided he would ask Dan point blank what he thought when he was back in town. Or maybe he would ask Ione, or even Carl. Someone would have to tell him the truth. Right?

GREG ARRIVED home and found the door ajar and food boxes littering every available surface. He would've been more concerned, but he heard the large booming voice of Ione yelling at the TV.

"How did you get in here?" Greg asked accusingly of his best friend. Ione shrugged.

"Grabbed your spare key while I was here Monday night."

"Um, why?" Greg asked, exasperated. "You have your own home, Ione, a whole house in fact."

"Eh, I like your TV better and Uber Eats delivers better stuff here." Ione motioned to the mountain of takeout boxes on the table.

Greg huffed and grabbed the trash can, angrily grabbing boxes and stuffing them in. The bag filled quickly, and he had to grab another just to make a dent.

"Did you even go to work this week, Ione?"

"You know it, Bro." Ione flashed a smile over his shoulder before turning his attention back to the sports game he was engrossed in.

"In fact, I found out what happened to your little friend, Marie." At the mention of her name, Greg dropped the trash bag he was holding.

"Really? What?"

"Internal transfer. she's up north in Reno now." Greg furrowed his eyebrows. "Are you sure?"

Ione smiled. "Yep. She came into the office yesterday to get the rest of her things. I guess she had some family issues she needed to address, and Reno's been hurting for a while, so, they were all too happy to take her."

"Wait, you saw Marie yesterday?"

"Yeah, Bro, why the nth degree?"

Greg shook his head. "It's nothing. I just—"

Ione had now turned his full attention away from the TV and to his best friend.

"You just what?" Greg slumped on the table.

"Ione, I need to ask you something."

"Yeah?"

Greg took a deep breath. "Do you think I'm crazy?" It was Ione's turn to look confused.

"Dude, you sound like a chick asking a question like that. No, I don't think you're crazy. Why?"

"The officer investigating the explosion in Arizona insinuated it." Greg shrugged and resumed collecting the trash that was cluttering his apartment. Ione shut off the TV.

"Explosion? What explosion?"

Greg sighed. "While I was chasing Ava down in Arizona, I was led to this one location and there was a slight explosion."

"Slight explosion?" Ione's mouth hung open in disbelief.

"I thought it was a bomb but the officers who investigated the scene said it was fireworks and they accused me of setting them off."

"Man, you do all the fun stuff without me!" Ione whined. "But really, man, I'm glad you're okay whether it was fireworks or a bomb or whatever. Maybe, if you sleep on it, it will help you remember. You look tired."

Greg nodded and tied up the bag he was holding. Maybe this whole situation would be clearer in the morning. He placed the two full garbage bags by the door and headed for his bedroom. Ione had turned the TV back on.

"I assume you can let yourself out?" Ione held up a full beer in his direction with a smile. Greg took that as a yes.

32

THE NEXT MORNING

Greg awoke to the sound of his phone ringing from where it was plugged in on the side of his bed. For a minute he was confused, as he didn't remember plugging it in last night, or even bringing it into his room with him. Maybe Ione had put it there for him. He picked the phone up and looked at the screen with a groan. Great, now he had to answer.

"Hi, Mom."

"Greg! What's this I hear about an explosion?" his mother practically screamed into the phone.

"Ugh, I'm fine, Mom. Who told you?"

"Your little friend, Ione, called me last night. Thank God, otherwise I would never know anything that's going on in your life!" Greg almost laughed out loud at his mom referring to Ione as "little friend" but he didn't want her to think he was laughing at her, so, he let it go.

"I'm an adult, Mom, you don't need to know every little thing that happens in my life." His mom sighed, obviously calming down.

"I know, you just know that I worry, Greg. Especially after what happened."

Greg waited for the usual pang of sadness and regret, which hit whenever anyone referenced Ava's disappearance. But it never came. Was he officially over her?

"Mom, I'm over what happened to Ava." Speaking it out loud solidified any doubt he'd had in his mind. He was over her.

"Greg, I'm not talking about Ava. I'm talking about you."

"Wh . . . what?" Greg shot straight up in bed. If he wasn't fully awake before, he was now.

"Did you forget again?" His mom sounded concerned on the other end of the phone.

"Forget what?" His heart was racing and his headache from the day before started to come back.

"That you were hospitalized after Ava disappeared."

"Hospitalized?" Greg stuttered, his headache becoming a blinding pain, "What do you mean?"

His mother sighed.

"Maybe I should come down there."

"No mom," Greg argued.

"I'm fine, just tell me what you mean by hospitalized."

"Greg, honey, after Ava disappeared, you stopped sleeping and started getting delirious. You were seeing things that weren't there. I tried to help you, but you wouldn't take the sleeping pills they were prescribing you. Finally, you got so out of hand they had to check you into the hospital so they could give you something to sleep."

Greg's world spun, the phone dropped from his hand. He faintly heard his mom calling his name from the other end. He stumbled over to the mirror, touching his reflection. Had he been having trouble sleeping lately? Maybe. He'd slept well last night, he could feel that. Had he slept in Arizona? Maybe not. He walked back over to the phone and picked it up.

"Mom?"

"Oh, Greg, thank God. I was just about to get in the car and drive over there."

"Am I crazy?" Greg's hand shook in fear with what her response was going to be.

"No! Of course not, Greg! When you were in the hospital they diagnosed you with stress-sleeping hallucinations. When your body undergoes stress, you stop sleeping. Most people crash after a few days of no sleep but, since you get just enough to keep you going, you're able to function but you start becoming delirious after about a week. Remember? They gave you sleeping pills to take when you start getting stressed . . . "

Greg walked back over to his bathroom mirror and opened it to reveal the cabinet. The bottom shelf was lined with bottles of medicine. Two of which were prescriptions and, when he picked them up, sure enough, they were sleeping pills. He set them back down and wracked his brain, why couldn't he remember this hospital visit?

And, if he hadn't slept well in over a week, how much of what had just happened had been a delirium? How much of it had been true? Had he even really found Ava? Or had he imagined the whole thing?

Greg's mom was still babbling on the other end of the phone, but he was no longer interested in what she was saying. He pulled the phone away from his ear and went to his notes app where he had been making notes while talking to the woman in the Mexican restaurant. When he opened the app, there wasn't a single note.

In a panic, he ran to his computer and began digging through all his files on the Ava case. There was the original file he had scanned in from the police station, and a page of his own notes from when he interviewed Kyle a few weeks before. But nothing since.

Where had he been the past few weeks? What had happened to all his work? He would call Dan, Dan would have copies. He placed the phone back up to his ear, his mother was still talking on the other end. Greg debated on listening to what she was saying, but he heard the words knitting club and promptly hung up. It would be awhile before she even noticed.

With a shaking finger, Greg scrolled through his contacts, until he came to Dan's name. He pressed call. It rang once, then twice, then a third time, just as a ringing sound came from Greg's bedside table. He rushed over and opened the drawer, pulling out a cell phone that he remembered buying when Dan asked him to set up a separate phone line. He pressed answer. The phone at his ear stopped ringing.

Greg laid on his bed, staring at the ceiling, a cell phone in each hand. He was crazy. He really was. He laid there for what felt like hours until he heard a key turn in the front door.

"Greg?" It was Ione. Greg didn't answer, he just continued to lay there on the bed not moving. The apartment wasn't that large, and Ione found him fairly quickly.

"Yo, Dude, your mom called. You okay?"

"No." Greg answered shakily. "I'm crazy."

"What do you mean?"

"Ione, do you even have a brother named Dan?" Ione raised his eyebrows.

"Of course I do. You met him at my house just recently."

"And I've been working with him on the PI business for weeks, right?" Greg asked hesitantly. Ione looked even more confused.

"What do you mean, man? Dan told me he met you in that coffee shop a few weeks ago, then didn't hear from you again. He's been trying to call you but figured you were busy with your girlfriend's disappearance." All Greg's fears were being confirmed.

"So, the past three weeks, I haven't been working with your brother?"

"No, man, he said you went AWOL, so, I came to check on you that one day. Figured you were having personal issues with the Marie thing, too, so I let it rest and figured I would broach the topic when you returned from Arizona." Ione cocked his head to the side like a confused dog. "Did you think you were working with my brother?"

Greg ignored the question.

"Was Marie real?"

"Is all this about Marie, Dude? I know it didn't work out between you and her, but it was just a fling, man, you'll find someone else."

"It's not about Marie. I'm losing my mind, Ione, and you told me last night I wasn't." Ione sat on the edge of the bed and reached for Greg's hand, pulling him into a sitting position.

"Your mom was right. Maybe I should take you to the doctor."

Greg tried to pull his hand back, but his friend was too strong. "I'm fine."

"You're clearly not, so, let's go. Honestly, you haven't been fine since Ava's funeral two months ago and I should've said something then, but I didn't ,so, I'm doing something about it now. Grab your shoes and let's go."

Ione let go of Greg's hands so he could slip on his tennis shoes and tie them. He thought about refusing to go, but he'd seen Ione lift weights and knew it would be futile. If he refused to go, Ione would just fireman carry him out.

They headed down the stairs to Ione's car and Greg slid into the passenger seat. Ione started babbling on about something, but Greg wasn't interested in listening or responding. The only things he could think about were what he had been doing the past three weeks. And how he was talking to himself and hadn't a clue. He really had gone crazy.

Greg had no idea how Ione managed it, but when they arrived at the hospital, Greg's mother was there waiting. It was Saturday, so the doctor's office hadn't been open. As they went through the check-in process, Greg briefly thought about how he was going to pay for this. If what Ione was saying was right, Greg hadn't worked for weeks and didn't currently have a budding PI business. He began to wonder about the case of young Jeremy. Had he imagined that, too? Or was that a real case he had found when he was looking online. What about following Phyllis's husband? Had he really done that? And if he did, why?

Ione and his mother filled out all the intake documents and Greg was led into a private room. He was happy to note that he wasn't immediately placed in a straightjacket. Then again, maybe those were just things people did in the movies. He wasn't sure.

Greg's mother and Ione sat in the corner of the room, gabbing like old friends, while Greg laid quietly on the bed. He didn't feel sick enough to be in the hospital, but he didn't have any other ideas, either. Within a few minutes a nurse came in and Ione excused himself saying he would check in on Greg later. Greg vaguely remembered saying "okay" as the nurse prepped his arm for an IV. She placed it with ease and then began talking to Greg. He remembered vaguely listening before he completely lost consciousness and fell into what could only be a dreamless sleep.

He was groggy when he awoke. And it took him a minute to remember where he was. Looking around, he took in the waiting chair, TV, and counter before he remembered he was in the hospital. The IV bag attached to his arm was almost empty, and Greg lifted his other hand to inspect it. There was no label to let him know what it was they were giving him. He looked around the room some more and noticed there was a window covered by blackout shades, so, he had no idea what time of the day it was, or even what day it was.

He looked around for his cell phone, which had been in his jean pockets when he had arrived, only to realize he was now wearing a hospital gown. *When had that change happened?* he wondered. He looked around on the table by his bedside and on the counter. Nothing. But he did see the nurse call button, and he decided to press it. Within a few minutes, a young blonde woman in bright pink scrubs poked her head in his room.

"Ah, I see you're awake." Greg nodded.

"What day is it?" She pulled the chart out from the end of his bed.

"Tuesday." He felt his eyes widen.

"I came in on Saturday! I've been asleep the entire time?" The nurse nodded. "Yes, but it looks like your body needed it. We took your blood when you came in and, while we can't truly measure sleep deprivation yet, the levels of stress cortisol in your blood were extremely high, which usually indicates either an infection or lack of sleep. You don't have any infection so it was definitely the latter." She placed the chart back in its spot.

"So, what happens now?" The young nurse smiled.

"My guess is you'll begin outpatient therapy just like last time." Greg searched his memory, still not finding recollections of "a last time."

"You'll have to forgive me, but I can't remember what happened 'last time' Miss . . . " He trailed off realizing there was no name tag on her scrubs.

"I'm Kailey." She smiled sweetly back. "And, no worries. I'm sure your psychiatrist will explain everything. I'll go talk to your doctor and work on getting you discharged." With that she left the room.

Greg once again wondered just how he was going to pay for all this. A three night stay in the ER could run into the six digits. He wanted to check his bank account but realized he hadn't asked Kailey about finding his phone and didn't know where to begin to look. He sank back into the pillows on the bed and looked at the ceiling.

A few minutes later, a young, thin, dark-haired doctor came into the room. She was tall for a woman, almost five-foot-eight. Her hair was pulled back into a tight bun. She had high cheekbones and dark brown eyes. Greg surveyed her familiar face for a moment before he placed her as one of his high school friends. "Samantha?" he asked in disbelief.

"Greg!" she said with a laugh.

"Never thought I would meet you like this!"

"So, you're a doctor now?" Greg asked as she picked up his chart.

"Not yet. I'm in my second year of residency, but I should be a doctor soon if I play my cards right." She flipped through his chart.

"This is embarrassing for you to see me like this." he mumbled as he looked down at his backless white hospital gown and compared it to her nicely pressed black scrubs. She shrugged.

"Don't worry about it." She flashed him a white smile.

"Nobody's perfect. And honestly, there are many more embarrassing things you could be in here for other than sleep deprived delirium." Greg wasn't sure if she realized just how crazy he was, but he decided not to inform her now.

"So how's life been for you?"

"Great." She smiled but it didn't stick, "Well, mostly great. Never thought I would find myself already a single mother."

"I'm sorry to hear that. How many kids do you have?" Her face immediately brightened and the smile returned.

"Just one daughter. She's four. I always wanted more kids but I started my doctorate and then, with the residency, it never happened. And now with the pending divorce, I'm glad it didn't." Suddenly, Greg realized he didn't even know who Samantha had married. He was about to ask but it was as if she read his mind. "It's no one from high school or anyone you know. It's a guy I met while I went to college in Illinois."

"I guess I never realized you went to college out of state." Samantha shrugged.

"I didn't, the entire time. Started out at the local community college but then transferred out the beginning of my third year. I think that's right about when you and Ava broke up so you probably don't remember." Then as if realizing she just said a bad word, she clamped a hand over her mouth. "I'm sorry, I know it's still a tough subject."

"Actually," Greg corrected, "I don't think it bothers me anymore. Not sure I can talk about her at length, but I definitely don't feel the need to be defensive like I used to."

Samantha smiled sadly. "I am still really sorry for how I acted on the phone when you called."

Greg held up a hand. "No hard feelings. I probably did much worse when I ignored you in high school. I'm sorry about that by the way." She shrugged.

"Young love is a beautiful thing, I don't blame you." She glanced back at the chart and, as if suddenly remembering where she was, her tone shifted to be much more serious.

"You have an appointment with a psychiatrist tomorrow, and I'm prescribing you some sleep medications. Make sure you take them for at least a few weeks until we can reevaluate your stress levels."

Greg agreed, afraid and embarrassed to ask one of his high school best friends about the cost of the psychiatrist. He didn't want to admit he was a fool with no job.

"Anyway, I've got other rooms to stop by so I'll have the nurse come in with your clothes and get you all set up for discharge, all right?"

"Sounds good to me." Greg smiled, about to stand up, but then he realized he was still in the backless gown and decided to remain seated instead.

"Do you know what happened to my cell phone?" Samantha pulled open a drawer on the counter and handed it to him.

"I think it's dead, but here." She pulled a business card from a holder in her pocket. "Here's my number. Send me a text when you get it charged back up and I'll buy you that coffee I owe you."

Greg smiled and accepted the card. "Thanks, Samantha"

"No problem." She smiled back as she stepped out of the room and closed the door behind her.

33

WEDNESDAY

The psychiatrist's office ended up being just up the hill from Greg's apartment. It was so close, in fact, that he decided to walk.

It was small office, owning one of the center sections of the shopping center. If he had to guess, he would say it wasn't more than a thousand square feet. The front room was a waiting area, complete with a water cooler and a single gender-neutral bathroom. There was no reception, simply a closed door on the other side of the room that said, "Session in progress, be with you shortly." Greg took a seat on the green couch beside the door.

After getting home from the hospital the night before, Greg had been too tired and scared to dig through his computer to tell what was real from what was fake. He also had a message from Ione and had been too embarrassed to call him back. It's not every day that you have to drive your friend to the hospital because he can't tell what's real from what isn't there. Greg resolved to dig through his computer after the appointment with the psychiatrist.

The door on the other side of the room opened and a woman in her early forties stepped out. She was dressed in a white pantsuit and wore black large-rimmed glasses. The typical psychiatrist dress code.

A younger woman stood behind her, not making eye contact with Greg. The woman in the pantsuit smiled when she saw Greg.

"Well, hello, you must be Greg Sanders, let me get her," she motioned to the young woman behind her, "—all checked out then we will start your session." She stepped aside as did the young woman following her. "Go ahead and head on in. Make yourself comfortable and sit wherever you like."

Greg did as he was told and he heard the door close behind him. The room was small, just as he had anticipated, and was filled with a variety of seating options. There was a desk in one corner with chairs on either side, as well as a reclining leather chair and matching sofa nearby. On the other side was a plush blue cloth sofa as well as a rocking chair. Greg thought they had almost every seating option available to offer. He chose the leather couch because it had a decent view out the window. Granted, there wasn't much to see in the rear parking lot, but it helped calm his nerves for some reason. It wasn't long before the psychiatrist came into the room. She walked over to where Greg sat and offered her hand.

"Hello, I'm Dr. Fauna."

"Greg," he said, although he was sure she already knew his name.

"Now, Greg, why don't you tell me a little about yourself."

"That's not how I thought we would start but, uh, I'm Greg, obviously. I'm twenty-eight, and I used to be a police officer but now I'm unemployed . . . anything else?" Greg looked up to see her eyes trained on him. "Don't you take notes or something?"

Dr. Fauna tapped her head. "All my notes are in here. I'm a bit of a progressive psychiatrist and I think physical note taking has little benefit and makes my patients more antsy." Greg nodded. "So, tell me about your family, Greg."

"It's just me and my mom." He shrugged, finding it hard to be confident under her glare. He had to disagree, he thought note taking would have definitely helped him be less nervous.

"And what happened to your dad?" she prodded. He shrugged again.

"I'm not sure. My mom never really talked about it and I never pressed for more information."

"You seem like a go with the flow kind of guy, Greg. Would you say I'm correct in saying that?" Greg thought for a minute, a little thrown off by the subject change. But then he remembered how he let Ione inhabit and make a mess of his house at every turn.

"Sure . . . I guess you could say that."

"But you don't fully agree. Why?"

"Well, I guess that leads us to why I'm here. About eight weeks ago my first girlfriend was buried and, well, let me specify, they had a funeral for her but no body." Dr. Fauna waited for him to continue. "You see, she disappeared five years ago and the police think she's dead and her family agrees so they closed the case and held a funeral."

"But you don't agree, do you?" Greg shook his head.

"Not at all. That's why I'm here. I spent the past eight weeks investigating, or at least I thought I did, only to realize that I didn't and now I'm really confused as to what was real during that time and what wasn't." Dr. Fauna gave him a sympathetic smile.

"We may never know for sure, but you and I can try to weed through it if you would like." Greg thought about discussing Ava with this woman. How would she know what he did or didn't do over the past eight weeks?

"Um, well, I guess . . . "

"Only if you want, Greg. We can discuss whatever you want." He decided to get some pressing questions off his chest.

"How long do I have to come here?"

"A while. I think you're booked for twice a week for six weeks and then we can discuss how you are doing after that." She folded her hands in her lap, neither offended nor surprised by his questioning.

"And . . . how much is it going to cost me? You see, I don't have insurance—" Dr. Fauna held up her hand.

"Your mom is taking care of it. You can discuss money matters with her." Greg let out the breath he didn't know he had been holding.

"So do you want to talk about Ava?" He was taken aback.

"How do you know her name?"

"I research all my patients before they come in, Greg."

He nodded and glanced around the room, still quite nervous, even more so now that he realized this woman knew things about him that he hadn't said. He fixated his eyes on a painting on the wall, trying to get up his gall to ask a question.

"You want to ask me if she really disappeared?"

Greg's eyes snapped back to her face. How were all these women able to read him so easily? His cheeks flushed in embarrassment but he nodded, yes.

"Yes, she really did disappear. Five years ago, just as you thought."

"And she was never found, right?" Dr. Fauna's smile never faded.

"That's correct."

"And I quit my job as a police officer over it?"

"I'm not sure why exactly you quit your job. That's something I don't think you told anyone but, yes, you quit almost six weeks ago." Greg nodded, soaking it all in.

"Did I go to Arizona to find her?"

"Yes, you did. However, your movements around Arizona are hard to follow. Your mother gave me permission to pull your credit card statements. However, legally she can't do that. If you give me permission, I will go ahead and have them for our next session."

"I give you permission." Greg was dismal. Here, a stranger was about to comb through his life because he couldn't tell what was real from what wasn't.

"Any other questions?"

"Have I really been acting as a PI these past few weeks? I remember working a couple cases . . . " he trailed off. Dr. Fauna gave him a sad look.

"I'm not sure, Greg. How about you bring in your phone and your computer next time and we will go through things together? It will be easier for you to see what is or isn't real with me here guiding you."

"I can do that." Greg looked down at his lap.

"In the meantime, make sure you are taking the sleep medication they prescribed for you, okay? No more delusions." She said the last part in an almost patronizing manner—which really got on Greg's nerves. She stood and led Greg out of the office, opening the front door for him.

"I'll see you Friday, all right?"

Greg hated being talked to like he was a child, but he agreed regardless. Then he turned and began the walk home. It only took him a few minutes before he was once again standing at his front door. He twisted open the knob to a dark apartment. With a sigh, he didn't bother flipping on the lights and made his way to the bedroom.

He opened his laptop computer and began to click around in his files. He quickly located a large file about Jeremy Reed and a bunch of small files. Curious, he pulled up a browser and headed to google. He typed in 'Jeremy Reed' and his screen was immediately filled with results. So, he hadn't imagined young Jeremy. In fact, the articles he had read were all there. He pulled open the folder and saw that his notes were intact. But, if he hadn't really been working with Dan, how had he received the interrogation footage?

Opening his email, he scrolled through the inbox, skipping over all the advertisements until he found it. An email from Dan. He opened the email to find a short message, "I hope this case might interest you." Along with all the attachments. Greg clicked on the name, only to see an unfamiliar email address. He typed a quick response, asking who the email address belonged to, thinking it might end up on the email account he had opened on his second phone. He had discovered the second email account earlier today when he had been looking through his phone. He was pretty sure he had made if for the PI business as he had aptly picked the address 'DandGinvestigations.' He pushed send. He checked the email on the phone. Nothing. He checked the email address he had made versus the one he had just sent a reply to, and they were similar, but two of the letters had been reversed in the one with the Jeremy Reed videos. Had he created two fake emails during his crazed state? He minimized the window and looked for any applications he didn't recognize on his desktop.

He found he had downloaded an app that could do background checks. So that part had been real. Even if he hadn't been working with Dan, he had certainly meant to. He enlarged the window with his email open and composed another email to the person who had sent the videos.

"Hello. My name is Greg Sanders and I received video footage on a criminal investigation case from you. Would you mind telling me who you are? I seem to have misplaced your information." He signed it with his information and then pressed send.

He returned to clicking around in his files to see what else he had been up to. He found PayPal receipts for services, which he double-checked with his bank account, and he had indeed been paid for a tail on Harvey. So that had been real. And he did have the background check app, so he had been working as a PI. At least he wasn't totally crazy. He clicked back into the window where he had sent the email, only to see something odd. The email he had just sent had bounced back. The note said, "This email address does not exist."

But wait, Greg had sent two messages. The first one was a simple, "Who is this?" and it had not bounced back. That meant that whoever that address belonged to had seen his first message and had immediately closed the account. Who was he dealing with here? Whoever it was, they really wanted him to look into the case about Jeremy Reed, and they thought it would be a good case for him. For some reason, he felt the same way.

Pulling open the list of last known phone numbers Jeremy had contact with, Greg also opened his tracing app and began typing in the numbers one by one. Many of them returned with names and addresses. Now, the police had probably already followed up on these, and had found nothing, otherwise the case would be solved. What Greg was looking for were numbers that didn't bounce back with any information.

There was only one. Assumedly, it was a prepaid cell. But it did list a carrier. Greg was sure the police had already visited the locations of the carrier in the city. Probably didn't find anything. This was all too easy. What could he possibly find that the police hadn't already found?

What if I didn't want to be found?

Ava's voice echoed in his head. Greg pinched the bridge of his nose. Why was her voice back now?

Because you never really found me.

Greg groaned. He picked up his bottle of sleeping pills from the desk next to him and considered taking one now. But he knew Ava's voice had echoed in his head long before he'd gone crazy and a pill probably wouldn't do much. He slammed down the pill bottle and turned back to his computer.

Could Jeremy really have run away? How would a sixteen-year-old boy make it on his own without help? Who would let him stay with them? Obviously, he wouldn't be able to pay rent . . . and that's when it struck Greg. What if he had been saving money, just like Ava? And hidden it where his parents and the police hadn't known about?

Greg clicked back to the strange email that had been sent. Who would send this? Suddenly, he had an idea. He opened a new Google search and typed in 'how to trace an IP address' and began looking at the articles that explained how to do it. It honestly didn't look too hard and he was sure he could do it. He began following the steps, most of which just involved typing information into the site he had found. It only took about ten minutes before a result popped up.

Greg couldn't believe his eyes. The location where the email had originated was familiar. It was the credit union he had visited in Arizona.

34

FRIDAY

"So, Greg, what do you want to talk about today?" Dr. Fauna asked as she led him into the back room.

"I really want to figure out what parts of my trip to Arizona were fact and what parts were fiction." Greg carried his laptop under his arm as well as a printout of his credit card statement. He wasn't sure if it was any help having Dr. Fauna in the mix. But he figured maybe she could shed some light on things that hadn't made sense.

"All right. Well, let's start at the beginning. Where did you go first?" Dr. Fauna sat down behind the desk at her computer. Greg made himself comfortable on the leather couch.

"A credit union." Greg gave her the name, which she typed quickly into a search engine.

"It exists. Did you talk to anyone there?" He nodded.

"An employee named Karena."

"All right, I will call later and verify she works there but, at this point, we will assume you were 100 percent living in reality."

"Uhh . . . " Greg rubbed his forehead, "there's a chance I also went there the week before. Maybe as Dan. Or maybe I called with the name Dan." Dr. Fauna turned to face him.

"Do you think you suffer from multiple personalities? Are you missing chunks of time in your life?" Greg shook his head, no.

"I'm never missing chunks of time, I just always remember not sleeping well. So, I think I must sometimes do things in my sleep."

"Now, Greg, I can't say for certain, but I don't believe you suffer from multiple personality disorder. And driving down to Arizona would be quite the feat to do without remembering or while sleeping. So, I'm just going to assume you talked to this girl on the phone. Maybe you did introduce yourself as Dan, I'm not sure. But you don't have the characteristics of someone with a dissociative identity and we are going to operate under the presumption that you don't."

"Okay. Well, then I did call with his name or something. But I went there as my first stop."

"And what next?" Dr. Fauna turned back to the computer.

"I checked into a motel." Greg shuffled through some papers and pulled out his credit card statement. He had highlighted the motel charge in yellow when he had printed it off the night before. He handed it to Dr. Fauna.

"Which you did." She typed something into the computer and said, "the name matched, as well, so, I would confidently say there weren't any delusions at this time."

"Oh, wait." Greg suddenly remembered Mrs. Atkinson, "I did go to speak to an old lady about whether she had seen Ava." Dr. Fauna grimaced.

"I have no way to check the authenticity of that unless you happened to get contact info for her?" Greg shook his head.

"Well, I'm still leaning towards you being in your right mind at this point, so, let's say that you did go to her place until we find out otherwise. What happened next?"

"I went to the Mexican restaurant in the parking lot." Dr. Fauna squinted as she looked over the credit card bill that was still in her hand.

"Did you take cash with you to Arizona?" Greg hung his head.

"I don't think so."

"Do you remember the name of the place?" Greg did not. Dr.

Fauna did some typing on her computer, then looked over at Greg, removing her eyeglasses and placing them on the desk next to the keyboard.

"I looked at Google Maps and I don't see a Mexican restaurant anywhere near that motel, Greg."

"Figures." Greg huffed.

"So, now we will assume you are in a delusional state. What happened next?"

"The next day I went and visited more properties. Two to be exact." Dr. Fauna looked at the credit card bill.

"You did purchase gas, so, we will assume you did actually go visit properties. I would disregard any conversations you had with people, though, as I cannot be sure they actually exist." Greg nodded.

"Then I went to the Mexican restaurant again. Then back to the motel. That brings us to Thursday, which I spent mostly doing research, and that does exist on my computer." Dr. Fauna didn't say anything, waiting for him to continue. "Then I went to the Mexican restaurant again. And then back to the motel. On Friday, I checked out of the motel, bought a Red Bull at a gas station, then headed up north."

"And that's where the police found you," Dr. Fauna finished for him. Greg nodded in agreement. She responded by pulling out a document from another folder off to the side. She slid her glasses back on, then began reading.

"On the date in question, suspect Gregory Sanders was picked up near the Kaibab National Forest. Suspect was outside of his vehicle, seemingly in shock. Upon further investigation, it seems a small structure, perhaps an outhouse, in the area had been destroyed. There were fragments of wooden planks, but not many. There were no signs of an explosive device, but ash was present, leading the officers to believe fireworks had been set off inside the dwelling, leading to its destruction." Dr. Fauna stopped reading and put the paper down. Greg didn't say anything.

"I found Ava," he whispered finally.

"Did you really?" Dr. Fauna asked patronizingly, obviously knowing the answer.

"No. It was an illusion."

"Good! Greg, I think we've made great progress. I'd like to stop our session here for today, unless you have any further questions."

"No, that's it." Dr. Fauna handed him all the credit card documents as well as a copy of the police report.

"We will see you Tuesday, okay? If you start not sleeping again, though, please call immediately. I'm reachable twenty-four/seven on my mobile." She held up what looked like an ancient flip phone.

Greg gathered up his things and headed out the door. He had once again chosen to walk to his appointment and he walked briskly back to his apartment. During the walk, he made mental plans to go back to Arizona on Monday. It seemed risky, but something was going on at this credit union and he needed to figure out what. He knew everyone would tell him not to go, so, he would just have to tell no one of his plans. As he reached his front door, his cell in his pocket started ringing. It was Ione.

"Hello?" Greg asked tentatively, afraid talking to Ione would be awkward.

"Greg! Beer! Food! Sports! My house! Immediately!" Ione shouted into the phone. Greg winced at the volume of Ione's voice but figured it would be good to get out of the house.

"Sure, I'll head over."

"See you in a few!" Ione yelled back and then the line went dead.

Pushing open his apartment door, Greg realized he hadn't asked if he should bring anything. Ah, well, a six pack of beer was never turned down. He opened the fridge to find it barren. He hadn't gone to the store since before his trip to Arizona.

Well, then, he would just stop at the liquor store on the way over to Ione's. He grabbed his truck keys and headed for the door. It would be nice to have a normal guy's night for once.

35

MONDAY

The weekend passed in a blur for Greg. He spent Friday night hanging out with Ione and Andy, then most of his weekend was spent researching further on the disappearance of Jeremy Reed. Although he knew now that his confrontation with Ava was imagined, he still felt as if he couldn't look into her disappearance anymore. He felt as if she had asked him to stop.

But she didn't. Maybe she still really needs your help.

Greg rolled his eyes at the suggestion of his subconscious. It was going to get him into trouble, again.

He hadn't discovered any major breaks in the Jeremy case, but he did have a few leads. He had made a map of all the phone numbers Jeremy had contacted. And, as it turned out, a number of them were in Kingman, Arizona. The same city as the credit union where he had received the email asking him to look into the case. Something very weird was going on here. And Greg felt like he was close to an answer but, for some reason, it wouldn't formulate. The sleeping pills had been helping him sleep, but he felt they also decreased his mental performance. He was going to continue to take them, all the same.

On Sunday, Greg met up with Samantha for coffee and they spent time catching one another up on their lives. Samantha talked a lot about her young daughter, and Greg could clearly see her life revolved around her. They'd parted ways with plans to meet again later in the week. He'd also had to call his mother to keep her updated on his "condition." It was annoying, but it was the only way to keep her from driving down to check on him Sunday afternoon.

Greg spent the rest of his Sunday preparing for his second trip down to Arizona. This time, he carried posters of Jeremy with him, rather than the faded ones containing Ava's beautiful face, as well as printouts of the email he had received and the reverse IP tracing. He'd also packed an overnight bag, slipping his sleeping pills into the side pocket. He didn't really plan to spend the night there, but he also didn't want to be caught unprepared if the trip took longer than he thought.

It was only five a.m. when Greg left his apartment, securely locking the door behind him (not that it was going to stop Ione). He took a step back and glanced at his homely apartment door. He'd been living here for almost ten years. Maybe it was time for him to move on and look for something new when he returned to town. He made a mental note to check out Zillow, then turned and headed for the truck.

The drive seemed to drag on. He wasn't sure why, maybe because this was now the third time he had done it, but it no longer held any anticipation for him. And, although he was involved in the Jeremy case (unofficially), all the same, his heart wasn't in it.

Greg arrived at the credit union just after nine in the morning, hoping to catch the young Karena he had spoken to last time. He was in luck. When he walked in the door, he quickly recognized the young woman behind the desk. He walked up and leaned over, trying once again to put on his most charming smile.

"Hello, Karena."

"Hi, how can I help you?" she responded back. Her tone indicated she was unsure, maybe even skeptical of him, and Greg suddenly realized she might not actually remember him. He pulled out his PI badge.

"I'm a private investigator. I was in here a couple weeks ago." Her face broke into a smile.

"Ah, yes. Did you find the girl you were looking for?"

"No, actually, but I'm here now on a different case." He took out a picture of Jeremy and placed it on the desk. She regarded it nervously.

"Have you seen this boy around here?" Karena bit her lip nervously. She didn't respond.

"I promise this won't ever come back to your boss."

Karena tilted her head to the right and Greg followed with his eyes. There was a camera setup in the upper right corner of the room.

"Okay, I get it. Do you have a lunch break?" She shook her head 'no' while whispering.

"Yes, at noon. I'll meet you at the Wendy's down the street." Greg made sure to keep his face neutral.

"All right but, if you think of anything, be sure to give me a call." And with that, he turned and walked back out to his truck.

It was a bit odd that Karena seemed more willing to talk to him about Jeremy. Maybe because she was the one who sent the email? When he'd asked about Ava, she'd given him next to nothing. He checked the time on his phone and saw that he had just over two hours before he needed to meet Karena at the Wendy's and, honestly, he didn't have much else to do. He decided he might as well fill his truck up with gas and then head to the Wendy's parking lot and wait.

While he was sitting in the truck, he decided to send a text message off to Samantha, telling her he hoped she had a good day. He debated over finishing the message with a smiley face, or if that would appear too feminine. He decided a neutral smiley would be okay. He pressed send. She responded with a surprising amount of speed.

Samantha: "Thanks! You Too!"

Greg: "Wow, that was fast."

Samantha: "Yeah, I'm on my lunch break. Glued to the phone, per the usual."

Greg smiled at her response. He knew he was different, in the way he wasn't glued to his phone, but he was strongly attached to technology, in general. So, he couldn't blame her, honestly. Everyone was attached to the internet these days. His phone buzzed again.

Samantha: "I scare you off?"

Greg: "Nah, just distracted."

Samantha: "Back on the case?"

Greg: "One of them. Yes."

Greg wasn't really sure what to say beyond that. After all, she'd seen him in the hospital so she already knew he'd been experiencing some delusions. He just hoped his mother hadn't embarrassed him by telling her all the details.

Samantha: "Awesome!"

If she knew, apparently she was polite enough not to say anything.

Samantha: "Want to plan to meet for dinner on Thursday night?"

Greg: "Sure!"

Samantha: "Cool. I'll touch base with you Wednesday!"

Samantha closed her text with a smiley face like the one Greg had used, making him feel much less awkward. He smiled, scrolling back through the texts. She never referred to it as a date, but Greg was pretty sure it was.

He glanced at his clock to see he had a half hour before meeting Karena. He decided he was hungry enough to head into the Wendy's and order lunch while he waited. He wasn't big on fast food, but Wendy's was much more acceptable than some other fast food locations people liked to frequent. He ordered a baked potato and some chili, then took up residence at a table in the corner where he could see the entire room, more specifically, both doors. He didn't want to miss Karena or risk her not recognizing him.

She was prompt, and walked through the door at five minutes after twelve. Greg waved her over. She glanced around nervously, before walking over and sliding into the chair across from him.

"Thanks for meeting me, Karena," Greg started, trying to make her feel less nervous.

"Sure . . . now listen, I don't have much time," she paused, glancing behind her, "but I've seen that boy before. Multiple times, in fact."

"Does he come into the credit union by himself?" Karena shook her head. "Sometimes. Other times there's a guy with him."

"A guy?" Greg prodded.

"Not like that. I mean, they're friends, at least I think so. They look to be about the same age." Greg raised his eyebrows.

"And what age would that be?"

"I don't know, college?" Karena glanced around again.

That made sense. Jeremy was only sixteen, but tall for his age. He could probably easily be mistaken for a college student.

"Does he show an ID when he comes in?"

"Yes. An Arizona driver's license. We require one for all withdrawals."

"Do you happen to remember the name?" She leaned forward and pinched the bridge of her nose.

"I'm so going to get fired for this," she whispered under her breath, "it was Joe Roberts or something. Can't remember exactly." She glanced around again and stood up. "I have to go."

"Wait. Just one more thing." Greg pulled out the printout of the email he had received. "Why did you say this would be a good case for me in the email?" Karena looked down at the paper, her eyes wide.

"I never sent you an email." Greg cocked his head to the side.

"But this came from the IP address of the credit union and, if you didn't send it, who did?"

"I don't know. But I never sent you any email. I haven't seen or spoken to you since you came in asking about that girl. Now, I definitely have to go." And with that, she turned and hurried out.

Greg sat at the table looking down at the printout of the email. If Karena didn't send him an email, who did? This case was getting more confusing by the minute. It was time to call in a favor. He picked up his phone and dialed Ione's number. His friend answered almost immediately.

"And to whom do I owe the pleasure of interrupting my workday?"

"It's me, Greg."

"Duh, I have caller ID. I'm just wondering why you're calling me during work, not that I'm complaining," Ione chuckled on the other end.

"Do you have any hookups that can look into the Arizona driver's license database for me?" Greg really hoped Ione could help him.

"Maybe. But it's going to cost you."

Greg could just picture Ione spinning around his desk chair, trying to draw out the phone call as long as possible. Ione hated paperwork.

"Can I pay in beer?" Greg asked.

"You're in luck. That's one of our most highly-accepted currencies. Text me the info and I'll get back to you."

"Thanks, Ione. You're the best!"

"I know," Ione responded and the line went dead.

Greg quickly sent a text with the suspected name and zip code range he expected young Jeremy to be located in. He felt like he was close. Ione sent a text back letting him know he probably wouldn't have the results until the next day. Greg was a bit crestfallen because that meant he would have to head back up north without an answer. He felt it was a bit too soon to start canceling psychiatric appointments. Plus, his mom would kill him.

He climbed back in the truck, pausing for a minute, but then decided, as embarrassing as it was, he would do it. He pulled out his phone and dialed the original number he had been given for Dan before he had gone off the rails.

"Hello?" The Dan who answered the phone was much more businesslike than the one Greg had imagined himself talking to.

"Hey, it's Greg, we met for coffee a few weeks ago."

"Ah! Yes! Greg! I spoke to Ione about you just earlier today. He said you were still eager to work with me, just experiencing some minor health setbacks." Wow. Ione had actually been very respectful in that excuse. Greg was surprised.

"Yes, I am still interested in working with you. I got the PI badge, as we talked about, and I also," he internally winced before he said the next part, "got a separate phone line for the business.

My crazy ass has just been using it for my delusions, his subconscious added. Greg shook his head to clear the thoughts.

"Oh, perfect, you really hit the ground running," Dan replied, giving no indication that he knew about Greg's brief descent into madness.

"Yes. And I decided that my girlfriend's case really isn't what I want to feature as our first case. I'm working on something now that I believe could be high profile enough to gain us some traction." The heat in the truck was starting to get to him, so, he quickly slid the key in the ignition and turned it to the start position.

"That's great. What case, may I ask?"

"I don't know if you remember, back in January, when there was a manhunt for a sixteen-year-old boy," Greg paused and Dan was silent on the other end of the line, "his name was Jeremy Reed." Dan was quiet, quiet enough for Greg to hear the keyboard sounds coming from the other end of the line.

"Ah, yes, I see now. Well, do you want to pursue this one solo?"

Greg paused for a minute, thinking, did he want to pursue this case solo? Or should he ask for help? I mean, he'd already done most of the legwork and Ione was supposed to have the ID information for him tomorrow.

"I think I'll stick to it solo, if that's okay."

"Yeah, seems fair. You're too far along to catch me up, I'm guessing." Dan spoke in a very understanding tone. It made Greg feel comfortable.

"Yes, I mean, I'm in quite deep at this point."

"No worries. Listen, I'm going to look into getting some advertisements out for us. Since you took so long to respond, I had kinda figured you weren't interested in working with me anymore, so, I haven't been doing too much with the business since we last talked." Greg felt bad when he heard Dan apologizing. It was all his fault really.

"Are you still working your tech job on the side?"

"Sort of. I'm a freelancer with that, so, I'll probably continue to pick up tech jobs unless the PI market starts to really boom." Dan laughed.

"Sounds fair to me. What do you need me to do?" Greg asked. He felt weird continuing to sit in the Wendy's parking lot, so, he decided to start the long drive home. He quickly transitioned to his Bluetooth pairing, then turned and pulled out onto the main road.

"Uhh , , , " Dan obviously wasn't prepared for Greg's question, "I'm not sure. Listen, again, I wasn't prepared for you to call today. Give me a day and then I'll get back to you."

"No problem," Greg answered calmly. In fact, he was surprised by how calm he sounded.

"All right, I'll call you back tomorrow. See ya." And with that, the line went dead.

Greg glanced at the clock as he merged onto the highway. It was only one-thirty in the afternoon. The drive back was long, but he would still be back at a reasonable time.

During the drive, Greg pondered his romantic history. Really, he hadn't put any effort into a relationship since Ava. Even with Marie, he had only dated her because it had been convenient. I mean, she had been cute but, if she hadn't had an interest in him, he would never have pursued her. He had been off the radar so long, the romantic side of him was a little rusty.

As he neared closer to home, he came up with an idea. It was a bit out of character for him, but he was feeling daring. On the way home, he stopped and picked up takeout food from a nearby restaurant. He had debated long and hard over the type of food to pick up, but had finally settled on an Indian feast—something that they would need to eat together and it would be hard for her to push aside. Then he gave himself a cautious sniff—he was still somewhat fresh, thank God—and he turned and headed towards the hospital.

Greg parked his car in the normal hospital lot, and headed inside to the reception desk. As he was walking in, he realized he didn't know Samantha's last name. He took a seat on one of the benches outside and pulled out his phone.

Greg: "I forgot to ask the other day—what's your last name these days?"

Samantha didn't respond as instantaneously as she did before, and Greg figured she was busy. He waited about three minutes, and was about to just head inside and try his luck with reception, when his phone buzzed.

Samantha: "Rivera. Why?"

Greg smiled and slid his phone into his pocket. She would find out shortly. He walked into the hospital, approached the large wooden front desk, and asked the young receptionist to page Dr. Rivera. She smiled sweetly and did as he asked.

"Is this an emergency, sir?" Greg shook his head, no, and held up the bag of food.

"Nah, just bringing her dinner."

"Greg!"

Greg turned towards the sound of his name and saw Samantha walking toward him. She looked just as put together as the last time he saw her. Her black hair was pulled into a nice bun and her scrubs were freshly pressed.

"To what do I owe this visit?" Samantha embraced him in a friendly hug. Greg held up the food as she pulled back.

"Do you have time to have a quick dinner with me?" Samantha checked the small black watch on her wrist.

"You know what, I have one patient I need to check on but then I can meet you in the cafeteria."

"No problem," Greg answered, "point me that direction and I'll go get set up."

Samantha pointed to a door down the hall and to his left. Greg headed that way, walking through the door to find an extremely modern cafeteria. There were pictures on the wall promoting all sorts of hipster food and coffee options. The tables were wooden with a mismatch of artistic but maybe child-hand-painted chairs. Greg chose a table in the corner, setting down the food, then asking the cashier if he could borrow silverware and plates. He also ordered two bottles of water. By the time he was finishing setting up the meal, Samantha was sliding into the seat across from him.

"Wow, did you buy the entire Indian buffet?" she asked, her eyes wide.

"No, but there is a lot, so, I sure hope you like Indian food." It had been a risky choice, he had to admit. But the Samantha he knew in high school hadn't been too picky. He hoped that hadn't changed.

"I love Indian food. Thanks." She began to dig in, piling her plate high with tikka masala and saag paneer. Greg passed her a Styrofoam box filled with naan.

"I'm glad you had the time to eat with me," Greg said as he tried to start the conversation.

"Of course," Samantha answered smoothly. If she noticed his awkwardness, she didn't say anything. "Thanks for bringing food! I usually eat cafeteria food, or sandwiches from home, so, it's a nice change." She dug into her food with gusto.

"You can't go and pick up takeout?" She shook her head.

"Uber Eats has really revolutionized the medical business because I can use that to order food and, during my thirty-six-hour shift, I have to stay on the property the entire time." She was eating as if she hadn't seen food in years, but Greg didn't mind. He was a messy eater himself.

"I can't believe you're a doctor now. The last I remember, you wanted to own your own business." Greg watched as a blush crept up her pale neck. It was actually pretty cute, he had to admit.

"I wasn't sure what I wanted. I mean, how many of us really knew back then anyway? I guess I honestly thought I was never good enough at science to be a doctor, but then I learned that it was more memory and people skills than anything and that it suited me. Well, I pursued it and here were are." She motioned to the near empty cafeteria. Greg checked his phone. It was six-thirty, a perfectly normal dinner time.

"Where is everyone, anyway?" Samantha politely covered her mouth as she chuckled.

"There are no normal meal times around here. I'm actually quite spoiled today to have a moment to sit down at a normal time. As a doctor, you have to put everyone's needs first and that means skipping a lot of meals and eating at weird times." Greg nodded.

"I guess in the TV shows it seemed like everyone in the hospital sort of ate together." Samantha leaned her head back and let out a hearty laugh.

"Are you talking about the TV show, Scrubs? Because that show has almost no reality basis to it." Now, it was Greg's turn to blush.

"I guess you can say that I really know very little about the medical industry." Samantha had resumed eating her food and paused long enough to reach over and pat Greg's arm.

"Don't worry," she said between bites. "You're not the only one who thinks those shows are reality, I promise." Greg smiled, feeling the most comfortable he had in years.

"So, Thursday, is it okay if we, uh," he hesitated, "make it a date?" He nearly choked on the last part. Samantha smiled.

"Is Greg Sanders asking me on a date?"

"I guess, if it's, uh, okay with you." He smiled sheepishly, he could feel the blush creeping up his neck.

"Of course. But, um . . . " now it was her turn to pause, "full disclosure, my divorce isn't final yet, so, uh . . . "

"I get it," Greg nodded. "We can move as slow as you need." For the second time that night, a smile spread across Samantha's face just as a beeping sound erupted from her pocket. She groaned.

"That's my cue to go."

"No problem." Greg stood up just as Samantha did.

"Want me to leave any of this as leftovers?" She surveyed the smorgasbord of boxes littering the table and frowned.

"I don't think I have room in my office fridge for this much food. So, I'll have to decline. But thanks, again. This was really fun." She leaned over and gave Greg a hug. Then she began to briskly walk away

"I'll text you later," she called over her shoulder.

Greg smiled as he watched her retreating form. Then he turned to the food, combining what was left into as few bags as he possibly could, and then he headed back to his truck. Although he hadn't solved the Jeremy case, he had a good feeling about the next day. In fact, he hadn't felt this good about anything in a long time. He wasn't sure if it was the combination of the fact that he felt the case was about to break, or if it was the meal with Samantha, but all he knew was that the day had been a great day.

36

TUESDAY

Greg was walking back to his apartment after his appointment with Dr. Fauna when his phone rang and Ione's number popped up on the screen. Greg could barely contain his excitement as he pressed talk.

"What'd you get, Ione?" Ione scoffed.

"Well, hello to you, too." Greg rolled his eyes.

"Since when do you care about formalities?"

"Since never," Ione laughed, then his voice quickly switched over to business mode, "anyway, got some driver's license records for you, but you aren't gonna like them."

"And why is that?" Greg questioned as he approached his front door and inserted his key into the lock.

"I got three hits on the name, Joe Roberts. The buddy I called in for a favor wasn't sure if it was short for Joseph, either, and we have two Joseph Roberts to add into the mix."

"You've got to be kidding me." Greg was quite dismal, thinking of scouring homes in the countryside only about a week and a half before.

"I know, Dude. But, on the bright side, maybe the kid used his real picture and you can find him by matching that up." Ione was trying to remain optimistic.

"Yeah, and maybe I'm Santa Clause," Greg whispered under his breath. He was nowhere near as optimistic as Ione.

"Hey! No comments from the peanut gallery!" Ione snapped but Greg could hear the humor in his voice. Then Ione said, "Oh, by the way, I'm coming over to your place."

"You've got to be kidding me, Ione. I just cleaned up from your last visit," Greg groaned as he placed his keys on the table by the door and began to turn the lights on in his apartment.

"But I want to order from Burger Bar and they don't deliver over here," Ione whined.

"Ione, have you ever thought about driving to Burger Bar and picking up your food?" Greg walked over and opened the fridge, observing the buffet of Indian food leftovers he had planned to eat tonight. He really didn't want Ione crowding this place with anymore food.

"Ugh. Why are you always right," Ione huffed, "fine, I'll email you the results of the driver's license search and then I'll drive to Burger Bar." His mood seemed much more somber than before. Greg almost felt bad for a second. He knew he was going to regret it, but he couldn't leave the conversation with Ione in a dismal mood.

"How about we meet up on Friday for drinks and food instead? That okay?"

"Friday?" Ione said like a dog who had just received a treat, "you bet! See you Friday, Greg! We will be having a whole night o' fun!" And with that, the line went dead.

Great. Just great. The last thing Greg wanted to do was to find out what a "night o' fun" was. With a sigh, he collected one of the boxes of food from the fridge and transferred it to a plate so he could microwave it. He began scouring the rest of the boxes to find the one with the naan.

While his food was in the microwave, Greg set his laptop on the table with the email program opened. Ione wasn't always the most serious guy but, when he said he was going to email something, he usually meant immediately. By the time his food was warm, and Greg had sat down at the table with a fork, there was an email waiting for him. He opened it up while simultaneously pulling up a picture he had saved of Jeremy Reed. He scrolled through the email attachment nervously, looking for the matching photo.

Of course there wasn't one. Greg scrolled back up to the top and began looking at the details on the ID's. One of the Joseph Roberts was pushing sixty and his picture looked like it. Well, at least Greg could eliminate that one. One of the addresses was pretty far from the credit union, but Greg felt that he couldn't eliminate it based on geographic location as he wasn't sure how far Jeremy was willing to drive. For all he knew, it could be a long way.

Greg printed the document with all of the driver's licenses. He would just have to ask Karena if she recognized any of them when he went back to Arizona the next day. In another window, Greg typed in the name of the credit union, trying to get some background on it. It was very odd that both Ava (supposedly) and Jeremy had opted to keep their money there. Why?

Greg looked through all the testimonials of the credit union, but could find no indication of anything that would make it special. Then, suddenly, he had an idea. Clicking back to Google, Greg typed in the words, "How to disappear," into the search engine. What came up, surprised him. He had been expecting to find one of those wikiHow articles, with step-by-step instructions on how to become a new identity. Instead, he found website after website offering *services* to help someone disappear.

Greg scrolled through site after site, his jaw hanging open. Some of the sites offered all new identities, including a new social security number, for a nominal fee. Others seemed to be more charitable in nature, offering protection services for women escaping things such as abuse or cults. Some of the websites looked like invitations into cults. He skipped over those.

As the sun started to set, Greg looked through many, many sites. When he found one that seemed legit, he would send an inquiry asking for price and what he needed to do. Some of them looked phony right from the get-go, asking for money and personal information, so, he didn't waste his time on those. After about three hours of sending emails and reading about how to disappear and start a new life, Greg glanced at the clock and decided to call it quits. He took his sleeping pill and set his alarm for early the next morning. Hopefully, he would get at least one email back before he had to start his drive.

As he laid down in bed, Greg glanced at his clock and realized Samantha would be just finishing her thirty six hour shift. He'd never been the type of guy to do this, but something about her made him feel like a different man. Before he went to sleep, he typed out a quick message.

Greg: "I hope your shift went well. Get some rest."

He set the phone down, not waiting for the reply, and rolled over, falling asleep within minutes. After all, they weren't called sleeping pills for no reason.

37

WEDNESDAY

The sounds of Greg's shrill alarm filled the room before the sun was even peeking over the eastern hills. He groaned, rolling over, blindly trying to shut it off. He sat up in bed, vigorously rubbing the sleep out of his eyes. He remembered now why he had stopped taking sleeping pills in the first place. They made it too hard to wake up after a short night, while also making it difficult for him to remain alert.

Greg had never been much of a coffee drinker, but he now wished he had been enough of one to own a coffee maker. He didn't want to drive this groggy, but he also didn't have a Red Bull handy. Trying to give his body a moment to wake up, he shoved on some pants and headed to the kitchen to check his computer. He stopped by the fridge to see if there was an egg he could fry, only to be reminded he still hadn't had a chance to head to the store and all he had was left-over Indian food. He wrinkled his nose and resolved to stop at a gas station on his drive.

Since food to wake him up wasn't an option, he decided to turn on the water in the sink and wash his face with the coldest water possible. It helped some, but he still didn't feel fully alert. He slid into his chair behind his computer and waited impatiently for his computer to boot up. It wasn't a dinosaur like the ones he had used at the station, but it still made him impatient when it took a while like this.

He logged into his email and was shocked at what he saw. There was an email after email response from what seemed like every single site he had visited the night before. He knew it couldn't be every site because he hadn't contacted each one but, man, he did not realize just how many sites he *had* contacted.

The emails all contained different content. The first one he opened was clearly a scam:

"Dear Mister Gregory: We will help you disappear. Please wire ten thousand dollars to the address below via Western Union or MoneyGram."

Greg didn't even bother reading the full email. He deleted it. The next one was slightly more realistic, but seemed to be catering to the wrong audience. It mentioned running and hiding from abuse. Definitely not something he thought Ava or Jeremy would reply to. The third email was quite interesting.

"Gregory, We don't care to know your personal or religious reasons for disappearing, but we are happy to help. Our services will cost ten thousand dollars and we suggest having at least that much left in the bank after our fee to get you started. If you are serious, please go and purchase a prepaid cell phone. Send us the number, and we will give you a call. Please note: we will only call numbers registered to prepaid phones."

That email was signed by a strange name but Greg felt that it was decently legit. There was only one problem. While Ava might have had ten thousand dollars tucked away, he was almost certain Jeremy didn't.

The fourth and fifth emails he opened also looked like scams— asking for wire transfers before services were being rendered. Some of the emails were just adds, he deleted those without reading them. He also had an email from Dan containing some information about registering for a business license. His inbox contained two more emails from disappearance services, but Greg quickly realized they were some sort of virus because they wanted him to click on and download something to his computer. It figured that some of those sites were scam sites.

Greg saved the one email asking for ten thousand dollars. Maybe, after he visited the credit union, he would get a prepaid cell and give them a call. It was certainly worth a shot. He packed up his laptop and his overnight bag and headed for the truck. He really hoped this would be the last time he would do this drive to Arizona. He felt decently awake after the computer time, but still stopped by a gas station on his way out of town to grab a Red Bull, just in case he started nodding off later.

Greg pulled into the all-too-familiar credit union parking lot at ten in the morning. Grabbing his printouts of the driver's licenses, he headed inside. He stopped dead in his tracks as soon as he walked through the door.

The woman behind the desk wasn't Karena.

"Hello, how can I help you today?" the middle-aged woman behind the desk asked politely.

Dammit. This ruined everything. Greg thought about turning and walking out, then trying again tomorrow, but he realized it would make him look extremely suspicious

"Hello," he cleared his throat, "I actually came to see Karena. Is she in?" He tried to resist the urge to glance around nervously. He'd always had such a bad poker face. The woman smiled.

"She doesn't come in until the afternoon on Wednesdays. Is there something I can help you with?"

"Uh," Greg scrambled to think of a reason why he would need Karena and not this woman's help, "I was in the middle of opening an account with her on Monday, but then I had to leave in the middle of the process. I'll just come back this afternoon."

"What's your name, sir? I can pull up your application process and we can finish it now." She turned to the computer at her right, posed to begin typing as soon as he said his name.

"Well, we didn't actually get an application started. Karena was just explaining my options to me and we had decided on one but then I had to leave. And, well, I have other errands to run, so, I'll just come back because I don't have time to have it all explained again." It was a dumb excuse, and he knew it. It sounded even more dumb out loud than it had in his head. But it was the only reason he could think of as to why he wouldn't want this woman's help.

"All right, sir," the woman regarded him carefully, "if you're sure."

"I am," Greg interjected.

"I'll let Karena know you were asking for her. She'll be in around one."

"All right, I'll be back then."

Greg quickly turned and hurried out of the building. He couldn't explain it, but he'd never felt so nervous lying to someone before. He stepped back into his truck and drove around the corner. He put his car into park and pulled up his email inbox. He was happy to see that there was one more unread email. This one was extremely short.

"Dear Greg, We will be happy to help you with your assignment. Please purchase a prepaid phone and call the number below."

And, oddly enough, there was no signature. Greg was intrigued, though, as this was the second service that had asked him to buy a prepaid phone. He quickly searched for a location nearby where he could buy a prepaid phone. He was in luck. There was a place only about ten minutes away.

GREG WAS SHOCKED at how easy it had been to buy a prepaid phone. He had gone in the store thinking prepaid phones were only available in the brick-style Nokia phones or the flip phones of the previous era. He had no idea you could get a prepaid smart phone these days. He had browsed the selection and decided on a low-quality touchscreen phone for sixty dollars. He had then added an hour of minutes and five hundred texts for an additional twenty bucks.

The cashier seemed shocked that he hadn't wanted to buy a plan that included some data, but Greg insisted he just wanted to make phone calls and send texts. He was sure it looked very suspicious in the age of the internet. He walked back to his truck, spending the next twenty minutes setting the phone up. For some reason, he had assumed you just bought the phone and started making calls. But, like everything else these days, you had to register and give private info. However, it would be very easy to give a fake name and email if you were trying to stay off the grid.

After he was done registering, he called the number on the email. Someone picked up, but there was no hello on the other end.

"Hello?" Greg said hesitantly.

The person didn't answer, but he could hear the sound of breathing. He quickly referred back to the email, then tried again.

"This is Greg. I was told to call."

"Ah, yes. Greg." The voice was calm and in a monotone. It almost sounded as if the other person was trying to disguise their voice. Greg couldn't be sure if it was a man or a woman but the voice said, "I can help you with your journey." Man, this person was either weird or purposefully trying to be cryptic.

"How much?"

"Depends on what you want."

"Uh," Greg thought back to the articles he had seen the night before, "new social, new birth certificate, new identity. Doesn't matter where."

"Easy enough," the voice responded, "that'll be five grand." Five grand? Almost half off from the other email he had received.

"That's fine. But, just curious, if I wanted to disappear and didn't want the new identity, how much would it be?"

"Five hundred." Hm. Affordable. Greg quickly pulled up the notes section in his phone.

"What do I need to do?"

"You will hear from us on the identity documents. For now, start slowly pulling money out of your bank accounts. No large amounts, and you can't take it all, that's too obvious. Stash it away in a credit union somewhere." Greg's ears perked up at the use of the word 'credit union.'

"Okay."

"The smaller the town, the better. You can only take one bag of items with you. Decide now. Everything else stays. Don't call us. We will call you." Then the line went dead.

Greg could hardly believe his luck. Five grand, one bag of items. This sounded way too familiar. Now, he wasn't sure that Jeremy had the five grand, but he knew the kid had some cash on him when he disappeared, and he figured the kid might have only ordered a driver's license. After all, Arizona was one of the states with the easiest driver's license to fake.

He still had plenty of time before he headed back to the credit union, so, Greg decided to look into something that was bothering him. He drove to the motel where he had stayed when he had been here two weeks ago. It was just as he remembered it. Short, squat, outdated. But the real reason he had come was to see the parking lot. As he turned the corner, he couldn't believe his eyes.

There *was* a Mexican restaurant there. Greg slammed the truck into park, not caring if it was properly parked in the empty parking lot, and jogged inside. A young woman, who looked vaguely familiar as the server who waited on him last time, greeted him.

"Hello. Table for one person?" she asked.

"Uh, no actually," he ran a hand through his hair nervously, "I know this is awkward, but I was here two weeks ago, and uh—"

"Ah, yes," the woman smiled, cutting him off, "I remember."

"Great. Do you remember how I paid for my meals?" She looked at him funny. "Meals? You only came one time. And the strange woman you annoyed paid for your meal." Greg could feel his eyes becoming wide as saucers.

"Okay, um, thanks."

Greg returned to his truck and pulled up Google Maps. Zooming in to his location, sure enough, the restaurant didn't show up. He tried typing in the name, but it gave a location across the state. So, Dr. Fauna had thought this place didn't exist, but it did. However, Greg was pretty embarrassed that he had thought he had come here three times and it had only been once. And what woman had paid for his meal? His thoughts were interrupted by his prepaid cell phone ringing.

"This is Greg," he answered quickly.

"Yes. We have your documents ready. Please proceed to the pickup point we will send. What date can you have the money?" The voice was the same as before, however, it seemed as if they were not trying as hard to disguise it now.

"Cash?" Greg inquired.

"Yes, cash only. When can you have it? Remember, you cannot look suspicious." Who had five thousand dollars sitting around in cash?

Ava, who'd been working as a stripper, his subconscious reminded him. Greg quickly pushed the thought away.

"It will take me a couple of weeks," he hedged.

"Okay," the voice replied, "text this number with only the number five when you have it. Then we will call with further instructions." The line once again went dead.

Greg quickly got on his computer and began documenting everything that had been happening with these phone calls. He wasn't sure what he was going to do with this information yet, but the whole thing seemed fishy. Glancing at his watch, he realized it was about time for him to head back to the credit union. He emailed himself a copy of his document for safekeeping, then stowed his computer. Hopefully, Karena would have the answer he was looking for.

The drive back to the credit union was quick, and Greg arrived a few minutes early. He made sure his documents with the driver's licenses were ready, and then he sat and waited. It didn't take long before a small red car drove up and parked in the lot. He immediately recognized Karena behind the wheel. She stepped out of the car and headed into the credit union without a glance in his direction.

Greg waited for Karena to get settled, hoping that the older lady would leave. About fifteen minutes passed until finally he observed the older woman he had spoken to that morning exiting the building and heading to her car parked on the other side of the lot. He let out a sigh of relief, at least she was out of the way. He grabbed his papers and headed inside, giving Karena a friendly wave as she looked up from her desk to greet him. Her smile faltered slightly, as she clearly recognized him, but she was polite all the same.

"Hello, nice to see you again. What can I help you with?"

Greg walked up to the counter and pulled out his manila folder with the papers. Conscious that he was being recorded, he slid them across the counter towards her.

"I have a few documents for you to look over here. If you could just mark the one that is correct, that would be a big help." He hoped it looked like he was opening an account.

Karena cautiously opened the folder and began to flip through the papers. If she was surprised by the amount of information he had been able to attain, she didn't show it. She paused on a couple of pages, but eventually came to the end. He was tempted to lean over each time she paused, but he restrained himself. He needed to make this look as inconspicuous as possible. After coming to the end of the documents, Karena flipped back towards the front, going through them a lot more quickly the second time around. This time, she did draw a circle on a document, then she closed the folder and slid it back over to him.

"I'm pretty sure that's the one I've seen." She bit her lip.

"Pretty sure?" Greg asked, sliding the folder of documents under his arm. She nodded.

"I can't be one hundred percent sure because I see so many, but he has come in here quite a few times, so, I'm pretty sure."

"Well, I guess that's good enough for me. Thank you, Karena."

Greg turned and headed for the door as she called a 'you're welcome' at his retreating form. He was eager to see which one she had identified. He climbed back in his truck and started the ignition so he could turn on the air-conditioning. It was still much too hot to sit in a truck without it.

With a shaking breath, Greg opened the folder and flipped through the documents. When he came to the page she had marked, his breath stilled in his throat. He pulled out the picture he had of Jeremy and held it up next to the photocopied ID. Not an obvious match, but he could see some similarities. He quickly typed the address listed on the ID into his phone. Hopefully, Jeremy was one of those people who kept the address on their ID up to date. With his fingers crossed, Greg backed out of the parking lot and began to follow the GPS instructions.

Greg began to wonder what he would do when he got to the address. Obviously, he couldn't arrest anyone. At this point, he doubted the boy had been kidnapped, but there was still a small possibility he was being held against his will. As he drew closer to the address, Greg decided to park down the street a bit, just so he could surprise whoever he was about to find. Before turning off his truck, Greg set a time-delayed email and attached all of the notes he had made. At least, if something happened to him, this email would send and let everyone know what he had been up to. He once again put the missing poster for Jeremy Reed in his pocket and slid his firearm into the small of his back. Here goes nothing, he thought to himself, as he stepped out of the truck.

Greg walked down the block and around the corner, looking for the house number listed on the ID. He found himself standing in front of a small red stucco house. It was ranch style, with a six-foot chain link fence surrounding the yard which was mostly rocks and cactus in true Arizona fashion. The gate stood open, leading Greg to believe there probably wasn't a dog on the premises, but still he proceeded with caution. There was a doorbell, but the light wasn't on and wires were sticking out of the sides, leading him to believe it was most likely broken. He knocked on the door.

It took a few minutes, but the door was opened by a young man dressed in boxers and a T-shirt. His hair was disheveled, and it looked like he hadn't shaved in a while. Greg squinted. It could be the boy on the missing poster.

"Joe?" Greg asked, unsure. The young man yawned.

"That's me." Greg decided not to waste time with small talk.

"Jeremy Reed?"

The young man glanced behind him as if there was someone else in the house who could be listening. Then he stepped out on the porch, closing the door behind him.

"How did you find me?"

"Your address is listed on your driver's license." Greg shifted his weight from one foot to the other. He felt very uncomfortable, and was unsure how this conversation was going to play out.

"But how did you know Joe Roberts is Jeremy Reed?" Jeremy asked, keeping his voice low, "and please tell me you didn't call the police."

"It's kind of a long story," Greg said, and he really didn't want to explain his process to this boy, "but listen, I didn't call the police, and I'm hoping you'll come back to Nevada with me." Jeremy shook his head.

"I can't."

"And why is that?" Greg asked, careful to keep his voice low as well.

"You wouldn't understand. I didn't belong there. I had no friends, everyone at school hated me, I was an outcast." His shoulders slumped forward and he hung his head.

Greg understood, he really did. Things had been tough for him in high school, too. Especially before he met Ava.

"I know Jeremy, trust me, things were tough for me in high school, too. But look at me now. I'm working a job I love and I've got a really great friend back home," not to mention a horrible obsession with finding an ex-girlfriend and a sleep hallucination disorder, Greg added mentally but didn't say out loud, "and, besides, you're only sixteen. You can't legally live on your own yet. Even if you could, I don't think it's wise to not finish school."

"Seventeen," Jeremy corrected, "and that's the age you can legally be emancipated. And I don't need school. I'm learning everything I need to know from the internet." Obviously, the pep talk was not going in the way Greg had planned. He did have one more thing to try.

"What about your mom?" As soon as Greg said the word 'mom' he saw all the rebellion and fight leave Jeremy's body.

"I miss her," he whispered so low Greg almost couldn't hear him, "she's the only person I miss."

"Then you should go home to her. You broke her heart," Greg pressed. Jeremy was silent. "You're her only son. How do you think she feels not knowing where you are or if you're even alive."

Jeremy nodded, his eyes looking slightly moist. "I know. But I can't go back to that life, I just can't. I'm so happy here. Please don't force me."

Greg took a long look at the boy in front of him. He saw many of his own qualities in the boy, but he also saw many qualities of Ava in him as well. For a moment, he imagined finding Ava in similar circumstances and dragging her back to the life she had left. The life she had hated. He couldn't do it.

"Well, Jeremy, listen, I'm not going to call the police, but I really think you should consider contacting your mom. At least, let her know what happened to you before this completely destroys her."

Jeremy nodded. Just then, the door behind Jeremy opened and a young man, who couldn't be much more than a couple years older than Jeremy, popped his head out.

"What's going on out here?" the young man asked as he surveyed Greg warily.

"Nothing," Jeremy quickly spat out, "just talking to an old friend, but he's leaving." He gave Greg a pointed look.

"Yep, I'm leaving."

Greg took one last look at the boy behind the partially open door, and at Jeremy who still stood on the porch, then he turned and began the walk to his truck. He was halfway down the block when he heard Jeremy call.

"Hey, wait!" Greg turned to find Jeremy running up to him. Panting, Jeremy stopped a few feet from Greg and leaned over to catch his breath.

"She, uh, left this for you."

Jeremy proceeded to hand Greg an envelope that had been scrunched up in his hand. Greg hadn't even noticed it was there. Cautiously, he took it from the young man.

"She? Who?" Jeremy shrugged.

"Some chick who came by the house the other day. Said a man would be stopping by and to give this to him." Jeremy straightened up and looked around nervously. Greg's eyebrows furrowed. Was he hallucinating again? He turned the envelope over a couple times in his hand.

"Can you describe her to me?" Greg asked as he continued to inspect the envelope.

Jeremy didn't answer and, when Greg lifted his head to see why, he noticed the young man was briskly walking back to his home. Greg slid his finger underneath the flap and delicately tore open the envelope. Inside was a handwritten note on a single sheet of paper.

Greg—

Now, I know I said no more breadcrumbs. But I realized that what I said to you was a little harsh when you last saw me. I want to tell you that, although I can't live on the pedestal you put me on, I know there's a girl out there for you who is dying to.

I wish you the best, Greg, in all that you do. And thanks for keeping my secret. I appreciate it, Greg. I really do. Everyone deserves a friend like you. And there's a small part of me that I suppose will always love you.

Thanks for doing the one thing I never had the nerve to do.

Greg finished reading the note, then immediately read it again. It was unsigned, but he knew immediately who had sent it. His head began to spin. So, he had really met Ava in that Arizona cabin. But what did she mean, 'thanks for doing the one thing I never had the nerve to do'? And what was she doing visiting young Jeremy Reed?

Ava must've been the one who sent him the email. She must've found Jeremy Reed. He stood motionless for what seemed like forever, wracking his brain about what she could possibly have meant by her last sentence. He reread the letter a third time. Then it clicked.

Ava had found Jeremy but didn't have the nerve to turn him in.

Greg debated for a minute. He had promised Jeremy he wouldn't call the police.

But he also knew how horrible it felt to be one of the people left behind when someone went missing. And Ava obviously wanted him to call. Who was he loyal to?

He thought about the pain of Ava disappearing. And the years he wasted searching for her.

He knew what he had to do.

Greg pulled out the missing persons flyer from his pocket, dialing the number listed. He pushed talk and held the phone to his ear.

"Hello, missing person's tip line, how may I direct your call?"

"Yes," Greg took a deep breath, "I've located a missing person."

EPILOGUE-THREE MONTHS LATER

Greg stepped out of his truck, slinging the insulated tote over his shoulder. The park in front of him was alive with activity. There were kids playing on the playground and in the sandbox, while others were running around the field kicking what looked like a soccer ball. Parents stood in groups around the playground, discussing and pointing out their individual children. Greg surveyed the scene for a minute more until his eyes zeroed in on the woman he had been looking for.

Samantha sat on a bench, wearing a beautiful red sundress and a straw hat, reading a picture book to the young girl sitting beside her who had to be her daughter. The girl had the exact same color hair as Samantha, but a skin tone that was slightly darker. She wore a yellow sundress and a miniature version of the hat her mother wore. Samantha looked up and Greg gave her a little wave as he approached. She stood, embracing Greg in a hug.

"Hi," Samantha said in a slightly breathy voice. Greg just smiled like an idiot. She looked away from Greg's face to the young girl next to her.

"This is my daughter, Ava Lee, but she goes by Lee." Samantha's eyes searched Greg's face as she said her daughter's name.

Greg was surprised by the name but, after months of searching, he had finally laid the idea of Ava to rest. The Ava he had known was gone. While she may physically still be out in the world, running around Arizona doing God-knows what, the woman he had loved in his college years truly was gone. He accepted that now. He leaned down so that he was eye-to-eye with the little girl.

"Well, hello, Lee. And just how old are you?" Greg inquired. The little girl bit her lip, focusing very hard on showing him four fingers.

"Four? Wow! That's almost as old as me," Greg joked. Lee smiled. He motioned to the bag on his shoulder.

"I brought us some lunch to share. Want to help me find a good spot to eat?"

Lee smiled and nodded vigorously. She began turning around and surveying the grass, looking for a flat spot to eat. Samantha and Greg trailed behind. Greg broke the silence.

"I'm surprised you named your daughter after her after that last fight you had." Samantha nodded.

"I felt horrible when she disappeared knowing the last words I had said to her were in anger. I guess you could say this was my way of making amends."

"Makes sense," Greg replied as he reached out and secured Samantha's hand in his. Lee had found a shady spot under a tree and was jumping up and down waiving at them.

"Looks like she found a spot."

"Yes indeed," Samantha replied with a smile as she looked down at their intertwined hands and back up to Greg's face, "so, guess what happened this morning?"

"What?" Greg asked nervously.

"I signed the final divorce papers. It's official. I'm no longer a married woman."

Greg couldn't control the massive smile that spread over his face. Without a word, he turned to Samantha and swept her up in a hug, planting a passionate kiss on her lips. They had been dating for the past three months, but Samantha had been hesitant to let things get too serious as her divorce was not yet finalized. She had especially wanted to wait to have him meet Lee. He should have suspected the divorce was nearing an end when she called him up last night and invited him to the park to meet her daughter.

Samantha was all smiles as they set up and ate their makeshift picnic. Greg had brought way too much food, but he hadn't been sure what Lee liked to eat. He was pleasantly surprised to find she wasn't picky at all, very similar to her mother, and she was willing to try everything he placed in front of her.

After they finished, Lee asked her mom if she could go swing and, when Samantha said yes, she had been quick to run off and join the other children. Greg placed his arm around Samantha's shoulders as they sat and watched Lee together.

"Well," Samantha finally broke the silence, "what do you think of her?"

"She's very precocious," Greg replied. Samantha laughed but agreed.

"Yes, she is. I was, too, at that age."

"I was surprised she wasn't a picky eater. I had asked Ione what four-year-olds like to eat, as I have no idea, and he had told me to be prepared and bring a lot of options." Greg motioned to the numerous bags of chips and containers of fruits that surrounded them. Samantha nodded.

"Ione wasn't wrong. Most kids are picky eaters. But I specifically don't allow it. If Lee doesn't want to eat what's served, she can choose to not eat until the next meal. We've always run the house like that ever since she was a baby."

"That a good tactic."

They both sat in silence for a few minutes, still watching Lee as she made a new friend by the yellow slide.

"How's therapy going?" Samantha asked hesitantly.

After he had returned from Arizona, Greg had been 100 percent honest with Samantha about why he had been in the hospital that day. Although he hadn't told her about his experience tracking Ava (he hadn't told anyone, in fact), he had been honest about his psychiatric visits. He didn't want to start a relationship filled with secrets.

Samantha had been completely understanding. She felt that perfection was a myth, anyway. Therapy had been good for him. He had started going because of his hallucinations but, the longer he went, the more he found it was helping with some of his deeply-rooted attachment issues. Dr. Fauna had helped him work them out. It was actually thanks to therapy that Greg felt he had finally been able to let Ava go. He only wished he had gone to get help sooner.

"I think Friday will be my last session," Greg answered triumphantly. Samantha smiled and looked over at him.

"Sounds like we will have to go out for a celebratory dinner on Friday night!"

Greg smiled in return and planted a kiss on her lips once more. How had he gotten so lucky to find such an understanding woman?

"Sounds good to me. I might have to work this weekend, though.

Greg had gained quite the reputation after solving the case of the missing Jeremy Reed. Although he felt he shouldn't be taking all the credit, he was the first to admit that he wasn't going to be able to explain how a second missing person had solved the case of the first.

The notoriety had come with a new job offer from a large investigations firm in Washington, DC. Greg had been hesitant to take it at first, as he wanted to remain close to home both for his therapy, and for Samantha, but they had eventually agreed to let him work remotely, and just fly in for occasional meetings, as investigations usually involved a lot of travel anyways.

It wasn't quite his dream job, but it was much closer than being a traffic cop. And although he really had wanted to pursue an independent PI business with Dan, it simply hadn't panned out as they had planned. Much of the money Greg had originally planned to put towards opening their firm had simply evaporated with his helping his mother with his medical bills and from not working for a few months. He'd hated to let Dan down, but the guy seemed to understand, as he also didn't quite have the capital they thought they needed. Ione had mentioned that Dan had received numerous job offers from technology firms, anyway, and it was more fiscally responsible for him to take one of those jobs than to open his own business.

Ione was still working as a traffic cop, with the same gusto as before, and he also continued to go out most Friday nights. He was always pestering Greg to come and to bring Samantha, but Greg explained that late nights were not necessarily conducive with working in the ER nor being the mother of a four-year-old who gets up at the crack of dawn.

Greg and Ione did continue to hang out on Sunday afternoons and watch football together. Well, mostly at Ione's insistence, since he still had a key and pretty much came over uninvited every Sunday afternoon and proceeded to order mountains of food that he wanted Greg to help him eat. Some things never change.

As the morning in the park turned to afternoon, Greg and Samantha began to pack up their picnic, calling Lee over from where she had been playing with her hoard of new friends.

"No, Mom, I don't want to leave," Lee pouted, sticking out her lower lip.

"I know, Hon, but it's getting late and we have things to do at home," Samantha replied. Lee continued to pout but didn't argue anymore. As they headed towards the parking lot, Lee slipped her small hand into Greg's.

"Are you coming to our house, Mr. Greg?" He looked over Lee's head at Samantha who smiled.

"Only if it's okay with your mom." Lee turned to look at her mom

"Can he, Mom? Can Mr. Greg come over?"

"Sure, I think that's a wonderful idea," Samantha replied, winking at Greg over Lee's head.

Greg smiled back as they climbed in their respective vehicles and headed off in the direction of Samantha's house. There had been a few really difficult years for Greg, and he'd had to face some cold, hard truths during his investigation of Ava's disappearance. Although some of them had been painful, he was happy with where he was headed. And he honestly wouldn't have wanted it any other way.

～

SHE SITS at the table in the quaint Mexican restaurant quietly stirring her margarita. A prepaid cell lies on the table next to her left hand.

He walks in and looks around. She nonchalantly brushes a strand of her red haired wig from her eyes to its place behind her ear. She's never seen him before.

He notices her and slides into the seat directly across from her.

"Do you have it?" she asks.

He nods and sets a paper grocery bag on the table. She opens it and peers inside. There are five bundles of hundred dollar bills.

She smiles, picking up the manila folder that was on the seat next to her. She slides some documents across the table and places the money on the seat. She flips over the freshly printed driver's license.

"Welcome to your new life, Roger Montana."

BIBLIOGRAPHY

Sources:

Bilich, Karen A. "Child Abduction Statistics for Parents." *Parents*, Parents.com, 29 Nov. 2019, www.parents.com/kids/safety/stranger-safety/child-abduction-facts/.

Kepple, Kevin, et al. "By the Numbers: Missing Persons in the USA." *USA Today*, Gannett Satellite Information Network, 25 Sept. 2014, www.usatoday.com/story/news/nation-now/2014/09/23/missing-persons-children-numbers/16110709/.

"NCIC Missing Person and Unidentified Person Statistics for 2013." *FBI*, FBI, 23 Jan. 2014, archives.fbi.gov/archives/about-us/cjis/ncic/ncic-missing-person-and-unidentified-person-statistics-for-2013.

ALSO BY HOPE E. DAVIS

If you enjoyed The Fate of Ava Miller, please take a moment to leave a rating or review and check out Hope's other mystery novels, Deceptive Perfection, Before Now, and You Can't Run! Available on Amazon.com in both paperback and Kindle!

ABOUT THE AUTHOR

The Fate of Ava Miller is Hope's second novel. When she isn't writing, she is busy traveling the world, trying new foods, or hanging out with friends. A graduate of Metropolitan State University, Hope grew up in Colorado but currently calls The Netherlands her home. To find information about her other novels, or future novels, follow Hope on Instagram or TikTok: @hopeedavisauthor.

www.ingramcontent.com/pod-product-compliance
Lightning Source LLC
Chambersburg PA
CBHW021147110726
47900CB00002B/466